FAÇADE

Zahra Owens

Dreamspinner Press

Published by
Dreamspinner Press
4760 Preston Road
Suite 244-149
Frisco, TX 75034
http://www.dreamspinnerpress.com/

Façade

Cover Art by Paul Richmond   http://www.paulrichmondstudio.com

ISBN: 978-1-61581-075-8

Printed in the United States of America
First Edition
October, 2009

eBook edition available
eBook ISBN: 978-1-61581-076-5

To the men-loving men who inspire me,
my fellow writing sisters who keep me on my toes,
and the girls at Dreamspinner who continue to give me a voice.

CHAPTER 1

JONAS HUNTER didn't take on new clients. He was no longer a young man and was making a very nice living thanks to the regulars he already had. He certainly didn't need a client whose assistant was as pushy and demanding as this one. Jonas had repeatedly brushed him off until a seductive but businesslike female voice had pleaded with him to give it a try. One visit and then he could decide whether to come around again. Jonas wasn't sure what had made him say yes. Maybe it was the fact she gave him the choice; maybe it was because the tone of her voice showed she cared for the man on whose behalf she had made the call. Or maybe it had to do with one of his oldest friends mentioning the man to him and telling Jonas he was going to recommend him.

He'd heard of Nicky Bryant, of course—had seen his antics on television, had even heard firsthand about the elaborate and often over-the-top theatrics Bryant loved to weave into his *haute couture* fashion shows. Fashion journalists loved to call him highly original, the bad boy of couture, unafraid to stick his neck out, but otherwise too shy to come forward without some sort of costume and covered in extensive make-up. He seemed to do everything imaginable and some things quite unimaginable, all in an effort to be as unique as possible. And he'd succeeded in being the toast of every fashion week all over the world for the last six years, despite the fact he was barely out of design school when he'd taken the most difficult road: starting his own label before he'd honed his craft by working for one of the large fashion houses first.

Still, to Jonas he was just too much, and most importantly, too effeminate and way too demanding. Jonas might be a body for hire, but that didn't mean he didn't have his preferences. He also had no idea why the man's assistant had picked him to call on.

Yet here he was in the downstairs lounge of a house that looked well-maintained and rather inconspicuous on the outside, but resembled the owner's over the top tastes on the inside.

The young man who had opened the door and shown Jonas inside looked like he'd walked off the pages of Vogue and had eyed Jonas with quite blatant disdain. Jonas wasn't bothered by his attitude. He was quite used to the scrutiny, despite the fact he didn't look like a man of his profession.

"Mr. Bryant will be right in," a different young man from the one who let him in announced, placing a flute of champagne on the table next to Jonas. "Traffic is murder on the Périférique at this time of night, but he would like to have dinner with you in his rooms later."

And then some, Jonas almost murmured. Instead, he took a sip of the champagne and noticed it was top-notch. This was going to be a long night, spent in the company of some spoiled rotten, full-of-himself girly brat. He was only doing Scott a favor, although he had no idea how his longest running client knew anyone in the fashion business.

There was a ruckus outside in the hall, and the doors to the lounge flew open. About ten fashion models, each one looking more androgynous than the last, waltzed into the room and miraculously parted when Jonas's client came in. To Jonas's amazement, he looked just like he did on TV: slim and elegant, in full make-up, wearing something resembling a pirate's costume. And bursting with ego, though some people would no doubt call it charisma. Jonas had to admit he did look like he could make heads turn. He was eyeing Jonas up and down.

"This him?" Nicky asked, pursing his painted lips.

The assistant who had stared Jonas down upon his entrance was now acting like a gibbering idiot. "Yes, sir, he is. Came highly recommended, sir. Very… talented and extremely discreet, sir."

Nicky didn't even look at the young man, who was bowing incessantly. He simply dismissed him with a wave of the hand.

"I'm sure he'll be to your liking, sir."

"Laurent! Assez!" Nicky shouted, his voice so suddenly loud it made the entourage scatter like a bunch of mice. The one person who didn't even flinch was a tall, slender and very elegant woman in a pantsuit, with legs up to her neck and flawless make-up and hair.

"Tanna, send them home. They depress me. All of them." He waved them away as if he was swatting flies. "I want dinner in my rooms upstairs and I want you to bring it in, no one else. Show him where it is."

Nicky pointed at Jonas, turned around, and paced out the room, leaving all of his painted entourage lost and clearly dumbfounded.

TEN minutes later, Jonas was led into a darkened room by the charming Tanna.

"Sorry about the lack of light. It's how he wants it," Tanna said, her voice as subdued as their surroundings.

"And I don't suppose you ever do anything he doesn't want?" Jonas replied.

"He's our meal ticket, Mr. Hunter. It would be foolish to throw that away."

At least she was polite and not half as condescending as the others. "Would do him a world of good," Jonas murmured.

"Excuse me?"

Tanna interrupted his thoughts, and Jonas realized he had spoken out loud. What did he have to lose? This job? It was a favor for someone, not *his* meal ticket. "You look like the only one he would listen to, and I think it would do him a world of good to be grounded."

She sighed. "I take care of him, Mr. Hunter, and believe me, he needs taking care of. If I give him reason to hate me, then he has no one." She turned around and returned with a trolley filled with food. "Try to get him to eat something, and then… well, I don't need to tell you how to do your job."

His eyes now adjusted to the half-dark, Jonas saw the soft compassion in her gaze. He'd expected something else, not her understanding, and it unsettled him more than if she had looked down on him.

"I'll leave you now. Please be patient; he may take a while to get here. If he asks, you can tell him that I'll be in my room and all the others have left." With that she silently left the suite.

Jonas sat down on one of the sofas, grateful that it was comfortably soft, worn leather, nothing like the antique chair he had sat on downstairs that looked as if it had come straight from Versailles. He waited a few moments in total silence. The only light came from the street lights outside shining through the creases along the sides of the heavy drapes. He felt around the side table and flicked on the small lamp he found there.

"Turn it off, please," a soft, low voice coming from the other side of the room asked.

Jonas was mildly startled, wondering how long he'd been there. He looked in the direction of the voice but saw only a doorway with a long dark shadow.

"Your assistant asked me to make sure you ate something, and I don't think we can do that in the dark."

"She's not my assistant," Nicky answered quietly, still not stepping out of his darkened corner. Jonas thought at first he was going to add something, but he lapsed back into silence.

"It's a little difficult to talk with me here and you over there. Why don't you come here, get comfortable, have a bite to eat, and then…." Jonas didn't finish his sentence, figuring they were both grown-ups and fully aware of why he was here.

"You're not paid by the hour, so there's no rush. Besides, I don't eat." Nicky's voice sounded high and mighty again, as if he'd regained some of the arrogance he'd displayed when he walked into the house, but it waned quickly. "And I don't like strangers seeing me like I am."

Jonas's patience was growing thin. "Listen, I'm not judging a beauty pageant here. Believe me, there's very little that throws me off about a person. A man," he corrected himself. He hoped a little humor would help break the ice. "I draw the line at trolls and werewolves."

Nicky didn't laugh. "Just turn off the light."

"No," Jonas replied, determined. Instead he got up and walked to the trolley, where he lifted the covers off the plates. "This looks good, Nicky; you really should eat something, you know."

"You're not my mother."

The source of Nicky's voice had moved around the room. "No, I'm not, but I don't think you're just a spoiled brat either." He started putting a few things on the two plates, some scalloped potatoes, green beans, and a few strips of roast beef.

"Just fuck me, okay? That's what you're here for, and all you're getting paid for."

"Like you said, you're not paying me by the hour," Jonas replied calmly. "This is all part of the service. Besides, I think it was Tanna who hired me, and she was the one who asked me to get you to eat something, so I suppose I am hired for this as well. And one of your boys told me that you had requested dinner with me first."

"It's still my money."

Jonas abruptly turned around and saw him standing there, near the light. On the one hand, he looked like a boy, innocent, almost angelic, not a trace of make-up left and his long hair flowing around his face in ringlets. On the other hand, the sleeveless top and jogging pants he was wearing did nothing to hide his obviously lean physique. The clearly trained body, complete with nicely curved chest, washboard stomach, and narrow waist and hips, made Jonas's body react, a feeling he hadn't had in a long time.

"You're the boss, but Tanna will like me a lot better if she sees you've eaten." Jonas took the plates and some cutlery toward the coffee table and placed them on it, one near where Nicky was still standing and the other one in front of him as he sat down. When Nicky didn't move, he started eating, trying to ignore the tension in the air. Eventually the young man sat down and picked at the potatoes with his fork.

Jonas finished his plate. "You know you don't have to pretend with me. Anything that happens between us, that is said or done here, won't leave this room. If I'm renowned for anything, it's my discretion."

For the first time, Jonas saw a smile play round Nicky's mouth. "You're known for a lot more than your discretion."

"Well, that would be what I'd hope for, you know, in my profession," Jonas replied, raising an eyebrow while he ran his fingers over the side of his mouth.

Nicky chuckled and the tension in the air lifted a little. "So whenever I'm ready…?"

"Yeah," Jonas said, trying to sound relaxed, and nodded. "It would be easier if you just told me what you wanted. No need to be shy; if you can think of it, I've probably done it at one time."

He saw Nicky tense up again, and then the young man seemed to regain his self-confidence. "Nothing exotic. I just want to be fucked, from behind, hard and fast."

"Okay," Jonas agreed, thinking that for that, Nicky could have his assistant pluck a guy off the street. He had no idea why he would ask someone to come from London to Paris for just an ordinary fuck. Jonas didn't want to jinx things, though. He had learned a long time ago not to question a client's motives. Usually there was no way he could figure them out anyway. Maybe it was just that this guy was used to getting only the best, just like his champagne.

He watched Nicky move to the bed, unceremoniously kneeling at the side of it and pulling his jogging pants down.

"Condoms and lube are in the drawer," Nicky whispered, his voice a little hoarse. He waited patiently while Jonas took off his suit and placed it carefully over the back of one of the chairs.

Jonas tried not to stare at Nicky's nice ass sticking out and at his hand moving between his legs to touch himself. To his own surprise, he was half hard by the time he took the supplies out of the drawer. He admiringly ran his hands over the globes of Nicky's ass, slowly massaging them. He always made a point of making it good for his client, so he leaned over to murmur, "Do you want me to rim you?"

"No," Nicky was quick to answer, "just...."

"Okay," Jonas cut him off, knowing what Nicky meant. He moved his hands down Nicky's long, lean back and continued prepping him, slowly trying to get him to relax enough to allow himself to be breached. This took time and Nicky was not very patient, telling Jonas to get on with it.

"I don't want to hurt you, Nicky," Jonas said softly, trying to add a second finger to the first. He heard Nicky's pained breathing and moved his other hand around Nicky's hips to touch his cock. Nicky was barely hard, so Jonas started working on two fronts, trying to get the young man aroused enough to relax and vice versa. Anything not directly aimed at Nicky's groin was met with disapproval so Jonas used every trick in the book. Luckily he'd never had any trouble getting it up himself, because the sheer mechanical quality of this encounter was enough to turn any man limp.

"Just take me," Nicky pleaded after a while.

Jonas cocked his head and sighed. Almost automatically he fisted his semi-hard erection to life and rolled on a condom, applying ample lube. As soon as he lined it up with Nicky's entrance, the young man pushed back and reached behind himself to pull Jonas closer.

"Now stop wasting time and fuck me. Hard and fast."

Clearly a man used to dishing out orders, Jonas thought. "You'll need some time to adjust," Jonas suggested.

"That's for pansies. Now fuck me like a man. Or are you a pansy too?"

Jonas pulled back and plunged in again.

"Fuck yeah, that's it," Nicky grunted.

Jonas knew it must have hurt and hoped Nicky wouldn't bleed as he continued the onslaught, urged on by the young man. He could tell Nicky was trying to hide the pain clearly visible in the way he held his body and hoped that he simply got off on it and that it wouldn't last very long. The knuckles of Nicky's hands were white as he held on to the bedding, and then Jonas saw him push one hand underneath himself.

"Don't stop now! Harder! Please!"

That last word was drawn out and Jonas felt Nicky slightly pull away from him, so he stopped thrusting. He couldn't be sure, but he thought Nicky had come, although there were very few indications. Nicky had stopped urging him on, and when Jonas let his hand caress Nicky's back, Nicky pulled away again, this time pushing himself to his feet and pulling up his jogging pants. Jonas let himself drop to the floor. He leaned against the side of the bed as he watched Nicky walk a bit unsteadily toward what appeared to be a bathroom.

Jonas rolled off the condom and didn't bother tying it in a knot since he hadn't come. He simply discarded it in a small basket that was next to the bed and got up to pull his boxer shorts on again. He wasn't sure if he should wait here and give Nicky some privacy, or if he should just knock on the door and ask if he could freshen up a bit before returning to his hotel, but his train of thought was halted when he heard a thump and then a loud curse. Before he could stop himself, he had pushed the door open and walked inside the bathroom.

Nicky was sitting on the closed toilet lid smoking a cigarette. His long hair looked messy and he was shivering. The only light inside the bathroom was what reflected off the mirror from the other room.

"You okay?" Jonas asked as he turned around to wash his hands. Just as he noticed the broken glass in the basin, he saw Nicky wipe the hair out of his eyes, leaving a dark smear across his face. "What the...." Jonas patted the wall for the light switch and flicked it on, illuminating the room with light that was way too bright. There was blood on Nicky's face, arms, and chest. Jonas tried to stay calm. "What did you do?"

Nicky shrugged and looked at Jonas with narrowed eyes as Jonas took hold of his wrists and examined them.

"Watch it," Nicky said, looking annoyed as he pulled loose the hand that held the cigarette. He took another drag and blew the smoke away from both of them.

"Did you cut yourself?" Jonas asked. He grabbed a wash cloth and wetted it. "Boy, you really like to hurt, don't you?" he asked, more to himself than to Nicky.

"It was an accident, okay!" Nicky shouted like a child caught doing something he shouldn't have done. "I forgot about the broken glass and it was dark and...."

Jonas started wiping away the smeared blood and couldn't find any large cuts, not even on Nicky's wrists where he thought he'd find the wounds. Instead, there was a relatively small cut on Nicky's palm, still bleeding quite heavily. Jonas took a dry wash cloth and rolled it up. "Here, squeeze that. It'll put pressure on the wound."

Nicky complied, but he was shivering more violently now, and Jonas saw tears running down his cheeks. He hesitated for a moment and then pulled the young man up and into his arms. "Let's get you to bed, warm you up a bit, hey?"

"No, no bed." Nicky resisted, shaking his head and wiping his cheek with his uninjured hand.

Jonas took the cigarette stub from him and threw it in the sink, and then he pulled Nicky into the bedroom again.

"No, don't want to lie down, can't sleep anyway," Nicky protested, tensing up in Jonas's arms. "The cupboard. There's a duvet in there."

Jonas let him sit down on the larger couch and opened the doors of the cupboard.

"You can use the bathrobe if you want," Nicky said in a soft voice. "If you're cold too, I mean."

Jonas took Nicky up on the proposal and donned the soft robe that was hanging on a hook inside the door. Then he grabbed the blanket and draped it around Nicky's shoulders before hiking his feet up onto the couch and tucking them safely under the warm duvet.

"Better?"

Nicky was not shivering so badly now. He shrugged, but then a smile appeared on the young man's face and he looked fifteen again, innocent and shy. Jonas was intrigued by how Nicky was trying to hide behind this persona he'd created for himself but succeeding less and less as time passed. Despite the disastrous first impression, Jonas found himself curiously attracted to the young man.

"Thank you," Nicky whispered and cleared his throat. "Don't think this was part of your job description."

Jonas chuckled. "Well, you'd be surprised." He bit the inside of his lip. "Pretty much anything you can think of, I've experienced at one point or another. Having a client try to kill himself after sex with me isn't good for my reputation, though, let alone my ego."

Nicky sighed. "I didn't try to kill myself." There was annoyance in his words but not as much as Jonas was expecting.

Jonas reached for Nicky's injured hand and opened it, slowly removing the bloodied cloth. "Would be pretty stupid to try to kill yourself by cutting your palm." He pushed a wide leather band higher up his own left wrist. "It's much better to cut yourself there."

Nicky looked up from Jonas's scarred wrist into the older man's gray-blue eyes, not hiding his shock.

"I was sixteen and had just come out to my parents. No need to explain to you they were not impressed."

Nicky smiled compassionately. "I never came out to my parents. They still think it's because I'm 'artistic' and 'talented' and think this is the way I need to act because otherwise I won't be taken seriously as a world famous fashion designer." The sheer sarcasm in his voice wasn't lost on Jonas. "They'd probably go ballistic if they found out that their precious son likes to take it up the arse."

"There's a difference between liking that and what you made me do to you, though, isn't there?"

Nicky shrugged.

"I bet you won't be able to sit on a hard surface for a few days." Jonas knew he was trying to draw Nicky out of his cave, out of his safe place, but what did he have to lose?

"I like being sore like that," Nicky eventually answered after a pregnant pause.

"Sore like that is amazing if you've been fucked, slowly and thoroughly, for hours. Not after a three minute pounding." Jonas paused too, waiting for the words to sink in. "You know you can ask for anything you want. This is your time, you're paying for this." Again silence. "Seriously, if you can think of it, I've probably done it."

Nicky smiled, a hint of mischief in his face, and Jonas felt a surge of excitement hit him. He tried to hide it, not wanting to frighten Nicky and make him crawl into his shell again. The young man didn't speak, though, so Jonas continued. "Want me to make some suggestions?" Nicky didn't answer. "Just nod yes or no."

Nicky nodded. Yes.

"Do you want to be tied up?"

Nicky shook his head. No.

"Spanked?"

No.

"Want me to call Tanna in and ask her to join us?"

Nicky raised an eyebrow and then gave Jonas a mock indignant look and frantically shook his head. No way!

Jonas chuckled, enjoying this game of questions immensely. He wondered what else he could suggest to the young man. Nicky seemed surprisingly vanilla, not interested in the more exotic games.

"You want to be gently stroked with an ice cube."

Nicky shivered theatrically and pulled the duvet closer around himself, smiling nevertheless. No.

"You want a hand job? I have very talented hands."

Nicky hesitated, but then: No.

"Blow job? I have a rather renowned mouth too, you know. I used to have a client who wanted nothing more than to fill my mouth with whipped cream and then let me blow him."

Nicky laughed out loud and Jonas's heart jumped. But again: No.

"You want to be made love to, not fucked. Slowly, lovingly and you want to feel like there's no one else in the world but you and your lover."

Nicky's face turned serious, but he was looking straight at Jonas. "You can't do that. You can't pretend to be my lover. You can't make me feel loved."

Jonas wasn't put off. There was a reason why he was still making a better living at what he did than he could have ever done with a real job. "Want to bet? What have you got to lose? Really?"

Nicky looked skeptical and didn't reply. With Nicky lying on the couch and Jonas sitting next to it on his knees, Jonas's hand was slowly making its way into the bundle of blankets toward Nicky's feet. He reached them and slowly stroked across the toes and the bridge of the foot, expecting Nicky to pull away any moment. He didn't, though, and Jonas started wondering if it was his imagination or if Nicky was moving into the touch. Jonas enjoyed the feeling of the warm, smooth skin. He explored the bones of Nicky's ankle, the nice muscle of the calf. He moved his hand up to the knee, making Nicky jerk when he tickled the hollow behind it. All this time they were looking at each other, Jonas's face soft and accepting, Nicky's teasing and teased.

Nicky bit his lower lip when Jonas's hand moved even higher and his thighs parted, inviting Jonas to proceed. Jonas was almost completely stretched out now so he scooted a little closer, never losing contact with Nicky's leg. He slowly stroked the softest skin on the inside of Nicky's thigh and used his other hand to pull the duvet away from Nicky's chest, admiring the well developed muscles, nicely trained but still consistent with his lean physique. He couldn't resist running his fingers over the large, dark nipples and felt Nicky react.

Jonas wanted to say something, tell Nicky how beautiful he was, but was afraid of breaking the spell. He didn't want to hear Nicky put himself down again because it would defeat the purpose of making him feel loved. So he didn't say anything, didn't tell the young man that his presence was making him hard, couldn't tell him that he truly wanted a man for the first time in years. Instead he leaned in closer, nuzzling Nicky gently. To Jonas's surprise, Nicky turned his way, and Jonas felt his soft lips against his temple.

Jonas's left hand was still near Nicky's hip, touching the smooth, hot skin. He encountered the curly pubic hair and purposely avoided moving closer. He used his other hand to wipe the hair away from Nicky's face and then softly kissed him on the lips. To his considerable surprise, Nicky took over, deepening the kiss and moving a hand to the back of Jonas's neck. Nicky tilted his hips and his rock hard cock nudged Jonas's hand. As he started stroking it, Nicky broke the kiss.

"Please stop," Nicky whimpered. "You're going to make me come like a school boy if you don't."

Jonas looked away from Nicky when he realized he was blushing and sat back on his heels.

"Can you fuck me again already?" Nicky asked, not in the least bit embarrassed about his question. "I mean, I know older guys need more time in between and—" Jonas stopped him from saying more by kissing him again. He'd been happy he wasn't wearing a pair of his tighter boxer shorts for some time now and didn't need to look to reassure himself.

"How do you want to do this?" he murmured against Nicky's mouth.

For a moment, Nicky seemed to lose his new-found confidence. "I don't know. How do we do this? In bed?"

Jonas chuckled. "Let's never go there again." He kissed Nicky quickly. "Stay here." He got up and retrieved supplies from the bedside table, took off the bathrobe and his boxers, and then pulled Nicky to his feet and sat down in the middle of the couch. Jonas wasn't the type of man to be embarrassed about his nakedness, but Nicky staring at his erection while standing there with the duvet wrapped around himself did make him a little self-conscious.

"Can I…?"

Jonas cocked his head and spread his knees, making space for Nicky to move closer. A blowjob was a rare treat in his profession, and he was definitely not denying himself the pleasure. Nicky was hungry and certainly not a novice at this. Jonas held Nicky's hair back so he could enjoy the view. Seeing his cock disappear into Nicky's mouth was a delicious sight, but he didn't want to come this way. It just wouldn't do. A soft tug at Nicky's hair was enough of a hint for the young man to stop.

As Nicky looked up at Jonas, his eyes dark with lust, he let the cock pop out of his mouth. "Fuck, Mr. Hunter, you've got quite a tasty log there."

Jonas chuckled at the undignified term, but he didn't want to lose momentum. "Come here," he said, gesturing with his finger. "Straddle me." He hadn't touched Nicky's cock yet. "You're not so bad yourself."

"Flattery will get you everywhere," Nicky teased.

"I just want you to ride me," Jonas replied, and then he realized he was in no position to issue demands.

"Oh, you do?" Nicky asked, defusing the situation.

"Yeah," Jonas said, their bodies now close together. "I think it would be good for you too. You'll be in charge, do exactly what feels good."

He saw Nicky think about it. "Talk me through it."

"I'll need to prep you," Jonas said, happy that Nicky was still eager.

"I'll be okay, I'm pretty relaxed now." Nicky pulled the duvet around the two of them as he settled down on Jonas's thighs. "Nice and warm like this."

"You like that little bit of pain, don't you?" Jonas asked, almost rhetorically.

"Yeah, but I'm in charge, right? So allow me." Nicky ripped open the condom packet with his teeth and rolled the latex onto Jonas's cock, and then he added the lube, making Jonas inhale sharply as he spread the gel.

"You know what you're doing, don't you?"

Nicky smile was cocky. "Of course I do."

The young designer pushed up and reached between his legs to lift his tackle out of the way, giving Jonas a view of how he was impaling himself while Jonas steadied his latex-covered cock. Little by little, he felt Nicky's tightness sink around him and watched the young man's face for any signs of discomfort. To his surprise, all he saw was ecstasy.

When Jonas was totally inside Nicky, the young man slowly relaxed. "Fuck, I can't believe how well we fit together."

Jonas smiled and pulled Nicky closer, trapping the young man's cock between their bellies. They started kissing, slowly and sensually, and Nicky started rocking his hips back and forth. Jonas couldn't help stroking the long, lean back and kissing down Nicky's neck toward his chest and those enticing dark nipples. Nicky reacted to having them licked, just like Jonas had anticipated, and sped up his movements as he started riding Jonas in earnest. The duvet was forgotten as it fell around Nicky's back, and Jonas guided the young man's moves by resting his hands on his hips.

"Oh fuck, this feels so good. Never... before—" Nicky was breathing heavily and was barely coherent. The young man's cock was so hard it barely bounced despite his rigorous movements. It was leaking copiously, painting wet streaks along the olive skin of his stomach. Jonas was trying all his tricks to last longer than his lover, but he couldn't tear his eyes away from the incredible vision in front of him.

"Look at me," Jonas asked. "I want to see your eyes when you come."

"Can't... close! Oh fuck, I'm gonna... come!" Nicky sank down hard, tilting his hips as he did, and Jonas felt the hot seed splatter between their bellies. Nicky kept riding up and down erratically, and the friction, together with the ecstasy on Nicky's face, were enough to make Jonas's groin contract as well. He came with Nicky in his arms.

Their breathing and heartbeats slowly steadied enough so they could start kissing once more, lazily this time, and Jonas pulled the duvet around them again.

"You're still inside of me," Nicky mumbled against Jonas's mouth.

"I know. You feel good."

"I do?" Nicky asked, shy again now.

"Yes, you do."

"We'll have to move eventually."

Jonas moaned in disappointment.

Nicky leaned back, retrieving the washcloth that had been used to bandage his hand and wiped their stomachs with it. As Nicky moved around, Jonas slipped out of him and got rid of the condom, tying it in a knot and folding it into the towel.

"Want to get some sleep now?" Jonas asked.

"You know, I think I could. Will you stay until morning?"

"Sure," Jonas answered. He didn't usually sleep over if he was only paid for the evening, but right now he was unable to deny Nicky anything.

"Can we just sleep here on the couch? You're right; I don't like that bed either."

Jonas snuggled Nicky closer, spooning with the duvet around the two of them.

Next thing he knew, Jonas was waking up still smelling Nicky's hair. He felt Nicky's hands on his body and the young man's ass push against his morning erection.

"No matter how great that feels, I need to go to work," Nicky said, clear regret in his voice.

"Can I take a quick shower?"

"Be my guest. There's another shower in the next room."

When Jonas stepped out from under the hot spray, Nicky was standing in front of the mirror, applying make-up and looking like a highwayman. "Jonas? Can I call you again some time?"

"Yes, you can. In fact, I'd like it if you did."

Despite the fact Nicky was in full working gear, he smiled that warm smile Jonas had discovered behind the façade.

AFTER putting on his suit again, Jonas walked downstairs with a spring in his step. Tanna, dressed to the nines, met him at the bottom of the stairs. "Your fee is transferred, Mr. Hunter, and I've taken the liberty of calling a car to take you to your hotel and then the airport."

"Thank you, Tanna," he answered.

"Could you please pencil Nicky in for London fashion week? But I'm sure we'll be calling you before that as well. If that is okay with you, of course."

Jonas didn't need to think about it. He'd seen behind the façade and hoped to be allowed that privilege again soon. He smiled at the gorgeous young woman. "Consider it a date, Miss Taylor."

CHAPTER 2

JONAS was uncharacteristically nervous when he walked into Nicky's Paris fashion studio. Not because he would meet the young, eccentric designer again, but because he wasn't here for Nicky. He was here with one of his other clients, a well-preserved fifty-something communications mogul named Christopher Price. The man had inherited a newspaper from his father and had turned it into a global media conglomerate with publications all over the world. Deciding to branch into television, Chris had just bought a commercial television station in England and had asked Jonas to accompany him to Paris for a little celebration. Although Jonas was well aware of Chris's tastes, he was surprised to be taken along for a shopping spree to his favorite designer. Most men of a certain age, when asked what designer could make them a suit, would go conservative and say Armani. Not Christopher, though. He'd always had that touch of eccentricity and frankly, plenty of money to indulge it. No, Chris wanted a Bryant, and although Jonas wasn't sure why exactly, he was apparently going to find out.

Nicky had kept them waiting in a small room adjacent to the studio. Jonas noticed it had the same uncomfortable chairs on spindly thin legs as the downstairs waiting room at Nicky's house. They looked like antiques and were probably meant to impress, but they only annoyed their occupants when they were kept waiting.

Several of Nicky's minions had entered, bringing fashion magazines and then, already some thirty minutes after their arrival, two glasses of champagne. Sometime after that a young man walked in carrying some sketches. Jonas recognized him as Laurent, the young man so sternly told off by Nicky the last time Jonas had met him.

"Monsieur Price," he bowed, greeting Chris respectfully and speaking his name with a French accent that seemed much heavier than the one Jonas had been treated to a few weeks ago. "Monsieur Bryant will be with you shortly, but I am sure he would like you to choose a style before he arrives, so you may save time."

"His time or ours?" Chris replied, smiling. He didn't even glance at the sketches. Jonas had known him long enough to tell that although his face and voice betrayed nothing, Chris was not amused. In fact, Jonas had seen the man fire one of his most trusted employees with exactly that same smile. Jonas also knew he had plans that involved the young designer or at least his studio, otherwise they would have left already; Chris simply wasn't the type of man to be kept waiting. He knew the media man liked the build-up, though, the anticipation of what was going to happen as much as the event itself. This didn't mean their time waiting had to be spent in boredom. Jonas was good at entertaining his patrons outside of the bedroom as well as in it, so he engaged Chris in small talk, letting Chris tell him about one of the editors of his New York magazine whom he'd promoted after the man had turned him down. Although Chris seemed relaxed, exchanging touches with Jonas that on the surface seemed casual, but that he would never bestow on a stranger, Jonas could tell his client's patience was stretching thin.

Chris had just asked one of the young men rushing around where the restrooms were when Tanna walked in. Just like last time, she was the epitome of calm and grace. She stretched out her hand.

"Mr. Price, Mr. Hunter, I am very sorry to keep you waiting, but Mr. Bryant is a very busy man, as I am aware you are too. Why don't I show you to the dressing rooms so you can try on the ordered suits and we can fit Mr. Hunter for his?"

Jonas looked at Tanna and then at Chris with some surprise in his face. Was Chris going to buy him a designer suit? He'd had suits with designer labels before. Armani, Paul Smith, Dries Van Noten, but never one made especially for him, and to get one by Nicky's hand was an added bonus. He was strangely turned on by the idea as they were led into the studio. From the corner of his eye, Jonas saw Nicky, in full peacock regalia, bent over one of the long, wide tables full of cloth and half-finished clothing. They walked toward the back where one wall was separated from the rest of the studio by off-white sheets draped over a curtain rail. Despite the seemingly bland color and fabric, Jonas understood it for what it was; the backdrop was meant to ensure the clothes shone above the surroundings. They were taken behind the curtains, and Chris was helped out of his clothes and into his new suit by nimble and clearly skilled hands.

Stepping out of the dressing rooms again, Jonas admired the charcoal grey trousers and jacket that truly looked like they were sculpted to Chris's tall, lean frame. Jonas's appreciative look was rewarded with a gesture to come closer. Chris put his hand on the back of Jonas's neck and pulled him into a kiss. It wasn't lost on Jonas that the minions looked away but Tanna didn't. Her gaze wasn't intrusive, but she was clearly not embarrassed by it either. Jonas was quite used to being put on display and barely blushed, letting his hand wander around Chris's waist to rest on the small of his back.

"Nice fabric, excellent cut," he said.

"Your turn now," Chris nodded as he stepped back. "Take your clothes off, so they can fit you with the test cut and Bryant can weave his magic. I bet he'll make you look brilliant in no time." Chris moved closer to Jonas again and lowered his voice, just enough to give a semblance of privacy. "Not to mention, those beautiful fingers of his all over your body will make me hard as a rock and that's just how I like it."

Jonas took off his jacket and started unbuttoning the pants he was wearing. He took his time, knowing how much Chris liked a good show. It didn't bother him that Tanna was there along with the two young male dressers. Jonas had nothing to be embarrassed about. All his life he'd taken good care of his body, and even now that he was in his forties, it still showed. Even the girl sitting at the far table, clearly trying to keep her mind on what Nicky was telling her and failing miserably, didn't prevent Jonas from doing what he had been asked.

However, once he had stripped down to his briefs and was being helped into a suit cut from muslin and held together by coarse thread and pins, he did worry about Nicky. He'd only been with the young man once and hoped he would get another chance, but Nicky hadn't called him yet and now he had probably squandered his chances all together. Most clients wanted to forget about what Jonas did for a living, wanted to feel that they were the only one. Chris wasn't as picky. His needs were different, and Jonas had no illusions that he was the only one getting paid by Chris to render his kind of services. Nicky was the needy type of client, though, and Jonas didn't think he would enjoy having it blatantly pushed in his face.

"Isabelle! Viens ici!" Nicky shouted at the young girl who had been sitting by his side. He left the table, making his way toward the dressing room, pacing quickly and closely followed by the young woman, who looked more than mildly intimidated. Jonas tried to look him in the eye, but Nicky wouldn't let him; instead he whirled around him at an astounding pace. "Regarde-moi!" he instructed Isabelle as he started to adjust pins along Jonas's body.

She was frantically making notes on her notepad, guided by Nicky's fast-spoken French. Although that language was one of many that Jonas had a working knowledge of, he barely understood more than a few words of what the young man was saying. He eventually decided that what he heard was mostly jargon, so he tried to relax. It wasn't easy. Despite his professional demeanor, Nicky's hands were all over him, stroking his sides, his back, his chest, grazing his nipples as Nicky smoothed out the cloth before fitting the seams. If Jonas hadn't known any better, he would have thought Nicky was trying to arouse him, but Nicky's apparent disinterest in him showed the contrary.

Jonas was pretty good at controlling his bodily reactions but he felt the blood pooling in his groin anyway. He inhaled deeply, trying not to let his imagination run away with him. He wanted to do all sorts of things to the young man who had his hands all over him, wanted to pin him to the wall and fuck him into oblivion, but despite

Chris's open-mindedness, he knew he had to keep his hands to himself. Chris was his client here and lusting after another guy in his presence was just bad for business. He gazed over Nicky's shoulder and saw Chris shift in his seat. The teasing smile meant they were doing a good job turning Chris on, but Jonas was happy that Nicky was standing between them because if Nicky didn't stop touching him soon, no pair of perfectly cut trousers was going to hide the evidence of his arousal.

Nicky moved into his field of view, and for a moment Jonas saw something change in the designer's eyes. For a moment it was Nicky again, who only wanted to feel loved. In that moment, he dropped his façade.

"Let's move over here for a moment," Nicky suggested, taking Jonas by the arm and pulling him into the dressing room, partially away from Chris's eyes. Then a lot more quietly, "We'll have to adjust the cut on these trousers at another fitting. Unless, of course, you intend to walk around with a flaming erection all the time." Nicky smiled broadly, and then the mask was back. "We're done, Mr. Hunter, you can take that off."

Jonas stepped out of the muslin garments as the designer walked away, careful to avoid the scratchy pins and delicate seams. He had barely discarded the trousers when Chris joined him in the dressing room, pulling the drapes shut behind him. Jonas felt a strong hand flat on his belly and the warm body of the slightly taller man behind him.

"Now I have you where I want you." Chris didn't even bother to whisper as he moved his hand down. "And apparently how I want you as well."

Jonas braced himself against the wall and pushed his shoulders back against Chris's chest. "Well, bring it on."

To Jonas's considerable surprise, by the time he was back at his hotel room there was a message from Nicky on his voice mail. Was Jonas interested in coming to his house if he was free?

Jonas took a quick shower and arrived less than an hour later, expecting pretty much the same routine as his first visit. To his surprise, it wasn't one of Nicky's minions who opened the door; it was Tanna herself. She was dressed more casually than that morning, heels less high, hair pulled up less tightly, but she still looked flawless and almost… innocent.

"Mr. Hunter, we're glad to have you here on such short notice."

She was smiling and speaking softly, stepping aside to let Jonas in. Jonas wasn't entirely sure if he felt at ease. He still had no idea what Tanna's function was in Nicky's life, while Jonas had the distinct feeling that she knew exactly what was going on between him and Nicky. Not that it was much of a secret, but her use of "we" instead of "Nicky" made him slightly suspicious.

"Nicky is waiting for you in his rooms. Would you like me to take you up there or can you find your own way?"

Jonas looked at her and paused for a moment. Then he nodded. "I know the way."

She winked at him and then turned around to retreat to one of the side rooms.

Jonas took a deep breath and walked up the staircase two steps at a time. He knocked on the door, but there was no answer and he wasn't sure if he should enter, so he waited. He knocked again, a little harder this time. Tanna had told him to go right up and that Nicky was in his room, and now he didn't answer. Jonas decided to be bold and opened the door slowly. The room was still fairly dark, but not completely. The small table lamp he'd lit last time was illuminating one corner of the room.

As soon as he poked his head inside, he felt strong hands grab him by the jacket and yank him through, the door closing with a loud bang. Before he could react, he was pushed against the wall and thoroughly kissed by strong but soft lips surrounded by equally soft facial hair that tickled. For a moment he tasted salmon and something peppery, possibly spinach. At least Nicky had eaten this time.

"You fucking bastard," Nicky groaned when they came up for air. "You're a fucking bastard for fucking my client in my dressing rooms."

Jonas could tell Nicky was angry with him, but it didn't stop the young man from almost ripping Jonas's clothes off. This wasn't an easy task, since Nicky didn't stop rubbing his obvious erection against Jonas's groin so Jonas could tell he wasn't just mad, he was horny too.

"Why did you bring him?" Nicky asked in between kisses.

"I didn't. He brought me," Jonas answered, helping Nicky out of his T-shirt.

Their bodies collided when Nicky lowered his arms again. "Why?"

Jonas chuckled. "I'm discreet, Nicky. I don't talk about my clients."

Nicky stepped back, indignation in his face. "You were having sex with him in my dressing room!"

"Technically it was our dressing room in your studio!"

"But you knew I'd hear every moan, every breath, every move you made!"

Jonas couldn't help being amused by Nicky's attitude. "I'm sorry about that…. What can I say? He got what he likes most, and I have a nice suit designed by you."

"Oh, flattery will get you everywhere."

They kissed again passionately and panted when they came up for air.

"He's my client too and likes sex with an audience. I aim to please," Jonas admitted, while he was trying to get Nicky more naked. "Besides, I didn't fuck him. He fucked me, which was quite welcome after you made me so horny."

Nicky stopped kissing and moved away, his eyes never leaving Jonas's as he got supplies from the bedside table. It was then that Jonas noticed that the rather opulent-looking Rococo bed had been replaced by a modern one, and that made him smile, remembering Nicky's bad memories of the old bed.

They were both naked now, and there was just enough light in the room for Jonas to see that any trace of make-up was gone from Nicky's face. He felt stared-at though, as Nicky prowled around him like a leopard ready for the kill. He expected Nicky to launch at him again any time and was grateful he was still close to the wall. To his surprise, Nicky sank to his knees in front of him and took Jonas's cock in his mouth, licking it, worshipping it with his tongue. Jonas groaned at the contact. He'd been hard since he'd heard Nicky's voice on his voicemail and had resisted jacking off in the shower. Fuck, where was his professional detachment now? Nicky clearly enjoyed what he was doing to him, and Jonas needed all his stamina not to come down the young man's throat. Just as he thought he could no longer hold back, Nicky stopped. He ripped open a condom, rolled it onto Jonas's erection and raised himself. The bottle of lube in his hand, he drizzled it abundantly over the condom before wrapping his arms around Jonas's neck and kissing him again.

"Now fuck me until we both see stars," Nicky commanded, pulling Jonas around until it was Nicky's back that was against the wall.

"I need to prep you," Jonas murmured against Nicky's mouth. "I'm not hurting you again."

"I liked still being able to feel you two days later," Nicky said coyly. Seeing the disapproval on Jonas's face, he added, "I prepped myself after I called you. I knew I wouldn't be able to wait once you got here."

"I would have loved to have seen that." Jonas smiled.

"Next time," Nicky whispered as he lifted one of his long legs, and Jonas hooked it over his arm. Pushing the young man against the wall with his chest, he lined up his cock and thrust inside in one long, slow push.

"Fuck yeah, that's it, Jonas," Nicky urged him on. "You feel so fucking good. Did Chris feel this good inside you?"

A little startled by Nicky's question, Jonas didn't move right away, telling himself it was because he wanted to give Nicky the time to adjust. "I don't talk about my clients with other clients," he said, realizing how cold it sounded. However, that was his policy. Discretion was a large part of his success.

Nicky urged him to move by fucking himself on Jonas's cock, and Jonas complied as it dawned on him that Nicky wasn't taking being called a client personally.

"You're one hell of a moaner, though. What does it take for you to moan like that?" Nicky asked unashamedly.

"All for show," Jonas admitted. "Chris likes it when he knows people can hear us. He likes to see their faces when we're all done and we walk outside."

Jonas felt Nicky's entire weight on his shoulders as the young man wrapped his other leg around Jonas's hips. He shifted his hands so he could cup Nicky's ass, directing their movements. It also gave Nicky more power. Despite the fact it was only their second time together, they soon found the perfect rhythm and, judging from Nicky's moans, Jonas was hitting all the right spots.

"Fuck, I'm so close," Nicky almost shouted as he sped up his movements, riding Jonas in earnest. "So close!"

"Can't do it," Jonas had to admit. Nicky was his height and, despite his slender build, quite heavy to support. They both stopped moving. "Don't want to stop; don't want to feel myself slipping out of you just yet."

Nicky's eyes lit up. "Good, because coming isn't half as good if I can't come around your cock." He became shy again all of a sudden. "Can you walk us to the bed?"

Jonas cocked his head as he thought about it and then nodded. He adjusted his grip on Nicky's ass and turned around, unsteadily walking the few paces toward the bed where he slowly lowered Nicky. He was amazed that they were still connected and let his hands run over Nicky's sweaty body while they kissed languidly. Jonas had never been a big fan of kissing.

His other clients rarely indulged in it, but with Nicky he didn't seem to be able to stop as he slowly started pushing into Nicky's tight heat again.

The young man moaned his appreciation, and Jonas directed his movements to those sounds, thrusting in more quickly and slowly pulling almost completely out every time. He could tell Nicky was zoning out when the young man's frantic hands stopped searching for more skin to touch and instead moved between their bodies. Jonas had no problem keeping Nicky from touching himself.

"Jo… oh fuck… gonna… need to come… so badly," Nicky murmured incoherently. Jonas thrust in three, four times in quick succession until Nicky wailed and came violently, splattering thick white strands of come between their bellies. Jonas barely registered it as the spasms wracking Nicky's body were enough to send him over as well.

Jonas continued moving in and out of Nicky's body, albeit at a more leisurely pace, while they both caught their breath. Nicky's arms were still around Jonas's neck, and as their heart rates slowed, they started kissing again, exploring each other's mouths.

"Mmm, that was the best fuck I've had in quite a while," Nicky confessed. "How long before we can do it again?"

Jonas chuckled. "I don't know about me, but you're still hard," he offered coyly.

Nicky blushed. "Are you asking me to top?"

"Only if you want to," Jonas conceded.

"And you like to bottom? You like to take it up the arse?"

"So do you, I believe," Jonas teased. He smiled and slowly pulled out of Nicky, holding on to the condom. He tied it in a knot and discarded it into the basket next to the bed before he got up.

"Where are you going?" Nicky asked. Jonas looked back and saw Nicky stretched out on his back, one arm over his head, his legs open and inviting, and his still semi-hard cock resting on his belly.

"I think that sticky boy there could do with being wiped a bit."

"Look in the bedside table," Nicky suggested. "There's more than condoms and lube in there."

"Baby wipes?" Jonas raised an eyebrow and then looked at Nicky.

"I hate getting up after I wank," Nicky replied matter-of-factly. "Now come here." He held open his arms, and Jonas settled into them after wiping off Nicky's belly.

Jonas wasn't used to the level of intimacy Nicky was offering. Despite his apprehension he couldn't resist pulling the lean and smooth body closer, enjoying the smell and feel of the soft skin.

"So you like to bottom, hey?" Nicky asked curiously.

"Why is that such a big deal?" Jonas replied. "In my line of work it pays to be versatile."

"Which do you prefer?"

Jonas thought Nicky looked like a schoolboy, eager to learn. "No preference. It depends on the partner. I wouldn't dream of topping Chris."

"Would you dream of bottoming for me?" Nicky was smiling.

"I would, but only if you wanted to."

His eyes narrowing, Nicky seemed to think about it. "Will you fuck me again later?"

Jonas sighed. "I can't stay, I'm sorry."

"Another client?"

Jonas nodded, a little hesitantly. He didn't want to leave, really, but he had another engagement that had been planned weeks in advance and he didn't like to cancel. "I didn't plan you, Nicky," Jonas eventually said, and then he realized his words could be interpreted in many ways, all of them correct.

"Yeah, right," Nicky spat out, getting up from the bed and walking toward the bathroom.

Remembering what happened last time, Jonas followed him to the ever-dark room. He was just in time to see Nicky light a cigarette and notice the façade was back. Jonas wasn't surprised when Nicky didn't offer him one as well.

"Go! Leave!" He waved his hand at Jonas, telling him to get out.

Jonas knew which battles he could win and which he couldn't. This one was lost before it started, so after one more look at Nicky, he turned around and walked out.

DRESSED in his suit once more he descended the stairs, not entirely surprised to find Tanna walking toward him.

"You don't have to wait up for me, you know," Jonas said, trying to make her feel at ease.

"It's okay," she replied softly. She placed a hand on Jonas's arm. "Nicky was a lot nicer to live with after you left last time. You have no idea what that means to us."

"Well, I'm not sure it helped this time. I think he's a little upset with me."

"Because you need to leave?" She looked despondent.

"Tanna, I'm sorry."

She kissed him on the cheek. "You probably don't want to hear this, but he really likes you. He's got a strange way of showing it, I know, but...." She inhaled deeply. "Very few people get to see the real Nicky, and I'm one of them. He's told me he lets his guard down around you too, so you know what I mean. There's a beautiful person behind that façade, Jonas."

Jonas nodded. Of course he knew that. He just wished he got more chances to see it. "You have my number."

As he walked out into the dark night, Jonas realized that he too had his own façade.

HAPTER 3

AS HE had predicted, Jonas didn't hear from Nicky for quite some time. Even Tanna didn't contact him to confirm the fact she'd asked him to pencil in London Fashion Week. Maybe she meant next London Fashion Week? Jonas was surprised to find he had been looking forward to seeing the eccentric designer again. He was too old to fool himself, though. To Nicky he was just a hired hand, someone on his private payroll, and it wasn't as if Jonas sat at home waiting for Nicky to call.

Life went on and Jonas saw his regular clients. He arrived back in London from Los Angeles one Monday morning and was pleasantly surprised to find a voice mail message from Tanna telling him he was invited to Nicky's catwalk show that afternoon at the Natural History Museum. Flying first class at his client's expense had its advantages, and Jonas had slept well during his direct flight, so he went home for a quick shower and a change of clothes before making his way across London.

At the museum, he was picked out of the endless queue by Tanna herself.

"I can't tell you how happy I am you're here," she admitted as she ushered him through the crowds toward the backstage area. "He's nervous as hell and snapping at everyone who crosses his path."

Jonas raised an eyebrow, but didn't answer. What could he say? That this was how Nicky always behaved anyway? Tanna knew that.

"I know," she sighed. "I should have called you earlier and confirmed our appointment, but he didn't want me to. For weeks, every time I mentioned you, he'd bite my head off. Of course now he's changed his mind."

Jonas smiled, silently happy that Nicky seemed to struggle with their relationship as well. Or maybe he was just reading things into it. Maybe Nicky was simply the spoiled brat he so loved to show to the outside world, used to having his employees at his beck and call.

EVEN behind the scenes, Jonas was surprised at the amount of people running around. He'd suspected there would be order and calm, much like how the models looked when they stepped out on the runway. Instead, there was utter chaos. Tanna was her usual self, exuding her comforting presence, but as they walked through the rows of clothes, make-up and hair stations with ungodly tall, anorexic models running around in near-hysterics, Jonas was happy he was quite a calm person himself. Somehow over all the noise, he heard Nicky's voice, although he couldn't see him anywhere.

"Sybilla, if you burn a hole in one of my frocks with that cigarette, you'll never work in fashion again."

Jonas smiled at Tanna, who was throwing him an apologetic look. "Nerves are on edge. Every show is a war zone. There is nothing more important for a fashion designer than a runway show, and he does about thirty of these every year. Paris, Milan, New York, Tokyo, London. Spring and fall collections, Couture, and Prêt-a-Porter. Men and women's lines. It never stops."

"It's a good thing he has you, Tanna." Jonas bowed to her slightly.

She smiled back shyly. "And yet, I'm not enough for him. Obviously."

Jonas didn't have time to respond. A male make-up artist with two painted girls in tow accosted Tanna.

"He doesn't like the make-up," the man stated arrogantly.

"I'm not surprised," Tanna answered curtly. "He asked for porcelain dolls. These girls look like Paris street walkers. Think transparent skin, long eyelashes and tiny, red mouths. You are the make-up designer; you should have done your research. Now get to work!"

Jonas had to admit he was impressed with Tanna's strong voice and determined words, and in that moment, he understood her strength.

Her face softened when she looked at Jonas again. "The next hour will be chaos here. After that, we'll have to move out quickly, but there are other people to do the clean up."

"Can I see Nicky now?" Jonas asked her.

She shook her head. "Believe me, you don't want to be anywhere near him now. He'll snap your head off for no reason." She looked a little ashamed of admitting it. "Afterward, he'll be tired and needy. He'll really need you then. Look, if you'd like to watch the show, I can get you a seat at the side. If not—"

"I'll stay in here," he interrupted her. "Out of sight. Until the dust settles."

"Well, if you change your mind, right through there," she pointed at a curtain, "you can sneak out into the show hall. Now I'm sorry, but I have some fires to put out."

Jonas nodded and watched her walk away. He sauntered between the chairs and make-up tables, picked up a flute of champagne along the way, and moved in the general direction of where he'd heard Nicky's voice earlier. It didn't take Jonas long to spot him.

Tensions were rising as the stage manager announced that the show was about to begin and that everyone should quiet down.

Nicky was moving between the models as they lined up, adjusting how the shirts and gowns were draped on them. His touches were professional, yet intimate. He bared their shoulders, glued garments to their breasts, told them to show more skin or less, and patted them on their non-existent asses as he sent them on stage. He wasn't too shy to lift skirts or peer down trousers to see why they didn't flow as he'd intended, and the models let him, their facial expressions vacant as they prepared to step out on the catwalk.

At the end of the show, as all the models lined up to go back on stage one last time, Jonas walked through the curtain and found a place to stand near the back. He saw them all march onto the stage, spreading out across the space. As the applause broke out, Nicky stepped through them and walked out front. He had shed the white shirt he'd been wearing and was now just clad in tight leather trousers, his bare chest only covered by thin braces and several trinkets dangling from leather strips. His hair was long and messy and, with minimal make-up, he looked entirely sexy. Jonas saw him look out at the crowd, nodding to some of the people in the front rows and applauding his models as he accepted the standing ovation. As he turned around, he put his arms around two of the girls and wiggled his ass at the crowd.

Returning to the backstage area was another thing, though, and it took Jonas a good fifteen minutes to make his way through all the people leaving the hall. It gave him a chance to hear them talking about what they'd seen, and he was secretly proud to hear words like "highly original," "quite imaginative," "innovative," and other gushing terms.

Once back behind the curtain, Jonas walked into the still-chaotic room, but this time the atmosphere was one of elation, not nervous tension. He didn't see Nicky anywhere but barely had the time to find himself another glass of champagne when Tanna took it from him.

"Come with me. I promise you'll get another glass in a minute."

She guided him out of the room and down the corridor, where she opened a door to the outside and a waiting limo. "Have fun. I'll see you boys tomorrow!"

It was no surprise that Nicky was inside. He looked tired but calm, laid back in the corner of the seat.

"Mmm, you're a sight for sore eyes," he moaned, holding out his arms. As Jonas settled next to him, Nicky's hands felt up his back and over his chest. "You can't believe how sick I am of boobs."

Jonas laughed.

"What? You know I like a nice hard body." Nicky almost pouted.

"Yes, I do," Jonas answered coyly. "It's just funny, because those models don't have boobs either. Or any other curves for that matter. Now if you were a Beverly Hills plastic surgeon, you'd have reason to complain."

Nicky pushed his body closer to Jonas's and kissed him passionately. "Tell me," he demanded.

Jonas shrugged and shook his head. "I've already said too much, and you know I don't—"

"Talk about your other clients, yeah, I know." Nicky let his hand move down to Jonas's groin and he squeezed the bulge. "But you're growing hard just thinking about him, and that's where you came from before you arrived back here, right?"

Jonas sighed. He never talked about his other clients; it just wasn't done in his line of work.

"Come on, Jonas," Nicky teased seductively, his hands down Jonas's trousers by now. "I was practically in the room when you let one of your clients fuck you."

"You *were* in the room, Nicky."

"So what's the difference? Tell me about your plastic surgeon! Change his name for all I care, just tell me about him. Is he gorgeous? Tall, hard-muscled body? Come on, Jonas."

Nicky was a hard man to resist. Jonas was turned on by him physically; the fact he was holding his erection in his hand and rubbing it in the back of a limousine was just part of it. He also possessed everything that Jonas found attractive: narrow hips, broader shoulders, a nicely maintained set of muscles without looking like he worked out every day, and to top it all, a nearly hairless chest. Nicky still wasn't wearing a shirt and those dark nipples of his were just begging to be licked. As soon as Jonas made a move toward them, Nicky brushed him away.

"Later," he demanded, extracting his hand from Jonas's pants. "Now, tell me about Mr. Hotshot Surgeon."

Jonas sighed. Part of him felt blackmailed, another part of him enjoyed being able to share his life with someone. He'd never done anything like that, but then he'd never found anyone who was willing to listen. "Let's call him Clay," he eventually said. And that wasn't even that far off.

They had arrived at what was apparently Nicky's London apartment. The limo stopped in the underground car park near the elevator, and Jonas tucked himself neatly into his trousers again before exiting. As soon as the elevator doors closed, Nicky's mouth was all over Jonas's, but his kisses were lazy, more aimed at creating intimacy than eliciting passion. Jonas went along with it, enjoying the change from Mr. Fast-Paced Lifestyle and I-have-exactly-fifteen-minutes-for-sex-tonight. Now why was he thinking about that, when he had this delicious creature in his arms?

To Jonas's surprise, the loft was dark and devoid of people. Jonas had somehow expected the minions or at least some inconspicuous staff, but there was no one. Nicky was flicking on indirect lighting as they moved along the walls, kissing languidly. It gave the place a slightly eerie feel, but Jonas had become used to seeing the young man in half-light, and as soon as his eyes got used to the dark, it suited him just fine.

Nicky was responding quite vocally to the way Jonas let his tongue and mouth stray to Nicky's chin, neck, collarbones, and then over those chocolate nipples. They tasted every bit as sweet as they looked and peaked nicely when Jonas sucked on them.

"Fuck, you're making me hard," Nicky moaned as Jonas continued paying attention to his nipples. His hands were in Jonas's hair, more as an anchor than to lead the older man's attentions, and Jonas moved his mouth higher again, kissing and nibbling until he was standing face to face with Nicky. "You're not the only one who prefers a hard male body over a soft one, you know."

"Do you ever sleep with women?" Nicky asked, his facial expression full of childlike innocence again.

"Rarely," Jonas stated determinedly.

"But you do sometimes?"

Jonas squared his jaw. "You're too curious for your own good."

Nicky wrapped his arms around Jonas's neck and, aided by the fact they were still pressed against the wall, hitched his legs around the older man's narrow hips. "Yes, I am." He kissed him quickly. "I want to know everything! Now take me to the couch. Please?"

Jonas, not easily caught off guard, grabbed Nicky's buttocks and carried him down two steps toward a sitting area with a large, plush sofa, where he sat down with Nicky in his lap. Nicky looked down at him sheepishly. "So, the women you sleep with?"

Jonas sighed. He really didn't want to tell Nicky about that. "I thought you wanted to know about Clay?"

"Oh yes, your Beverly Hills plastic surgeon who doesn't like boobies!"

Jonas rolled his eyes. "How old are you?"

Nicky giggled. "As old as I want to be!" His face was softer, though, and he got up from where he was sitting. "Why don't you get naked while I get us something to eat?"

Jonas watched him leave. Nicky eating without being told to? He shook his head, quietly happy, and started taking off his clothes, hanging his jacket over a chair and carefully folding his pants. He was still unbuttoning his shirt when Nicky walked back into the semi-dark sitting room, carrying a large plate. He was naked as the day he was born, and Jonas could see the shadows play over his slender body.

"Mmm, delicious," Jonas moaned as Nicky brushed passed him, showing him the contents of the plate.

"Yes," Nicky acknowledged seductively. "And so is the fish."

Nicky placed the plate of fish on the table near the couch and walked around Jonas, their bodies somehow always touching. "You're wearing a jock strap?"

"Yes," Jonas admitted. He tried to take his shirt off, but Nicky, leaning against his back, prevented that. "It makes your ass look better when you're wearing a suit."

Nicky slowly lifted Jonas's shirt away from his shoulders and let the older man pull his arms out. He threw it over the chair that held the rest of Jonas's suit and wrapped his arms around Jonas's torso. Jonas felt Nicky's nimble fingers weave through his dusting of chest hair and down to his stomach so he leaned back, savoring the contact of the warm body behind him. He felt Nicky's erection rub against his ass and a vision of being taken by the young man flashed before his eyes.

"Am I turning you on?" Nicky whispered in his ear.

"God, yes," Jonas uttered, quite a bit louder. His eyes were closed, trusting Nicky. He was slightly surprised, then, to be pushed in the direction of the couch and made to sit down.

He opened his eyes, looking up into Nicky's defiant face.

"Tell me the story of your plastic surgeon. Clay, right? Or at least that's what we'll call him." Nicky was tempting him, coaxing him to lower his guard even more. "I promise I won't tell anyone. Besides, you could be making it all up for all I know."

Jonas tried to keep his face neutral. He could do just that, make it all up, if he wanted to. Nicky was clearly in the mood for an erotic story, and he always catered to his client's needs.

"Clay's in his thirties. Buff body, a little more muscled than you and I. Works out almost as incessantly as he works to sculpt the bodies of all those Hollywood stars who need to look good on the red carpet. It was the start of awards season, the busiest time of the year for guys like him." Jonas watched how Nicky straddled his thighs, the plate of raw and smoked fish in his hands. Nicky offered him a strip of smoked salmon.

"Is he tall? Or one of those short, stubby guys?"

Jonas enjoyed the taste of the fish, but eventually swallowed. "Tall, taller than you, and dark too, with short, unruly hair and beautifully bright eyes. Amber almost." He watched Nicky eat, smiling because he was clearly enjoying it. He shared, though, feeding Jonas whatever he ate as well.

"Handsome," Nicky stated more than asked.

Jonas nodded.

"Hung?"

Jonas shrugged. Nicky wasn't exactly hung like a horse. Not that Jonas was complaining, because Nicky had a nicely balanced body and a huge cock would just look out of place, especially for a consummate bottom.

"Or does he have a little one?" Nicky wiggled his little finger and held out another piece of fish, this time raw tuna, for Jonas to eat.

Jonas took his time thinking over his options, pretending to chew really thoroughly.

"Come on, Jonas," Nicky urged seductively. "You know I like big cocks. Please tell me Clay has a big one."

Jonas chuckled. Decision made. "It was quite impressive before he was hard." He paused for effect. "But once he got going it grew even more. Long and thick." He drawled out those last words and seemed to push a lot of buttons where Nicky was concerned.

"Oh fuck," Nicky murmured, placing the plate with what was left of dinner on the side table and rubbing his bulge against Jonas's. "Can I make yours long and thick too? Will you let me suck it?"

Jonas swallowed. In all his years of sleeping with men for professional reasons, he'd never been so turned on by a client. Nicky's neediness combined with his shameless sexuality made him irresistible in Jonas's eyes. "Yeah," was all he managed to utter as he watched Nicky slide down until he was seated between his legs. Seeing Nicky lick his fingers and push them between his buttocks made Jonas scoot down to give him better access. The black jock strap was still covering his growing erection, and Nicky didn't seem to have any intention of releasing it. Instead Jonas felt the probing fingers rubbing over his entrance and the thickness of Nicky's hand pushing against his perineum.

"Tell me, did he fuck you with that big cock?"

"Oh yeah," Jonas said, sounding rather strangled. He could barely believe how much the memories of Clay together with Nicky's teasingly seductive look and ministrations were bringing him closer to coming with each passing moment.

"Tell me, Jonas," Nicky demanded.

Jonas took a few deep breaths, averting his eyes from the far too enticing sight in front of him. "He loves to fuck me again and again with that big cock of his. Sunday's his day off, and we don't even bother getting dressed." Jonas inhaled sharply as he felt Nicky's fingers breach him. "During the week, he doesn't have a lot of time, what with surgery and working out and seeing patients." It was becoming increasingly hard to focus now that Nicky was fucking him with his fingers. "So I'm just there for a quick fuck in the morning. And maybe at night before he goes to bed." Jonas spread his legs wider, by now almost completely on his back. Nicky was rubbing over his prostate, and he was achingly hard, feeling every seam in the silky cup still covering his now impressive bulge. Near the top seam, a wet patch was visible, and just as Jonas dared to look down, he saw Nicky licking it, making it even wetter. "Yeah, suck me, please?"

Nicky looked up. "Tell me what he does to you on Sunday?"

Jonas waited a moment and then started pushing down on Nicky's fingers. "We fuck five, six times. He's got pretty good stamina and recuperates quickly." They both knew the heat was rising between them, and Jonas needed all his willpower to not come.

"Where does he fuck you?" Nicky asked eagerly and then continued blowing Jonas through the silky fabric of the jock strap.

"Everywhere you can think of. Everywhere but on the bed."

"Tell me!" Nicky demanded as he moved from between Jonas's legs to sitting next to them. He slowly lowered the strap and Jonas's cock sprung free.

"In the shower, then at the kitchen counter. Later on in the dining room, over the back of the sofa. Fuck, Nicky, you're making me come! In the afternoon in the gym, and then in the Jacuzzi. I don't—"

Jonas didn't need to look to know that Nicky's mouth had enveloped his cock. With his right hand, Nicky was fucking him, pistoning his fingers in and out of his ass; with his left hand he was holding the base of his shaft and massaging his balls. Jonas didn't know what to do with his own hands, but he didn't dare touch Nicky, afraid he would hold the young man's head down while his groin thrust uncontrollably into the hot mouth and he really didn't want to make Nicky gag.

"Close!" Jonas cried out as Nicky's fingers pushed hard against that most sensitive spot inside of him at the same time as he swallowed around his cock. Jonas literally saw stars and felt his hips push upwards. For a moment he felt he couldn't breathe; then his body fell back into the couch and he opened his eyes. Nicky was staring up at him cheekily, still slowly licking Jonas's cock, lapping up the remainder of his release. Jonas twitched involuntarily from time to time, the head of his cock so sensitive now.

"Geez, Nicky, come here," Jonas beckoned, his breathing only just calming down. Nicky was still rock hard. "Let me take care of you?" Nicky straddled him again, snuggling into Jonas's arms. "Unless you prefer to fuck me? You know you can."

Nicky scrunched his face. "Can we just cuddle?" he asked, some embarrassment clearly visible in his expression.

"Sure," Jonas said, pulling him closer, "but don't you want to come too? It was pretty amazing what you did to me just now. I don't usually get treats like that." Nicky was pushing his body close to Jonas's, clearly eager for friction, so why was he so afraid to ask for it?

"I thought you liked being fucked?" Nicky asked innocently.

"I do, but it's for both of our pleasure. This was just for me."

"Oh," Nicky said, putting his head on Jonas's shoulder.

Jonas was waiting for something more but when Nicky remained silent, he kissed his hair. "Will you let me make it good for you too?"

"So Clay fucks you five times on Sunday, and then you get on a plane and fly back to London?"

Jonas chuckled and softly started stroking Nicky's still rock hard erection. "Well, there's always a parting gift." He kissed Nicky and felt the young man's repressed hunger. Nicky moaned into his mouth as he sped up the movements of his hand. "After he's made me come all five times, because he is an attentive lover after all, he lets me fuck him, on the bed. He wails and screams and begs for more, until he comes like a race horse. Hard and copious!" A few more hard strokes and Nicky was convulsing in his arms, thick white strands of come splattering between their bellies. Nicky held onto him as if he was drowning, and Jonas felt him shiver. "You're cold." He picked Nicky up and carried him to the bedroom, lowering his limp body onto the bed.

"Don't leave me," Nicky almost whimpered when Jonas got up again.

"Just getting the baby wipes," Jonas chuckled.

"I'm sorry," Nicky apologized, composing himself. "I... I'm usually not this needy."

"Oh, I think you are," Jonas rebutted, wiping his own stomach and Nicky's. "You've only just learned to ask for what you want."

Nicky looked up at him with large eyes.

"Tanna usually makes sure you have what you need, doesn't she?

Nicky nodded reluctantly.

"Well, I'm here for as long as you need me, even if that means all week."

"Will you tell me more stories?" Nicky asked, his self-confidence clearly returning.

"You're a little pervert, aren't you?" Jonas asked, tongue firmly planted in cheek.

"I thought you'd have caught on by now," Nicky answered, equally cheekily.

"Hey, I'm an old guy, give me some credit!" Jonas quipped.

"Well, come here, old guy, and keep me warm!"

CHAPTER 4

THE next morning Jonas woke up alone, the apartment eerily quiet. He got up and walked to the bathroom to relieve his more-than-full bladder and was just starting to see clearly when he noticed a pink Post-It note stuck to the wall opposite the toilet. He leaned in closer.

> When you're up call extension 11
> Dress casual and then call me,
> Love
> xxx
> Tanna
> P.S. There's a phone behind you.

After finishing his pee, he turned around and found the phone exactly where Tanna said it would be and dialed 11.

"Yes, Mr. Hunter. Can we bring you breakfast?" a fresh young voice said.

Jonas was a little startled at the personal approach. "Yes, please do," he answered, common courtesy taking over.

Fifteen minutes later he exited the bathroom from a nice, scalding hot shower, still drying his hair. In the middle of the sitting room was a trolley filled with every conceivable breakfast item from bacon and eggs, toast, sausages, tomato and baked beans to pancakes and waffles with maple syrup, fresh fruit, cereal, assorted jams, and orange juice, coffee, tea, and milk. Jonas raised his eyebrows thinking of all the food that would go to waste. At least four people could eat quite a hearty breakfast from what was packed, quite neatly he noticed, onto the trolley.

Since last night's meal of raw fish had been rather good for his waistline, Jonas decided to indulge himself this morning, putting a bit of everything on his plate and getting comfortable on the plush sofa with the three morning papers that came with the breakfast. He smiled when the images of the night before played out in his memory again and realized that for the first time, Nicky hadn't returned to being a morose, pouting brat after their lovemaking. Maybe he was feeling more relaxed about it, maybe he was just tired. Or was it that Nicky knew he'd better treat Jonas right since they were going to spend the rest of the week together?

Jonas wondered what the day had in store for him. He knew London Fashion Week was a high point for any designer, but he had no idea whether that meant Nicky would be pretty much busy all day long or whether he'd need company at some point. He knew Nicky didn't talk to the press much and had even turned down a personal call from Anna Wintour asking for an interview for Vogue. Jonas picked up the phone and dialed Tanna's number.

"Hello stranger," she answered in mock seductive tones. "Had a good night's sleep?"

"Quite nice, thank you," Jonas answered.

"Breakfast to your liking?"

Jonas couldn't help noticing her voice was subdued, as if she couldn't talk out loud just then. "Want me to call you back later?" he replied.

"No, that's okay," Tanna answered. "I just can't make too much noise because Nicky is fitting a young member of the Royal family with a gown for her first big ball and he's making quite a spectacle of himself." She giggled quietly. "Luckily the Princess is very beguiled by him. She's giggling and blushing. I swear he's making her feel that if she played her cards right, he'd be coming home with her tonight. Naïveté is such a sweet thing to behold."

Jonas was surprised to hear about another side of Nicky he hadn't seen. "I wish I was there to see that," he admitted to Tanna.

"I have something better for you." She giggled again. "Be ready by eleven, smart casual will do. I'll send a car to pick you up in front of the building."

Tanna didn't even wait for him to answer. Jonas heard her click the line shut and continued his breakfast, taking his time while flicking through the morning's news.

AT ELEVEN sharp he was downstairs in an off-white suit with a black turtleneck underneath. It wasn't a designer suit, but he figured that if Nicky didn't like it, he would make sure he got another one. He just hoped that his definition of casual was the same as Nicky's.

Despite the heavy traffic, the car took less than fifteen minutes to get to where they needed to be. The driver double-parked and stepped out to open the door for Jonas. Before he had the chance to look around to see where he needed to go, he spotted Laurent looking excited and eager. Jonas doubted it was because he was supposed to meet him here on the curb of one of London's most fashionable streets; there had to be more to his flurrying so Jonas waited patiently as the young man guided him into the small office of a modeling agency.

Jonas was glad for the relative quiet of the tiny cupboard of an office space, especially when Tanna came to greet him. She looked radiant as always, her hair tied back rather more artsy than usual, but still with an immaculately fitted dress and perfect makeup.

"I need your expertise," she stated enigmatically instead of greeting him, before placing a careful kiss on his cheek and wiping off the trace of lipstick it left.

"Expertise?" Jonas asked, eyebrow raised. He wanted to add that he only had one field of expertise and it didn't seem called for here, but he decided to keep his mouth shut.

"Nicky wants you to pick his models for him."

Jonas gave her a stunned look and then realized she must be joking. "I don't know the first thing about runway models," he told her.

"Well, he doesn't want 'runway models'," she replied. "He wants real men, who know how to walk. Don't worry; I'll do the first cut. I know the shape of the clothes and roughly the sizes we're looking for, and anyone who doesn't measure up gets dropped. Then they'll walk the runway in quick succession, and you can say which of them appeal to you."

"They don't have to appeal to me, Tanna, they have to appeal to Nicky and to the public." Evidently she wasn't joking!

"I know that, Jonas, and so does Nicky, but he says he keeps picking the same guys and wants a fresh look on the catwalk the day after tomorrow." She looked compassionate and a little amused. "He still has the final say. We'll pick more than he needs, and that way he can do the final cut."

Jonas nodded reluctantly and let Tanna wind her arm around his as she led him out into the crowd of young and quite tall men. She whispered something in the ear of a quirky, oriental, androgynous-looking possibly male person, who stepped on top of his chair and shouted, "Everyone inside. Look your best, girls! This is for Nicky's show at the museum!" in a thick South London accent.

Tanna tugged on his arm and dragged Jonas through the wall of male bodies toward the back. It became a bit easier to move once they all spilled out into the hall at the rear of the office, but Jonas was still amazed at the number of boys and men that had shown up. Luckily, Tanna seemed to know her way around, and he found himself following her like a puppy, afraid he'd lose her and never find her again. Jonas wasn't a short man but he hadn't felt this vertically challenged since Clay had taken him backstage at a Lakers basketball game.

"Watch and learn," the short, skinny, androgynous man told him. "Our Tanna's a pro at this and such a charm to work with!" He was carrying a stack of numbered cards and gave half of them to Jonas. "Hand one of these to every guy that gets a 'yes' from her."

Jonas nodded as the men lined up around them without being told. Obviously the models all knew what was going to happen even if Jonas didn't have a clue.

Tanna looked at him and winked; then she returned her gaze to the men and pointed her finger at each of them, stating either "yes" or "no." Jonas was amazed at the speed at which she made decisions; the two of them had great difficulty keeping up with her as she made her way around the room. "No, no, no, yes, no, no, yes, yes, no, no, no, no, no, no, no, yes, no, no, no, yes, yes, yes...."

Slowly the men who were not selected filed out. A smaller group carrying numbers stayed behind and began to get their résumés and head- and-body shots ready.

Tanna sighed and called Laurent, who came scurrying in carrying water bottles. She grabbed one and took a long drink. "Now that's over, it's your turn," she told Jonas, and then she turned to the short man. "Tau, dear, can you collect the 'folios and get copies to Nicky? Then let the boys strut their stuff?"

She wound her arm around Jonas's again and pulled him closer.

"I don't know what to do here, Tanna. What do I know about choosing models? I don't even know what they'll be wearing."

Tanna gave him a motherly look. "Nicky didn't ask you to do this because of your expertise, Jonas, but because of your taste in men. Listen, all the guys I chose will do just fine. It's up to you to find the ones with sex appeal, with charisma, and that doesn't take any sort of experience."

Jonas sighed. "So how do we do this?"

At that moment, Tau, the pint-sized organizer of the casting call, came in with a stack of portfolios with numbers attached to them and two clipboards, which he handed to Tanna and Jonas. He placed his hands on the lapels of Jonas's jacket and stroked down, a gesture that felt quite intimate coming from a stranger, but Jonas resisted the temptation to step back. The man's effeminate voice and posture made Jonas cringe when he said, "Do pick our Nicky some nice butch boys and let the losers down gently, Mr. Hunter. And you can send the hurt ones my way, because we all know what Nicky will do with the winners." He winked at Jonas and then left.

Tanna must have read his face because she leaned closer and whispered, "Tau loves to promote Nicky's image of being insatiable where men are concerned, and I do the same for the women. Of course you know the truth."

Jonas was a little unsure what that truth was.

Tanna straightened her back and instantly became the ray of sunshine she usually was. "Now let's look at how these guys walk."

About an hour later, after letting all the guys walk the makeshift runway numerous times and going through the portfolios with Tanna, they had narrowed it down to thirty-five models. To Jonas some of them had obvious sex appeal; others he really didn't care about. Because most of them had that vacant, disinterested look about them, none of them actually "did it" for him. He liked his men with a little more spunk.

Tanna held out the winners' portfolios. "Take these, walk through that door over there, up the stairs and show them to Nicky. Oh, and take these five as well. I think they're the runner-ups. I'm sure he'll veto at least one of those we chose."

"So why did we choose him then?" he asked Tanna, who had "tease" written all over her face.

"You'll see…." She winked and walked out in the direction of the main office.

Jonas sighed and turned toward the door. Then it suddenly struck him. Had Nicky been watching them all this time? He wanted to burst into the room upstairs but then realized it might save both of them some embarrassment if he just stayed in his role. Nicky was still his client and was paying him handsomely for their week together. He should knock on the door in case Nicky wasn't alone.

After a curt, "Yes?" he entered and realized he was actually happy to see Nicky sitting at what looked like a sound mixing board, large designs strewn all around him. He looked up at him, his brow furrowed with worry. "So. All done?"

Jonas nodded. "I didn't know you were up here."

Nicky held out his hand to take the bunch of folders from Jonas, and to the older man's considerable surprise, he dropped them on the floor next to his chair.

"Aren't you going to look through them?" Jonas asked.

Nicky shrugged. "Are you happy with your choices?"

"I'm no expert," Jonas admitted. He looked at Nicky and saw how tired he was. Would it be too forward of him to suggest that he take Nicky home for some rest? Come to think of it, it was way past noon and they hadn't eaten yet. After the copious breakfast, Jonas wasn't surprised he wasn't really hungry, but knowing that Nicky didn't eat much even when pressed gave him the perfect excuse to butt in. "Listen, I don't know what your plans are for today, but you look like you could use a nice quiet lunch and maybe a little nap? We haven't exactly been sleeping much these past few days...."

"I can't," Nicky answered curtly. "I need to pick the models, get word to my choreographer in what order I want them, then tonight I have to approve the set and the lighting for the show, and I have to make an appearance at a party."

Jonas stepped closer to the sound board, careful not to tread on any of the designs, and peered through the large window that looked down on the room below. There wasn't much he could say, except that it didn't look like he was needed any more today. Of course he couldn't just walk out; it was Nicky's place to dismiss him.

Suddenly he felt the young man's arms snake under his and around his chest. "I must admit your idea sounds nice," Nicky whispered in his ear.

Jonas covered Nicky's hands with his and leaned into the touch. "We can compromise. We'll look through the portfolios really quickly and you tell Tau who you want, then I'll take you to this nice bistro a friend of mine owns for some delicious food. It'll be quiet there now, since lunch hour is more than over, and...."

"I only have one objection to your choice of models," Nicky cut in.

Jonas smiled. Nicky hadn't looked at the folders he'd brought in, which meant he'd been watching them. "Tanna said you would."

"Don't you think Josh is a little past his prime? He rarely does runway shows any more, wants to make it as an actor." The mockery in Nicky's tone when he said that last phrase wasn't lost on Jonas.

"He fits the bill, Nicky. You wanted butch guys, not sissies. He walks the walk and talks the talk."

"Yeah, and fucks the arse and then tells everyone who wants to hear that he's straight!"

So Nicky had a history with one of the models. Jonas felt Nicky pull away. "Go on, you can tell me," Jonas urged him gently.

"There's nothing to tell," Nicky replied, the disdain in his face not quite hiding the anger. Nicky bent down to gather up the drawings and designs, and Jonas helped him. They didn't talk, since Jonas wanted to give Nicky the chance to gather his thoughts and maybe banish some of his own demons.

They made their way downstairs to the now abandoned hall and toward the front office. There were several assistants on the phone booking models, and Nicky shouted out for Tau. Jonas was amused to see how effortlessly Nicky slipped into his Fashion Designer persona, who demanded personal service and right now!

Tau looked like he was about to kiss the ground Nicky walked on, and Nicky treated him like that was exactly what he should be doing. He rummaged through the folders, took out Josh's, and then threw the rest over Tau's desk. "Book those," he ordered. He rummaged through the five extra ones and picked out one which he also threw at the talent agent. "And this one."

"No back-ups?" Tau asked him.

Nicky gave him a condescending look. "If they're not interested in working, then they shouldn't have auditioned."

"They may have found other shows to do." Jonas was surprised Tau was still smiling.

"There's only one show that's important and that's mine. No back-ups," Nicky replied calmly before walking outside to an empty curb. "And where the bloody hell is my car?"

JONAS was a patient man. After all, his job didn't just consist of offering sexual favors; there was usually some waiting involved as well. He'd been used as an ornament, a bodyguard, a companion, and even though he knew which one was his favorite, he got paid for his time, not for the nature of his services. Handsomely paid, he reminded himself every time the waiting began to drag him down.

Waiting for Nicky was usually interesting, though, especially when he was allowed to wait in the same room. Although Nicky's theatrics and tantrums would have driven Jonas up the wall before he got to know him better, now he was fascinated by them and endured them patiently because he'd seen the other side of Nicky. He'd seen the needy man who wanted to be loved, the boy-like creature who couldn't decide whether he wanted to kiss first or give a blow job or just lie there stroking a bit of skin and loved to be told what to do. Jonas imagined there was a charismatic god-like being behind that façade, full of sexual energy and totally in command of his own pleasure. Someday, he hoped he'd be allowed to peel off enough layers to see that person emerge.

They'd missed out on lunch because Nicky wanted the stage settings out of the way, fearing he couldn't relax until that was settled. So while Nicky was dealing with that, Jonas arranged for one of his favorite restaurants to cater to Nicky's house. They had a nice dinner of scallops and salmon with pasta in Nicky's sitting room. Nicky fell asleep mid-conversation, so Jonas carried him to the bedroom and crawled into bed next to him when Nicky mumbled "Don't leave me."

When he woke up several hours later Nicky was gone.

There was another Post-It note over the toilet, though.

> Gone to party.
>
> Will be boring but need to make an appearance.
>
> Pick me up in the car sometime after eleven?
>
> NB

Jonas looked at his watch and realized he'd better get a move on.

When Jonas arrived at the party and found Nicky, he was tipsy. Jonas didn't think he was downright drunk, but he was sort of giggly and clingy.

"Oh! My stalker was there too," Nicky suddenly said in the middle of his hello.

"Your stalker?"

"Josh the super-duper stud," Nicky elaborated as they made their way to the car. "Still thinks he can get inside my trousers. And he probably could have if you hadn't picked me up. Look! Feel!" Nicky took Jonas's hand and pressed it to his groin. Despite his inebriated state, he was rock hard inside his wide harem trousers. "You gotta fuck me tonight, Jonas, or I'll explode!"

Jonas chuckled. "Of course I will."

After arriving at Nicky's London apartment, Jonas had a hard time peeling Nicky off of him all the way upstairs. Not that he wanted to, because he was definitely getting quite turned on, but he wanted to calm Nicky down a bit so he would enjoy their lovemaking more. He thought about getting Nicky off before they started, but he didn't know what else other than alcohol Nicky had consumed at the party, so he wasn't entirely sure if that would do the job. Once inside the privacy of the apartment, Jonas decided to try talking to him, hoping the alcohol would make him less inhibited.

"So tell me why you can't shake Josh," Jonas asked as he was led into the bathroom by a swaying Nicky, helping to hold him upright while he peed.

"He's got the best cock and knows how to use it," Nicky answered, clearly a little surprised by his own admission. "I met him when I was still in design school. He was modeling even then and told me point-blank that he wanted to fuck me because I was going to have the best graduation show of the year and he wanted to be my star model. You know, a little like the girl who gets to wear the wedding dress at the end of the show, only for guys they don't have the wedding dress, of course."

Jonas chuckled.

"So I said he would be my favorite model and we fucked a few times, but every time, he said he was straight, that he didn't fuck guys. But Jonas, he was so good at it! We did everything! He would blow me, and believe me, I can tell when a guy likes to have a cock in his mouth or when he just does it because I pay him. And he would rim me even if I didn't ask him for it, and he was really good at it too! Oh God, and to be fucked by that perfect cock of his…."

Then suddenly Nicky seemed to realize that he was saying all this to Jonas. "Oh. I'm sorry, I didn't mean to say you didn't—" He pushed his body against Jonas's. "I like it when you fuck me too. You're much better to me than Josh was. At least you don't tell me girls fuck better than I do."

Okay, this conversation wasn't going the way Jonas had hoped it would. He could tell it was bringing Nicky down and that was no good. "You fuck much better than any girl, Nicky, trust me."

"I do?" Nicky asked coyly, his face lighting up.

"Yes, you do," Jonas answered, completely truthfully. He pulled Nicky even closer and whispered in his ear. "Will you prep yourself for me and let me watch?"

Nicky moaned. "Oh fuck yeah, would you? Watch me, I mean?"

"Of course I would," Jonas answered seductively, feeling his groin stir at the thought. He was surprised to see how eager Nicky was and how much it seemed to turn him on as he watched the young man shed his intricate harem costume and take some lube out of the cupboard. Nicky was still surprisingly hard and didn't waste any time. He covered two of his fingers with the clear gel and pushed them against his puckered opening as he bent forward, holding onto the washbasin for support. Jonas sat down on the closed toilet seat to get a better view, which made Nicky smile.

"You have the best view in the house, mister," Nicky drawled, looking over his shoulder.

"I have the only view in the house," Jonas corrected. "And I wouldn't miss it for the world." He unzipped his trousers and took his semi-hard erection out.

Nicky's eyes trailed down. "That looks good," he said seductively, licking his lips.

Jonas teasingly pulled his erection away from Nicky. "Uh, uh, later! When that hole of yours is nice and slippery and ready to take this mighty weapon, then you'll get some!"

Nicky giggled. "I want some now."

"Well, you can't." Jonas continued the teasing. "Not until you show me that you're ready."

In truth, Jonas wanted to prolong the enticing sight in front of him as long as he could. Nicky showing him his nice ass, two fingers slipping in and out of his entrance and bliss all over his face: Jonas thought he could look at that forever. He was quite hard now too, so he only stroked himself a little, just to keep Nicky's eyes on him.

Nicky scissored his fingers, stretching his hole. "See, I can take it, please fuck me now," he pleaded.

"I'll have to gauge if you're telling the truth," Jonas teased, leaning forward and slowly inserting his finger between Nicky's scissored ones.

"Oh fuck, yeah. Oh God yeah!" Nicky cried out.

Jonas felt Nicky shift, and his channel started pulsing around Jonas's finger. Before he could react, Nicky's knees gave out as he came hard and crashed to the floor. Jonas jumped up and knelt down beside him, taking Nicky in his arms, worried that he'd hurt himself. To his surprise, the face that turned toward him was one of sated bliss.

"Fuck, I came too fast! But it sure felt good!"

Jonas helped Nicky up and started wiping the come off his belly and thighs.

"I still want to fuck you... want you to fuck me," Nicky corrected himself, pointing fingers.

"Okay, baby," Jonas shushed him. "But let's do it in a bed this time, before you really hurt yourself."

Jonas led Nicky to the bed and took his own clothes off. By the time he slipped underneath the covers, Nicky was sound asleep.

IT WAS nearly dawn when Jonas woke up, realizing he was being manhandled. Not roughly, mind you, just soft and gently. He knew perfectly well where he was and what the mound underneath the sheet could be, and simply enjoyed waking up to quite a nice blowjob.

After a few moments he slowly lifted the sheets to gaze upon Nicky smiling around his swollen cock. With a pop the young man released the engorged erection and crawled up Jonas's body.

He greeted Jonas with a seductive "Good morning," and then kissed him lazily. "I think I need to apologize for last night."

Jonas shrugged.

"I was drunk and high and probably behaved like a bastard."

Jonas smiled and wondered if he should tease. Maybe not; after all, who was he to judge? "You were sweet, actually. Very horny and then very sleepy, but sweet nevertheless."

Nicky blushed. "You'd think I would know better by now not to mix vodka, Red Bull, and E, but thanks for rescuing me from the claws of the stalker."

Jonas was rather happy Josh's name wasn't mentioned this time and he wanted to keep it that way, so he decided to change the subject. "Before you fell asleep last night you said something about fucking me? And since you're rubbing up to me all needy right now, well, I'm game."

A wicked smile formed on Nicky's face as he raised himself up, letting the sheet fall from his shoulders. He straddled Jonas's thighs and was just as hard as his older lover.

Jonas raised himself up and kissed Nicky. "Let me prepare you?" he asked, murmuring against Nicky's mouth.

"No need," Nicky smiled. He reached behind himself and with some wiggling and a moan, produced a small, shiny black butt plug.

"How long have you been awake?" Jonas asked.

Nicky pretended to think about it and then said, "A while."

"Why didn't you wake me?"

Nicky looked away. "Because I like watching you sleep. It comforts me to have you sleeping next to me. Now I think we need a condom."

Not fazed by the change of subject, Jonas reached to the side table to retrieve the supplies. Nicky looked him in the eyes again as he expertly rolled on the condom and coated the straining member with lube. Jonas, still leaning back on his elbow, watched, mesmerized, as Nicky lowered himself slowly over his erection. Nicky didn't move right away, instead he stroked Jonas's chest as far as he could reach.

"I could get used to this," Nicky suddenly said. "I could get used to waking up with you next to me. You have this way of making me feel so good in the morning."

Jonas smiled at him. "That's what I'm here for."

Nicky slowly started rocking his hips back and forth. "I could forget the whole world outside."

Jonas pushed himself up, wrapping his arms around Nicky and hugging him tightly. "So forget. Nothing else matters right now."

"I wish I could," Nicky said, his breathing becoming a little heavier. "But then I'll come too quickly again. I'm such a twat sometimes; I can't even last long enough to give pleasure to my lover."

Jonas kissed Nicky thoroughly, and Nicky kissed him back with equal fire. Jonas leaned back again. "You set the pace then, learn to control it. When it gets too much, you stop moving and we'll talk, take your mind off it. Then when the fire dies down a bit, you start moving again and so on."

"We don't have all day, Jonas. I…"

"Shush, no real life until just before you think you're going to come!"

Nicky chuckled and started riding Jonas's cock, slowly and leisurely, until he stopped abruptly. "Oh fuck, that was close!"

"Okay, don't move anymore. You were saying?"

Nicky shook his head, unable to think, and grunted with frustration.

"Something about 'we don't have all day'."

"Oh… yeah. I have a rehearsal with the models, and before that I need to check the setup of the runway. Hey, this actually works!"

Jonas laughed out loud.

"Stop vibrating under me!" Nicky said, laughing along as he slowly started to move again.

They started and stopped a few more times until even Jonas thought he was reaching the limits of his self-restraint.

"Fuck! I don't think… I'll be able to hold it… again this time," Nicky moaned, riding the hard cock underneath him.

"Why not?" Jonas asked, his voice strained as well.

"Because I've run out... of things to say... and I really... really... want to come right now."

Jonas, flat on his back, reached for Nicky's leaking cock.

"Don't touch me!" Nicky pleaded desperately, so Jonas simply let it slide back and forth over his hand.

"Oh fuck! Man...."

Nicky's muscles tightened all over his body as he sank down over Jonas's cock two, three more times and then clamped down, his fists grasping at empty space. Jonas reached for Nicky with his free hand, grabbing his wrist for support as a shudder wracked through the young man's frame. His body, too, involuntarily thrust up into the tightness as they came together in a joint orgasm, Jonas filling the condom inside of Nicky's hot, tight body, Nicky shooting his release over Jonas's hand and their bellies.

Nicky sank down over Jonas's chest, completely limp until Jonas moved slightly and aftershocks rippled through them.

"Oh man," Nicky sighed. "I saw fucking stars, man!"

Jonas chuckled, making Nicky shudder again. "That's okay."

"Okay?" Nicky asked lazily. "That's like saying La Maison Bryant makes okay clothes." He looked up to kiss Jonas. "Thank you."

"No, thank *you*," Jonas answered, hugging the young man tightly. They were still connected and very sticky, but Jonas didn't want to move just yet, didn't want to break the connection. Not after the best sex he'd had in years.

HAPTER 5

JONAS slowly closed his cell phone and stared out into the darkness.

It hadn't been his work phone that had vibrated while he lay sleeping close to Nicky. In the company of a client, his work phone was off and his other clients knew that. He'd find a moment to check his voice mail at least once every twenty-four hours, but other than that, he was entirely there for the person who paid for his time, twenty-four/seven if that was what was required of him.

His private cell phone was never off but switched to vibrate-only. Very few people had that number and it was rarely called. It was only for emergencies really. This wasn't an emergency, but still it left Jonas with a hollow feeling in his stomach. Being given an ultimatum made all sorts of warning bells go off in his mind, and it went against everything he believed in.

None of his clients knew about Jonas's private life. He suspected most of them didn't even realize he had one. They made an appointment with him and he showed up, entirely at their beck and call. Jonas prided himself on giving his clients the illusion there was nobody else in his life. They knew what he did for a living, of course, but Jonas dealt in illusions so it paid to be discreet.

He took a deep breath and got up from where he had been sitting on the side of the bath. Careful not to make too much noise, he walked back toward the bedroom and smiled at the sight before him.

Nicky was sprawled on the bed on his back, arms stretched over his head. His long hair swirled over the pillow, eyes closed, mouth slightly open and completely lost to the world.

Jonas let his eyes wander over the long arm, the well-contained tuft of hair under the armpit, the lean side and then let them slide across to the large dark nipples and the immaculately tanned chest. It was sinful how much this man turned him on even as he lay there sleeping. It brought back memories of happier times when he still made the effort to have a complete private life to offset his professional activities. How strange that those memories were happy and sad at the same time. It made him melancholy and that was the last thing he needed, so he sat down on the couch next to the bed and focused on Nicky again. On the one hand, he wanted to lie down on the bed next to him, stroke the young man's satin skin, and lick his nipples until they grew hard. He already knew how the supple body would react, arching into the touch. He knew they'd kiss, and from just that and by running his hand over Nicky's side and stomach, they'd both get hard. And within no time they'd start making love.

But that would mean he'd wake Nicky up, and he didn't want to do that just yet. He wanted to enjoy the sight of him lying there completely oblivious to the eyes drinking in the sight of his beautiful body. Jonas smiled when he noticed the pubic hair crowning the semi-hard cock lying on Nicky's flat belly. The dark thickness of it was in sharp contrast to the near absence of hair on the rest of his body. Jonas had never seen him shave, yet his face always looked like that of a sixteen-year-old, proud of what little facial hair he managed to cultivate on his chin and upper lip. Come to think of it, the rest of his body didn't look much older either. Jonas ran his hand over his own chest in an attempt to satisfy his need to touch the other man's skin and then got up as he knew it was futile.

The bed dipped when he carefully lowered himself next to Nicky's supine figure. Instinctively the young man rolled on his side and ended up almost on his stomach lying against Jonas. Jonas held still, looking at his lover sideways to see if Nicky was awake. He even shifted a little so Nicky slid onto his stomach completely. Nicky continued sleeping. Jonas could feel the warmth of his body, the softness of his silky skin and couldn't resist turning to his side, his head resting on his hand. With the back of his finger, he caressed the rounded shoulder, which stuck out because Nicky had tucked his hands underneath himself as he'd turned in an attempt to cocoon himself. Jonas let his finger wander down over Nicky's shoulder blade toward his spine and heard him mumble to himself. It was warm enough in the room to lie there naked for a while before it started feeling cold to the skin, but Jonas saw goose bumps forming all over Nicky's back and arms. The young man snuggled closer and murmured, "'s cold, Jonas."

Jonas didn't know what made him happier, that Nicky had enough trust in him to not jump at the first touch or that he'd said his name while not being quite awake. The fact that he didn't already have an armful of fashion designer betrayed how far gone in sleep Nicky still was. Jonas carefully moved over Nicky's curled-up form so he could lie down on his other side, his chest against Nicky's back. "Better?" he whispered.

Nicky moaned slightly and instinctively pushed himself closer to the source of heat, nestling himself against Jonas, his ass against Jonas's already excited groin.

Half lying on his side, Jonas couldn't resist wrapping his arm around Nicky and feeling how well they fit together.

"Are you awake?" he whispered. No answer. Nicky's breathing was calm and his body was relaxed despite the earlier movement and despite Jonas's erection nudging his ass cheeks. At first he didn't dare let his hand investigate Nicky's nether regions for signs of arousal, and then he remembered that Nicky's cock hadn't been totally flaccid while he was asleep anyway. Although it went against his principles, the idea of taking Nicky while he wasn't fully conscious was curiously stimulating so he let his hand caress Nicky's side down to the crook of his hip in between his belly and the bed. As Jonas's hand touched Nicky's erection, the young man moaned and pushed down against the hand. Jonas followed, pushing his groin down over Nicky's ass. The movement was almost instinctive. Driven solely by what felt good, Jonas ground his hips down against Nicky's. He made sure he wasn't smothering his lover, keeping his chest resting only lightly against Nicky's back, but nevertheless the movements were directed toward one goal: getting both of them off.

Nicky's quiet moans were a good indication that between the hard shaft pressed into his cleft and the hand against his erection, Jonas was hitting at least a few of the right spots. He kissed the young man's neck and felt him lean into that touch too. Nicky's neck was slightly sweaty, and Jonas licked the salty skin between Nicky's shoulder blades. He sped up his movements, guided by his own growing need for completion and by the sounds Nicky was making. Another hand joined Jonas's underneath Nicky's groin, and Jonas felt the young man stretch his legs so he was flat on his stomach. Nicky was now actively grinding his hips as well, adding to the friction they were generating. Jonas knew he was close, but judging from the increasing volume of the sounds coming from the young man underneath him, so was Nicky.

Suddenly Nicky cried out, "Fuck, yeah! Yes!" and thrust his cock into their joined hands, hot spurts of sticky fluid shooting out over them. The sudden movements and Nicky squeezing his thighs together sent Jonas over as well, coating Nicky's ass cheeks with his release.

Jonas's eyes were still closed after his orgasm when he felt Nicky push him to his side and turn around, wrapping himself around Jonas. His mouth was invaded by the young man's tongue and locked in a searing kiss while aftershocks wracked his body because Nicky was rubbing their combined cocks with his hand.

"So sensitive," Nicky whispered against Jonas's mouth.

Jonas could only nod as he was still trying to catch his breath. He was relieved that Nicky had clearly enjoyed this uninvited little stint and that he'd obviously been well aware of what had happened.

Nicky's hands were caressing him as lethargy overtook him. "I never knew I'd enjoy this so much," Nicky murmured, his eyes still closed.

"Enjoy what?" Jonas asked languidly.

"Sleeping next to my lover, being woken up just because he was horny and wanted my body," Nicky answered. "I could very easily get used to this, Jonas."

Jonas knew he should answer "well, you better not get used to it too much," but he couldn't because his heart leapt when Nicky spoke those words. He wanted to get out, run, but didn't have the will as Nicky snuggled closer.

"Maybe we need to clean up a bit," he suggested half-heartedly, but Nicky didn't budge, his breathing now slow and his body limp in Jonas's arms.

Jonas was wide awake, though.

He couldn't lose his heart, not to a client. What kind of future did they have together? *Oh, he used to pay me for my services, but now I fuck him for free?* Besides, Nicky was a spoiled brat. Maybe he was just on his best behavior when they were together. Maybe he would show his true colors once the novelty wore off. Not to mention the fact that Jonas was almost old enough to be Nicky's father. What could a beautiful, talented, worldly young man like Nicky possibly want with a body for hire past his prime?

Jonas knew what had to be done. London Fashion Week was almost over. Later that day, Nicky would present his men's line, and then the circus would pack up and move back to Paris, leaving Jonas behind. His fee for this week would be enough for him to go on vacation for a few months, preferably somewhere half way around the world. He would simply not answer Nicky's phone calls, or maybe tell him he had other plans when he called to arrange a meeting. He needed to put some distance between himself and the young man now sleeping in his arms before it was too late.

CHAPTER 6

IT HAD taken Jonas some time to fall asleep only to be awakened by whispering.

Nicky was still partially in his arms, but he was moving around.

"Just give me a minute," Nicky said, trying to keep his voice down but obviously slightly annoyed.

"I wouldn't want you to be late, Nicky. You may come across as a spoiled child, but there's one thing they can't accuse you of and that's unprofessional behavior."

Was the other voice Tanna?

Jonas decided to pretend to still be asleep. Tanna had clearly come to wake Nicky up, and he was interested in the extent of their relationship. Obviously it extended right into Nicky's bedroom.

He heard Nicky giggle. "I'm sorry, Tanna, but I didn't get a lot of sleep last night. Apparently I'm irresistible." There was a pause and Jonas needed all his restraint not to open his eyes to see the look on Tanna's face. He heard Nicky speak even more quietly. "He woke me up in the middle of the night to make love to me."

Now Tanna giggled too. "Well, good for you; now get your lazy arse out of bed and get ready!"

Nicky moved away from him and Jonas contemplated "waking up" too. He decided against it. Being alone with Nicky meant they'd have to talk, and he wanted to postpone that for a while, so he rolled onto his stomach and tried to relax. He heard the shower and Nicky's electric toothbrush. The young man was apparently in good spirits as he was humming some song while moving around the apartment. It never ceased to amaze Jonas how quickly Nicky could get ready in the morning, and no longer than twenty minutes after waking up, he had left and the room became quiet again.

THE car to pick him up was waiting at the curb when Jonas walked out of the apartment building. He had taken his time this morning, grateful for the peace and quiet, to make some overdue telephone calls and other arrangements. He'd had a late brunch, not quite as elaborate as before, but then the little pink Post-It note over the toilet had said he could order whatever he wanted from the concierge downstairs, so he had some toast and jam, a few cups of coffee, and some bacon and eggs. Three newspapers and a shower later, he was on his way to Nicky's show in the suit Nicky had designed for him. This was the first time he'd had the occasion to wear it, and he had to admit he could tell it was made to fit him perfectly.

The Natural History Museum was every bit as busy as it had been last time, but even so he spotted the tall and divinely elegant Miss Taylor almost immediately. She kissed him on the cheek. "Well hello, stud," she whispered teasingly, winking at him.

"Hello, Tanna," Jonas answered reservedly.

"Did you sleep well?"

Jonas could tell she was fishing. "I've slept better," he answered, not wanting to show his entire hand right away. Though curious where Tanna might take the conversation, he knew she had work to do backstage. "If you know what Nicky wants me to do, then show me the way so you can go 'put out some fires'."

She laughed. "Nicky's walking on clouds today, but he's got everything under control. The men's show is always more relaxed backstage. Less hair and make-up, a lot less drama. They don't really need me today. Instead, you and I get to be in the audience this afternoon. How about that? Care to join me to watch some delicious bodies in some fabulous clothes?"

Jonas smiled. "Works for me." He held out his arm to Tanna and led her into the crowd. He saw her wave at an acquaintance or possibly a good client and nod to another.

"You know, you've really made a big change in Nicky's life," she told Jonas without changing her facial expression. "He's a lot less highly strung and so much nicer to be around."

"Well, he's enjoying the sex," Jonas offered. "I don't mean to toot my own horn, but from what I gathered, he hasn't had many satisfying bed partners before."

She looked at him with those large blue eyes of hers. "Most men don't tolerate my presence around him all the time. You, on the other hand, don't even blink when I show up in your bedroom in the morning."

"You showed up in my bedroom in the morning?" Jonas asked, trying to sound innocent.

"Oh come on, you may fool him, but there's no way we didn't wake you up this morning," Tanna said with a teasing smile. "Come on, you can tell me. Nicky and I keep no secrets from each other."

"So I gathered," Jonas answered evasively. He wasn't sure what Tanna was trying to accomplish here, but he almost felt as if he was being violated, figuratively speaking. He liked Tanna but still wasn't entirely sure what her position in Nicky's life was. Was she simply his right hand woman? His confidante? Were they like sister and brother or more like husband and wife? Without the jealousy of course, because that was one thing he'd never seen between them. Tanna had always been nothing but encouraging toward their "relationship," so maybe she felt more sisterly toward Nicky. She'd said earlier that Nicky needed taking care of, so maybe that's what she did.

"Miss Taylor! How nice to see you!" A well-preserved lady in her fifties walked over to them and held out her arms toward Tanna.

Tanna bent forward and air-kissed her. "Mrs. Swanson, we missed you at the women's haute couture."

She was one of those old money New York socialites with a nice figure and just the right amount of plastic surgery. "Well, I'll just have to come to the atelier in Paris then, so your better half can fit me with a gown of my own. I'm sure he'll work his magic."

Better half? So it was true that to the outside world Tanna was considered to be his wife?

"Call me whenever you're ready," Tanna answered, "and we'll make you an appointment. Oh, and may I introduce you to Mr. Jonas Hunter?"

Dragged from his disjointed thoughts at the mention of his name, Jonas extended his hand with innate civility.

"Mrs. Gilda Swanson, from the Connecticut Swansons," Tanna continued the introductions. "She is one of Nicky's most loyal clients," Tanna explained. For a moment Jonas wondered how Tanna was going to explain what he was doing here, whether she was going to make up some imaginary occupation, but once the woman knew his name, she clearly wasn't interested any more.

"Well, I must move on, dear. Expect me to ring you!"

Tanna smiled and nodded, and then she coaxed Jonas in the other direction. "Phew, that was a close call."

"It was?" Jonas asked.

"She's a terrible gossip. Not to mention very conservative and filthy rich. She's given Nicky a lot of business, so we tolerate her, but we're very careful around her."

"So you told her you were Nicky's wife?" Jonas fished.

"No, she pretty much figured that out all by herself." Tanna still looked cautious, despite their having moved quite some distance from the woman. Jonas thought she was going to elaborate, but she didn't. So was it all just a ruse to keep the conservative buyers from spending their money elsewhere, or were Tanna and Nicky really closer than Jonas liked to imagine?

They were nearing their seats and made it just in time for the lights to dim in the hall and the show to start. Jonas recognized many of the young men they had chosen the day before and found himself enjoying the rugged but imaginative clothes in browns and blacks. From time to time, he looked around to see who was in the audience. Here and there he recognized a celebrity or a socialite he'd seen on TV, all enthralled by the catwalk show. He felt proud of Nicky and exchanged looks of appreciation with Tanna.

Then suddenly two gorgeous boys walked out in nothing but extremely tight chocolate brown leather hotpants and large angel's wings. Between them was a tall, veiled figure dressed entirely in white; they each held one hand to guide this mock bride. Jonas didn't know much about fashion shows, but he did know it used to be fashionable to end a runway show with a perfect bridal gown. Nicky had told him earlier this wasn't the case with the men's show, though, so this had to be something else.

Jonas watched the angels unwrap the figure, removing layer after layer of organza, slowly revealing white flowing pirate trousers, then something that could only be described as a codpiece, then a tightly laced white corset. Just as it was dawning on the crowd, and on Jonas who it was, he threw off the large hat with the last of the veils and shook his hair free.

Nicky placed one hand on the back of one of the gorgeous angels and kissed him full on the mouth, and then he turned to the other and did the same, before turning to the crowd and bowing. Roaring applause broke out, drowning out the gasps Jonas had heard here and there. Judging from some of the faces, not everyone was impressed, but Nicky had certainly made sure his show would be talked about.

As the standing ovation continued and Nicky thanked his models and his audience, Tanna ushered Jonas out of the hall and toward the back entrance.

"Did you enjoy that?" she asked.

Jonas nodded. "He's very talented, and quite a shocker in some people's eyes, I think."

"Oh, they should be used to it by now. There's a reason why he's the bad boy of fashion, you know," Tanna quipped. "If he had a bigger cock he'd be showing that off too, I'm sure."

"Well, he is a bit of an exhibitionist," Jonas had to admit.

"You have no idea," Tanna laughed. "I don't think he even knows how far he would go. Maybe you could bring it out in him, Jonas," she suggested. Jonas wasn't entirely sure what she meant by that. Did Tanna want Nicky to break out of his public persona and become even more of a bad boy? Or did she want him to explore his own person? Did she want Nicky to show more of the person only certain people got to see and that was so elusive that Jonas didn't always know who he was looking at in any given moment? Maybe Tanna was using a roundabout way to tell Jonas about some of Nicky's fantasies. In any case, it gave Jonas a way to take a step back from the uncomfortable closeness between him and Nicky. Indulging Nicky's fantasies was what he was good at. He could do that.

They had arrived at the back door, and Tanna urged him to step into the limo. With a quick, "Nicky will be right here. I'll go see what's keeping him," Tanna left him alone with the driver, who discreetly stepped back after opening the door for Jonas.

Jonas had only just gotten comfortable in the back seat of the limousine when the door burst open again and Nicky crawled in, clearly in a hurry. He was still wearing the white outfit, complete with laced corset, and didn't even bother to sit down on the seat next to Jonas. Instead he straddled the older man, cupping his head and kissing him hungrily. Jonas felt the hardness of the corset against his chest and hardness of a different kind a little lower.

"I'll have to remember how much doing these shows turns you on," Jonas said as Nicky broke the kiss.

"It doesn't usually, but I had something to look forward to this time," Nicky admitted, placing small kisses along Jonas's jaw line and neck. "I've always wanted to have a hurried fuck in a moving limousine."

"We're not moving yet," Jonas stated the obvious.

Nicky turned around toward his driver. "Take the long way home, Marcus, and please close the partition."

The car pulled from the curb as the darkened partition between the driver's cabin and the back seats zoomed up.

"So what's with the corset?" Jonas asked, a little hesitantly.

Nicky chuckled. "That's another fantasy, but because we simply don't have all the time in the world, I figured we could combine a few." He obviously saw the not-entirely-sure look on Jonas's face. "We can take it off if you prefer."

Jonas shook his head. "It's your dime."

Nicky looked hurt. "Don't say that," he replied blankly.

Jonas realized how harsh it had sounded and he cupped Nicky's buttocks to pull the young man closer toward his own excited groin. "I'm sorry. Tell me what you want." He tried to sound genuine and seductive at the same time.

Nicky studied his eyes for a few moments before deciding it was okay. "I was all worked up before we started," he whispered against Jonas's mouth, just grazing their lips together. "Being laced into the tight corset…." His voice drifted off. "…But you can't hide a raging erection in these trousers, so I had to wank." By now, Jonas's hand was rubbing over Nicky's hard shaft, the soft cotton of the codpiece separating the two. "But I couldn't come. Not until I licked my fingers and pushed them inside of me." Nicky's hands were fumbling with the hidden fastenings of the codpiece. "Fuck, why did I have to make it so complicated?"

Jonas chuckled. "Because it needed to look good too?"

"Screw looking good! I want you buried deep inside me!"

Jonas tried to help, but gave up quickly, since it only seemed to make matters worse. "Just take off your pants."

"Can't," Nicky answered curtly. "It's a one piece, that's why I gave it the flap, so you could fuck me with it on!"

"Not to mention it gave it something special? You want codpieces to come back in style?"

Nicky giggled in frustration. "The idea was good, but they're too hard to handle in a crisis."

Jonas felt Nicky fumble with the zipper on his designer trousers and gasped slightly when Nicky's hand freed his erection, pulling the elastic of his boxers below his sac. Nicky leaned down and licked a bead of precome off the slit. Jonas almost came right there and then but managed to breathe through it as Nicky moved away to sit on the side seat, still trying to undo the codpiece. "Supplies are to your left."

As Jonas was rolling on the condom, Nicky managed to undo the fastenings and he sighed with relief when his purple cock sprang free. When Nicky grabbed the lube and started coating Jonas's latex-clad erection with it, Jonas kissed his forehead. "Let me prep you?"

Nicky shook his head and before Jonas could protest more, Nicky sank down over his thick, pulsing member with a loud groan. Jonas cradled him instantly, holding him still to allow him to adjust. Nicky was incredibly tight and Jonas knew it wouldn't be painless. "You'll hurt yourself this way, darling."

Nicky looked up at Jonas, the tears glistening in his eyes enough proof that he wasn't entirely comfortable.

"Let's take this slower, baby," Jonas tried.

"No," Nicky sighed. "No, you feel so good, Jonas. I wanted this last night, but you didn't come inside me, and then this morning we were running late, and...." He slowly started moving, pushing away the pain of the intrusion, and Jonas eventually felt him relax as they got into a leisurely rhythm. Never missing a beat, Nicky started unbuttoning Jonas's shirt and running his hands over the light dusting of chest hair. Jonas in turn ran his hands over the tight hardness of the corset, feeling his way around the soft ribs of the garment. It gave Nicky a clear waistline and broadened at the top and bottom to give him more hips and make his shoulders look bigger too. Despite Jonas's earlier misconceptions, it didn't make him look more feminine. The chemise that came over the top of the corset looked pirate-like and was devoid of lacy trimmings. Jonas tried to stick his hand inside, in search of Nicky's nipples, but the tightness of the corset halted his progress.

"Later," Nicky whispered as he continued rocking back and forth in Jonas's lap. "Later, when you fuck me in front of the mirror and take the corset off, one lacing at a time, then you can touch my nipples."

"Oh, so this fantasy of yours is more than just a fuck in the limo?" Jonas smiled, and Nicky nodded before leaning over to kiss Jonas.

"Do you like this? Do you like what you're seeing and feeling?" Nicky asked, his passion mounting as his breathing was becoming more labored.

"Oh yeah," Jonas sighed.

"Can I make you come like this, just from what I'm doing to you?" Nicky asked shamelessly.

"Oh yeah, you bet!" Jonas moaned. Nicky's tightness and the young man's rock hard erection pressing against his belly had him on the edge for quite some time. Their talking had kept his orgasm at bay, but he knew it wouldn't take much. He gently wrapped his hand around Nicky's dark cock and heard the young man gasp. "Come with me, Nicky."

"No, I want to see you come first," Nicky said, swatting Jonas's hand away. "I want to see your face when you come."

Jonas could feel Nicky work his muscles, relaxing them as he came down, pulling them tight when he raised himself up. Jonas threw his head back and closed his eyes, knowing he was so close.

"Look at me," Nicky commanded softly.

Jonas complied and felt his groin tighten, a sure signal of his impending release. With both hands on Nicky's corseted hips, he silently asked him to up the tempo a bit and finally thrust up reflexively as he felt the seed shoot out of him. He had the hardest time keeping his eyes open, but smiled back when he saw Nicky's eyes light up.

"Fuck, you're beautiful when you come," Nicky said, catching his bottom lip between his teeth.

"Your turn," Jonas panted. "Make yourself come."

Nicky seemed to hesitate for a moment, and then he took his leaking erection in his hand and fisted himself rapidly. He raised himself a little, inviting Jonas to thrust up into his body.

Jonas saw Nicky's eyes glaze over and thick white strands shot out of the young man's cock all the way up his chest as Nicky's movements became erratic. Eventually, Nicky collapsed on top of Jonas, panting hard.

"Was it what you wanted?" Jonas murmured into the young man's dark curls.

"It was more than I could ever have imagined," Nicky replied softly. "I wanted to make it good for you too, Jonas. You seemed so distant all of a sudden and—"

Nicky shivered and Jonas wrapped his arms protectively around him. Then he felt his cell phone vibrate against his hip.

"You're ringing," Nicky stated blankly.

Jonas shook his head. "It's nothing."

Nicky reached down between his legs to keep the condom in place as he slid off of Jonas's lap. "It must be important if it's allowed to interfere when you're with a client."

Jonas felt the full impact of the ice cold words, but he couldn't admit it. He didn't even have to look to know who it was and mentally kicked himself for not being able to keep his private cell phone turned off. "It's nothing," he repeated, more to convince himself than to persuade Nicky to not take it personally.

Nicky tied the codpiece again and knocked on the partition. "The apartment, Marcus."

LATER that night they had a nearly silent dinner, and then Nicky excused himself, saying he had a telephone interview to do. Jonas wasn't sure if that was just a ruse or if it was true, but it did afford him some time to check his cell phone and return the call. He was just saying goodbye when Nicky walked in.

"Client?" Nicky asked, surprisingly less morose than earlier.

"Yes," Jonas lied. "They do get a bit fidgety when I'm incommunicado for a longer period of time."

"Tell me about him."

Jonas had to think on his feet. That was the problem with lying. "He's a washed up eighties pop star. Made a huge killing with three albums and would have been bankrupt two years later if he hadn't had a financial adviser who invested his money in a certain Silicon Valley computer company. So now he's still filthy rich and terminally bored because all he does is get blind drunk or stoned out of his mind. In his own little world he's still the big rock star. He's had three wives, but really likes to watch guys who masturbate and come all over his chest."

"That's all you need to do?" Nicky asked. "Come all over him?"

"Yeah," Jonas nodded. "He hasn't been able to get it up for ages. He used to jack off too, but the equipment stopped working a while ago now. Not that he cares, really."

Jonas saw Nicky nod and couldn't help thinking the young man was planning something. He leaned over him seductively. "Will you help me take the corset off?"

Jonas shrugged. "Sure. Tell me what to do."

"It works best while you're fucking me," Nicky stated, fluttering his eyelashes.

Just minutes later, they were standing in front of Nicky's dress mirror, Jonas pounding into Nicky's tight body, slowly undoing the lacing eyelet by eyelet. Nicky moaned with every one that was loosened, until his patience gave in and he quickly undid the hooks at the front, ripping the bodice apart and shucking it to the side. The chemise was easily torn open as well and Nicky took Jonas's hands and placed them on his chest. "Touch me there," he moaned.

Jonas couldn't help but appreciate the view of Nicky's body jerking with every thrust, the white chemise hanging off his shoulders and his dark nipples reacting to Jonas's tweaking. When he looked down further he saw Nicky's cock, hard and dark, bobbing up and down with every movement. Suddenly Nicky threw his head back as he came, untouched, spattering his release all over the mirror. Jonas quickly wrapped his arms around Nicky's chest in an effort to keep him upright as he too felt his orgasm hit him hard.

Nicky regained his footing and they were both panting. "Are you going over there?" Nicky asked, with surprising eagerness.

"Where?" Jonas asked, leaning against the cupboard.

"The pop star."

"I told him I was with a client, so I couldn't."

"Can you take me with you? I'm sure two guys wanking are better than one."

Jonas tried to read Nicky's face to see how genuine his request was. "We can't tell him who you are. You'll have to pose as someone like me and get paid for it."

"Of course," Nicky agreed.

Jonas sighed. He had a phone call to make and he hoped Johnny was in for a surprise visit.

CHAPTER 7

JONAS wasn't quite sure how to handle this.

He'd hoped Nicky would be leaving for Paris soon, but the designer had told him that he and Tanna were staying on in London while the rest of the fashion circus travelled back to the atelier in Paris. This meant that he had to actually do what he had said he would and call Johnny, pretending that he was simply returning a call, and set a date for their encounter. He hoped Johnny would be put off by his suggestion that he bring Nicky along, so he would have an excuse to kill the whole idea.

Knowing Johnny was a creature of the night, Jonas had no qualms about calling him at two a.m.

"Oy!" the voice on the other side exclaimed suddenly after Jonas had let the phone ring for a considerable amount of time.

"Johnny?"

"Nobody else would pick up the phone around here at this bloody hour, mate," Johnny's telltale voice exclaimed.

"Jonas here."

"Not likely to be anyone else now, would it? Don't know anyone who calls people in the godforsaken middle of the night but you, padre."

Jonas smiled at Johnny's drawl. He was clearly happily buzzed, but not so far out of it that he couldn't get a coherent sentence together. Since Nicky was listening, he'd have to be careful of his words. "Listen Johnny, my, eh, client fell through...." He looked at Nicky to gauge the young man's reaction and was happy to see a smile spread across his face. "...So I can come see you after all." Nicky was clearly eager to find out what Johnny's answer was because he was sitting on the edge of his seat, elbows resting on his knees and looking straight at Jonas.

It was quiet on the other side of the line. Then Johnny started speaking hesitantly. "I haven't spoken to you in weeks, if I recall."

Damn, he was lucid enough to remember. Jonas knew he'd have to use all his talents of persuasion. "Well, you were rather pissed last time you left me a message, when I called you back and said I couldn't make it because I was with a client. You fell asleep during the phone call?" Nicky seemed to find this amusing, but Jonas feared Johnny wasn't quite there yet.

"Man, that must have been that night we were doing 'shrooms. I was pretty much out of it then."

"Well, you sounded like you were on another planet. Anyway, if the offer still stands...." Jonas looked at Nicky, who nodded eagerly.

"When can you get here?" Johnny asked, clearly in for a little fun and games. "'s been ages since I've been turned on," he added, probably only to himself.

"I have a little extra for you. A beautiful young man, who'd like to learn the ropes in the business." He left a silence, knowing Johnny's messed up brain would need some time to work through the possibilities of that suggestion by himself.

"He any good?" Johnny asked, clearly not entirely won over by the idea.

"The best," Jonas answered without hesitating. "He can do what your boys can't." Nicky's questioning face drew his attention, but he held up his hand to stop him interfering.

"That I'd love to see!" Johnny chuckled. "So when you coming over?"

"I'll call you back in five minutes," Jonas stated, before ending the call and closing his cell phone.

By now Nicky was standing next to him and he pulled the young man into his lap and kissed him passionately. He could feel Nicky not entirely giving in to it. "You think if I fuck you, you can come without being touched?" he asked, their lips never completely parting.

"You know I can," Nicky answered, pushing his excited groin against Jonas's belly.

"Can you do it while a guy's watching?"

Nicky nodded, not quite as confident any more though. "I think so, yeah. Will he want to touch me too?"

Jonas shook his head. "He doesn't touch, never touched the other guys he picks up. Some of the boys have complained about that to me. How he picks them up, lets them hang around his house, eat his food and drink his liquor, but how there's no sex until I show up."

"You fuck the boys for him?" Nicky asked. He sounded a bit disappointed.

"Yeah," Jonas admitted quietly. "He has them checked out for me, knows I won't touch them unless they have a clean bill of health. And even then I take extra strength condoms. Well, it's probably his manager who does that for him. Don't think Johnny's lucid for long enough to actually plan anything."

Jonas chuckled to make light of the situation, because he sensed Nicky was jealous. "None of those kids can come without being touched, though."

"How old are they?"

"Nineteen, twenty? They're not under age, Nicky. I'm not into young kids, you know that; besides, it's what Johnny wants, not me. And Johnny's usually too far out of it, but his manager is afraid of losing his meal ticket, so he makes sure they're not doing anything illegal."

Nicky seemed to be mulling it over in his mind. "He sounds weird, but at the same time very intriguing."

Jonas got close to Nicky and caressed him gently, his hand weaving into his hair. "You don't have to do this. I can just call Johnny and tell him the deal's off. He's not the type to harbor a grudge."

Nicky leaned closer, their foreheads touching. "You don't want to fuck me when someone's watching?"

Jonas nuzzled him tenderly. "I'll fuck you any way you want me to fuck you."

"Will you fuck me now, before we go? Because I've been horny ever since you told me about him."

Jonas smiled at how far they'd come since their first encounter. Nicky didn't just ask for what he wanted, he seduced him into wanting to give it to him too. "No, because then you won't be able to come again without touching in an hour's time. Think you can hold on for that long?"

Nicky bit his lower lip, but a smile was playing around his mouth. "I suppose. Call him. Tell him we're coming."

IT DIDN'T take them long to get to Johnny's in a black London cab in the middle of the night.

Still, they were a good hour later than they had said they'd be because Jonas insisted Nicky dress casually. One look at Nicky's wardrobe had made Jonas call in a favor from a friend of his. She owned a menswear shop and wouldn't have opened at this ungodly hour "for anyone else" other than Jonas, but after some emergency shopping, Nicky walked out of there in skinny jeans, a fitted midnight blue silk shirt, a tight leather jacket and a beanie, looking decidedly more ordinary than when he'd walked in. The movie-star sunglasses were still his own and the only thing Jonas would compromise on.

Jonas had seen the look of recognition and astonishment on his friend's face when Nicky walked in wearing his usual extravagant attire. Jonas had given her a reassuring look, which had stopped her reacting to the fact she had a world renowned fashion designer in her small boutique, but she was nervous nevertheless. She did manage to make Nicky look good while shedding his peacock feathers and for that Jonas was grateful, despite the fact that Nicky felt more than a little underdressed.

JOHNNY'S place was an ordinary looking Edwardian house with a few steps up to the front door. The man who opened the door looked like the love child of Guns and Roses' Slash and Cockney Rebel's Steve Harley. His bare chest and too-tight leather pants were enveloped by a large shag coat that had seen better days. He was wearing beads in clashing colors around his neck and had several large rings on his fingers and a cigar between them.

No words were exchanged. The man simply pointed up toward the first floor and walked off, leaving them to close the door behind them. As soon as he was out of earshot, Nicky pulled Jonas closer. "You wanted me to dress normally? That guy is worse than me! At least I have style. He's like a walking fashion history lesson!"

Jonas stopped his ranting with a kiss. "You're not here to be you, Nicky. You're just a guy who likes sex and doesn't object to being paid to have fun."

Nicky was silent now, looking Jonas in the eye.

"In fact it's probably a good idea to think of a name. Calling you Nicky sort of stands out."

"Jamie," Nicky answered. "James. It's my middle name."

Jonas kissed him quickly and then took his hand to lead him up the wide but cluttered staircase. The sweet scent that had hit them as they entered the house only became stronger the higher they climbed, but it didn't seem to bother Nicky, who was darting around looking at things left and right. Jonas held onto his hand, fearing he might wander into another room and he'd lose him. He just wished that the delay in their arrival meant Johnny would be blind drunk or passed out on the floor of his bedroom like he had found him more than once. Then again, there was always the chance that Johnny lived so far away from reality that he would never have heard of a young British upstart making it all the way to the top of the fashion world. In any case, if Johnny had ever seen a Bryant runway show, there was no denying that this young man was the genuine article and no nickname would hide that.

Jonas knew where to go. Johnny always seemed to be in his bedroom at this time of the night. He didn't bother knocking, simply opened the door a little hesitantly before walking in, Nicky close behind him. To his surprise, Johnny was sitting in a large wing chair strumming his guitar. At first hearing, the song he was playing didn't make much sense, but the two young women sitting at his feet were staring up at him in awe anyway.

Jonas started to walk closer, but was held back by Nicky. "Holy Fuck—I didn't know you meant that Johnny!" he whispered to Jonas. "I thought he was dead!"

Jonas raised an eyebrow and looked at the young man. "He soon will be. He's been trying to kill himself for years. Slowly."

"Jonah baby—great to see you, man." Johnny had put his guitar aside and was gesturing them to come closer. "And hell, you brought a friend. Yeah, you said you would, right? Great, man, just great. I get a show tonight, woo hoo!" His eyes didn't look all too clear and judging from his overly dramatic gestures, he was under the influence of something… or several somethings mixed together.

"Get it on, boys, come make an old geezer happy. You know what Johnny boy wants." He seemed to find himself incredibly funny, cackling with laughter as he slid down the chair until he was nearly horizontal.

"Ehm…." Jonas hesitated, looking at the two young women and then back at Johnny.

Johnny raised himself a little and motioned them to come closer. He kissed both of them on the cheek. "He gives a good show, our Jonah," he told them conspiratorially, "and I'm sure you'd all enjoy it too, but you see, he don't like girls much." He looked at Jonas as if he needed to confirm that and then returned his unsteady gaze to the girls. "Who knows, maybe these two beautiful boys," he rather grandly waved his hand in Jonas and Nicky's direction, "will help little Johnny feel good too, so there might be a little prezzie in it for you two."

The girls smiled at them as they retreated. They were clearly sisters, maybe even twins, but one of them looked at the men with contempt in her eyes while the other looked more like she'd prefer to stay and watch the show. In any case, Nicky's sigh of relief echoed Jonas's sentiments that they much preferred them gone.

"So who's the shy one you brought for me tonight?" Johnny queried, clearly not perturbed by the fact he was still on his back on the floor in a position that looked quite uncomfortable in Jonas's eyes. The shag carpet underneath him offered little support, no doubt.

"This is N... Jamie," Jonas answered, pulling the young man in front of him. He let his hand rest on Nicky's stomach and undid one of the buttons on the silk shirt so he could slip his hand inside to touch bare skin.

"Well, he's certainly beautiful, man, but can he perform? Like Johnny likes it?"

Jonas sensed how nervous Nicky was and wondered for a moment if the young man was going to chicken out. "I promise you he can," Jonas answered, more to give Nicky confidence than out of certainty. "Have I ever let you down?"

Johnny snickered. "You're a man of your word, Jonah. Now show me what that beautiful kid looks like."

"Patience, Johnny," Jonas cautioned. "He's not a seasoned pro." Then he buried his face against Nicky's neck and murmured, "You okay? Just relax, forget he's here."

Nicky tried, molding himself to Jonas's chest as the older man's hands caressed him underneath the seductive silk shirt. He turned toward Jonas and whispered, "But I like the fact he's watching. Think he'll get off on it?"

"Not likely," Jonas mumbled even more quietly. He let his hand wander down to Nicky's groin, but to his surprise, Nicky was nowhere near hard. "Relax," he urged him again. Jonas had no problem getting it up in almost any circumstance, and he'd never seen Nicky with anything less than a half-hard cock either, but it was still completely possible that this time the young man had bitten off more than he could chew. He could only hope that he could drag it out long enough for Johnny to lose interest or pass out. Luckily the aging rock star had his bottle of Jack Daniels within reach and wasn't afraid to use it.

After a particularly large swig, Johnny waved it at them. "Take his kit off, will ya? I can barely see him like that."

Nicky's shirt was unbuttoned already and Jonas pulled the sides apart to slip it off Nicky's shoulders.

"Now those are nipples!" Johnny exclaimed. "They're like a woman's, so big and dark! Does he like it when you lick them?"

Jonas made Nicky turn around and sank down to his knees, pulling Nicky onto his lap. He positioned the two of them so Johnny got a good view of both of them in profile and started kissing Nicky's neck before swiftly moving over his shoulder to his nipples. He knew he'd have to seduce Nicky, get him in the mood. He also knew this was one sure way of doing that. The wanton way in which Nicky started rubbing up against him, followed by one of the raunchiest moans Jonas had ever heard coming from the young man, made it clear he was well on the way there.

"You want help there, getting him out of those trousers, Jonah?" Johnny asked, giggling but clearly keeping his eye on the action.

"And who's going to help me?" Jonas answered, only half joking. "You've never touched any of the boys. I'm not letting you start with this one either."

Johnny pulled an exaggerated face and rustled around in his pockets before pulling out a pill and flushing it down with another large swig of whisky.

Jonas knew he couldn't let Johnny wait forever but since Nicky's kisses were becoming sloppy already, he thought he was ready to show more of himself. "Let's take those jeans off, baby," he murmured against Nicky's lips.

"You too," Nicky answered almost immediately, a seductive smile playing around his lips. They both got up and Jonas pulled down his jeans and boxers in one go before sitting down on the rug again. Nicky's skin-tight jeans were more difficult to take off, or was he simply making a game of it? Jonas helped him and noticed Nicky was looking straight at Johnny, seducing him with those chocolate brown eyes of his, which by now were probably almost black with lust.

Jonas saw Johnny's eyes wander south. "You sure he's not underage, Joe? He's not much of a shower, is he?"

The mocking tone with which Johnny put down Nicky's "assets" hit Jonas dead center in the chest and he pulled Nicky closer. "Guess I haven't done my job yet," Jonas replied, trying to make light of the situation. He put his hands on Nicky's hips so he could give him a blow job.

"Untouched, Jonah!" Johnny cautioned, way too alert for Jonas's liking. "That also means no blow job! Besides, I'd much rather see him blow you. Jamie?"

Nicky didn't immediately respond, and it took a look from Jonas to make him realize he was being spoken to.

"So Jamie, you like a big cock up your arse?" Johnny asked without even blushing.

"Yes, sir," Nicky answered, playing his role perfectly. He sat back on his heels like a good school boy.

"Tell me what you like about it."

Nicky hesitated and Jonas had to keep himself from smiling. Nicky was by no means naïve or shy about what he liked, so he was definitely playing it up. "I like how it hurts at first, but then it just feels so full and then—" He looked at Jonas and then back at Johnny. "…It makes me go all hard and tingly, and then it makes me shiver and shake, and I come really hard, much harder than when I wank."

Jonas buried his face against Nicky's neck to stop from laughing and then realized Nicky was still wearing his beanie and sunglasses. He pulled the cap off and Nicky shook his long hair free.

"And you've let our Jonas here fuck you before?" Johnny may have been drawling his words, but Jonas thought he knew exactly where he was going with this conversation.

Nicky nodded, biting his lower lip.

"You think you can come all over me, if I tell him to fuck you here, now?"

Nicky nodded even more eagerly.

"You better make him nice and hard then," Johnny suggested.

Nicky looked at Jonas with a much less naïve look than his earlier actions would suggest. Right then, Jonas knew Nicky was in control. He waited for a moment until Jonas got more comfortable, legs spread out in front of him and leaning back on his arms, and then bent down to take Jonas's barely hard cock in his mouth, his ass sticking up. Jonas knew how good Nicky was at blowing him and he knew how much the young man enjoyed doing it, so he tried to relax, even let himself fall back on his elbows. Nicky's mouth was hot and Jonas felt him pressing his tongue up to add friction. His heartbeat sped up and blood rushed to his groin as he allowed himself to enjoy the experience. Soon enough his erection was lying heavy on his stomach and Nicky was licking and sucking it as if it was a lollipop and he hadn't eaten or drunk in a week. Even though Nicky had been careful not to touch himself, making sure his hands were near Jonas's groin at all times, every time Nicky's head bobbed up Jonas could see the designer's cock grow bigger and harder until it almost looked like it was glued to his belly. It never ceased to amaze him how turned on Nicky could get from giving a blow job.

Suddenly Nicky stopped and crawled on top of him, grinding his body down and their erections together, while giving him a searing kiss. "Fuck! Can you just fuck me before I come?" he whispered as he came up for air.

Jonas nodded. "I'll prep you quickly."

Nicky nodded too, pulling back and panting hard, clearly trying to regain his self-control.

Johnny cleared his throat. "Well, he surely didn't stay small. Have to admit he had me worried in the beginning," he said, still smiling dopily. "So what's next?"

"Let us surprise you," Jonas replied, almost rolling his eyes at the ludicrous question. He fished some supplies out of his trousers, which he'd left not too far from where they were sitting, and threw them on the floor. Then he positioned both of them a little closer to Johnny, who was still half on the floor and half lying against his chair. Jonas made Nicky sit on his knees facing Johnny, and after opening the packet of lube and coating his fingers with it, he knelt behind the young designer. He wrapped his left arm around Nicky's shoulders and whispered, "Are you ready?" in his ear.

Nicky nodded, clearly calmer now than he had been a few moments ago.

Jonas gently smeared the warmed up lube into Nicky's cleft, feeling the young man react slightly when he rubbed over his puckered opening.

"Hurry up," Nicky mumbled softly.

Jonas shushed him, taking his time running his finger around the circular muscle before slowly sliding one digit inside.

"Oh yeah," Nicky sighed and Jonas didn't know whether this was Nicky's "porn" performance or whether the young man's passion was really welling up that quickly. Nicky was tight but clearly making an effort to relax, so Jonas added a second finger, feeling the muscle tense up momentarily only to soften again.

"Fuck yeah, stretch me," Nicky moaned. "Make me ready so you can fuck me with that cock of yours." Nicky was pushing back, leaning against Jonas's arm which was keeping him upright.

Jonas gently rubbed the muscle until it gave way and allowed him in, more and more with every movement.

"Fuck, yeah! God, that feels good, Jonas!"

Scissoring his fingers worked well, so Jonas added a third finger. At that moment Nicky pushed backward, impaling himself on the bundled fingers, and then thrust forward reflexively. Thick, white strands of come were shooting out of him and landing on Johnny's chest as Nicky wailed from the power of his orgasm. The rock star was clearly as surprised as Jonas was, but Jonas had his lucid mind to fall back on. He held onto Nicky and continued to pump his fingers in and out of the young man's body, making him convulse again and again until he started sobbing and Jonas pulled out. No tears were flowing from his eyes, though; his head was simply thrown back against Jonas's shoulder.

"I'm sorry, Jonas, I'm so sorry!" he cried out.

As Jonas wrapped his arms around Nicky, the young man turned his face toward him. "Now fuck me, make me come again," he whispered in a tone not at all consistent with his earlier charade.

Jonas looked over at Johnny to gauge his reaction. The aging rocker looked impressed and was lazily rubbing his fingers over his come covered chest. "You are a man of your word, Jonah. He comes like a rocket and shoots like a missile." He took a large swig from his Jack Daniels bottle and threw it away when he noticed it was empty. "Now will you add yours to his?" The look he gave Jonas could only be classified as amused—amused and loaded, but clearly amused.

"I think I can do better than that," Jonas said, looking at Nicky, whose head was still resting on his shoulder and turned toward him. Nicky's eyes lit up.

Johnny raised an eyebrow while Jonas grabbed one of the condoms. Nicky took it from him and with a gleam in his eye, proceeded to fist Jonas's cock a few times before rolling it on and coating it with lube. Nicky raised himself up to kiss his lover, and Jonas could feel the younger man's erection pushing against his hip. As they retook their positions, Jonas licked Nicky's ear and said, "I can't believe you're still hard."

Nicky just smiled and pushed his ass back, silently asking to be fucked.

Jonas teased him a bit, rubbing his erection over the sensitized opening a few times before slowly pushing in. Nicky pushed back almost immediately, impaling himself quickly until Jonas was fully inside him. Jonas wrapped his arms around him and sat on his heels, pulling Nicky down with him. He didn't need to tell Nicky what to do. The young man simply opened his legs, and resting his hands on his knees, started riding the hard cock underneath him.

"Oh, yeah. God, this is the best."

Leaning slightly to the side, Jonas could see Johnny's lustful look at what was going on, a mix of total enjoyment and slight frustration in his face. He couldn't blame the man. Seeing two guys getting off in front of him while knowing he couldn't make his own equipment work would annoy the hell out of him too.

"Fuck, Jonas, your cock is the best."

Jonas was close himself and started wondering if Nicky had just been overconfident or whether he could really come a second time. The fact was, Nicky's movements were becoming less rhythmical, so Jonas decided to meet him half way, thrusting up into the tight channel.

"Harder, Jonas, fuck me… gonna come again!"

With one last effort, Jonas raised himself and held onto Nicky tightly while he continued to piston in and out of Nicky's body at breakneck speed. He didn't need to see what was happening. He'd made love to Nicky enough times to read the signs the designer's body was sending out and knew he would indeed come again.

"Fuck man, you did it again!" he heard Johnny call out, followed by a nervous giggle. Jonas opened his eyes as Nicky slipped out of his arms. Before he could focus fully, he felt a hand on him—it could only be Nicky—pulling off the condom and fisting him rapidly. He barely managed to stay upright as his orgasm hit him like a white light, Nicky's arm supporting him. He panted hard, his eyes closed and his forehead against Nicky's temple.

It seemed to take forever for him to come down off his high, and if it wasn't for Nicky, he'd have probably passed out. He only really came to his senses in the bathroom, feeling Nicky's hands all over him again, cleaning him up. They quickly got dressed and were out of the door in no time, leaving Johnny behind, semi-conscious and with a near-permanent grin on his face.

"Hey, you okay?" Nicky asked.

The fresh air outside did Jonas the world of good. "You'd think it was me who'd come twice in a row," he quipped, pulling Nicky into a tight hug.

Just around the corner, they managed to stop a black cab to take them home.

"Was pretty intense, hey?" Nicky stated as they settled into each other's arms in the back of the cab.

"Yeah, it was," Jonas replied, still a little dazed. "And I think Johnny agreed."

"Oh, I'm sure he did," Nicky answered.

Jonas chuckled. "He hasn't been able to get it up for the last ten years, Nicky. I don't think we managed to get him off."

Nicky sat up and looked straight at Jonas. "You didn't see it, you were behind me, but when you were fucking me, he had his hand down his pants and I'm pretty sure there was something going on there!" Suddenly Nicky seemed to remember something and he started looking through the pockets of his jacket. "Look," he said, holding up a wad of cash. "Fuck, they're fifty pound notes! We're rich!"

Jonas laughed. "We were rich before we came here, Nicky. I don't think this amount of money will change that." Then a little more quietly, "I guess you really made him horny."

"Nah, it's you who made me horny." Nicky snuggled closer, hooking one leg over Jonas's thighs and rubbing his groin against his side.

Jonas looked at the young man snuggling in his arms. "Did you take Viagra or something? You came twice and you're still hard."

Nicky nuzzled Jonas's neck. "Who needs Viagra when they have you? Now take me home, lover."

CHAPTER 8

THEY had fallen asleep, their limbs entangled after a long night of lovemaking, the continuation of what had started at Johnny's house. Frankly, Jonas had been surprised by his own speed of recovery. He wasn't eighteen anymore, after all. Not that Nicky wasn't enough of a turn on, of course. In fact he was an incredibly sexual beast, open to anything and everything, insatiable and totally selfish at one moment, a completely slutty and incredibly giving man at any other time. Jonas thought he could easily get addicted to him but had no intention of succumbing. He was going to enjoy every moment of it as long as it lasted and when it was over, he'd walk away.

Sound was slowly filtering through to him. He sensed he was spread-eagled on the bed on his back, and he was slightly cold because Nicky seemed to be gone. He didn't want to open his eyes yet, knowing instinctively how little time he'd been asleep. The sounds coming from the room were curious, though. He vaguely heard Nicky's voice, far away or whispering, he couldn't quite tell. There was another voice too, higher pitched. It sounded like... a woman? Nicky had assured them they were alone in the loft, but there was a connecting door to Tanna's apartment. Could the voice be Tanna?

Jonas experimentally opened his eyes and felt around for a sheet to cover himself, knowing he was naked. When he didn't find one right away, he rolled over and his gaze stopped on the occupants of the sitting area sofa. It was indeed Tanna in the room. She was sprawled out on the couch, hips near the edge of the seat, endless legs spread wide. She was wearing grey briefs and a sleeveless shirt that resembled men's underwear and she was moaning quietly and whimpering. It took Jonas a few moments to realize that Nicky was next to her, butt naked and with his hand down her panties. He was the one making her moan. Jonas didn't need to imagine what Nicky was doing to her underneath the stretched fabric of the light cotton boxer briefs.

She wasn't wearing any make-up and her hair was loose, hanging around her face in long wavy strands. Nicky was kissing her on the neck and whispering to her.

"Wouldn't you like that great cock inside you? Pumping in and out, making that sweet wet pussy of yours feel soooo good?"

She nodded and whimpered, and then she clamped her hand over Nicky's and pushed down. "Faster," Jonas heard her demand of the hand inside her undies. Her moans became louder and Nicky shushed her. "Don't wake him up yet." He kissed her when she could no longer control the pitch of her moans, stifling the sound somewhat. Then she arched her back off the couch and came hard, convulsing. Nicky's movements didn't still right away, just slowed down somewhat until Tanna was relaxed on the sofa.

"I think we woke him," she whispered mischievously, breathing hard and looking unashamedly at Jonas while grabbing her bathrobe and swinging it around so she could put it on. "I better leave," she told Nicky before kissing him.

"I'll ask him," Nicky replied, watching her walk away.

Nicky wiped his hand on one of the ever present baby wipes before coming over to the bed. He walked slowly, seductively, and Jonas had plenty of time to admire the long, perfectly balanced body. Nicky was half hard and clearly horny as he moved over Jonas to kiss him. "Good morning, lover," he greeted Jonas.

"I'm sorry I interrupted your lovemaking with Tanna," Jonas replied. He was open-minded enough not to be jealous; after all, this wasn't the first time he'd had a client with a wife.

"What you saw was pretty much it," Nicky admitted matter-of-factly. "The fact that you woke up was a bonus."

"So you needed an audience? You could have just told me," Jonas said, trying to tease a bit. He gently took Nicky's erection in his hand and rubbed it. "Did I stop you fucking her? I wouldn't have minded."

"You wouldn't have minded fucking her or you wouldn't have minded watching me fuck her?"

"Watching," Jonas answered decidedly, pulling Nicky closer and feeling himself harden too.

"Too bad," Nicky quipped. "I don't fuck Tanna." Nicky's face was full of confidence. "I've fucked her in the arse, because for some reason she likes that, but never in her pussy."

Jonas raised an eyebrow. "Did you want me to fuck her?"

"Well," Nicky started, but then he paused. He looked a lot less confident all of a sudden. "When you said you sometimes did women too, I thought it would be a safe gamble to ask. You see, she really likes you. In fact I think she's got a bit of a crush on you. Don't worry, she knows nothing will come of it, she's not naïve or anything, but she has this one sexual fantasy and I think she'd like both of us to make it come true."

Jonas wasn't sure what to think of that. The only person he could think of who would suggest that he was up for something like this would be Ally, the wife of Scott, one of his oldest friends and his other married client. And now that he thought about it, hadn't Scott urged him to take Nicky as a client? He would bet quite a bit that Ally had been the one instigating this.

"So do I need to blame Ally for this?"

Jonas could tell Nicky was trying to hide the fact he'd been caught. He quickly recovered, though. "She's quite a lady, that Ally," Nicky said, rolling his eyes.

"Yes, she is," Jonas acknowledged. "Of course, I only fuck her husband."

"I've heard other things," Nicky replied teasingly. He didn't give Jonas much of a chance to rebut that statement when he kissed him, soft and slow, taking the older man's top lip between his teeth and softly teasing it. "Ally likes to watch you fuck Scott or Scott fuck you. She says it's incredibly sexy to see your two beautiful bodies get it on. She also told me that you and she have made Scott the meat in the sandwich, that you've fucked him while he was fucking her." When Nicky kissed Jonas this time it was hard and needy, and Jonas kissed him back, equally passionately.

When they came up for air, they were both rock hard and so turned on they were more than ready to continue the lovemaking.

"Tell me what you want," Jonas demanded, his body still pressed hard against Nicky's. "Or what she wants. I'll do it for you because you ask me and because you've made me so horny I could just fuck you through the mattress right now."

Nicky chuckled. "She wants you to make love to her and then for me to join you two."

"And what will you do then?" Jonas asked. He could imagine a few configurations and hoped Tanna and Nicky had thought up a nice one. Jonas didn't dislike women; he was just not very turned on by them. He preferred the male anatomy but wasn't blind to the advantages a woman's body offered.

"She wants both of us inside her," Nicky whispered, biting his lower lip, and still very close to Jonas. "We tried it with a dildo while I fucked her in the arse and she came a few times, really hard. Now she wants to try it with two guys."

Jonas raised an eyebrow. "I just wonder why she wants two gays?"

"Easy," Nicky was quick to answer. "She knows I don't get off just from fucking her, so she wants someone there who can make it good for me too."

Jonas was quite astounded by the level of disclosure between Nicky and Tanna. They obviously talked a great deal about what turned them on in bed and what didn't. "And what about her? Or does she like to watch too?"

Nicky smiled and shrugged. "She's curious about how we fuck, and I think she'd like to watch, yes. I think Ally whetted her appetite."

Jonas could envision it quite clearly: Scott and Ally and Nicky and Tanna around the dinner table, all polite, exchanging niceties about the lovely dinner and what a great house Scott and Ally lived in and how busy work was at times. He wondered how the transition would work, how that polite conversation would turn to what Ally and Scott liked to do in bed and how they had this other man who would come around to help them work out their fantasies. Jonas couldn't help but smile when he imagined being "highly" recommended by Ally.

"I'm just wondering how Tanna would feel when we get going and sort of forget there are other people in the room," Jonas wondered out loud.

"Well, Tanna offered to bring her girlfriend, but Maia isn't too thrilled about the fact that Tanna wants cock from time to time, and besides, I thought one woman at a time was enough for us, right?"

Jonas nodded slowly. "That was very considerate of you. Now maybe we should see what we can do for Tanna, hey?"

Nicky nodded and then kissed Jonas one more time before getting up from the bed and pulling his lover to his feet. They made their way over to Tanna's apartment, both still in their birthday suits. She opened the door for them, wearing pretty much what she had been wearing earlier that morning. Jonas noticed her long limbs, the curve of her ass and the perky breasts with erect nipples pushing against the thin cotton fabric.

She smiled and then giggled, her hand in front of her mouth. "Can you believe I'm nervous?" she asked. Contrary to what she was saying, she easily moved into Jonas's personal space. "I hope you're okay with this, Jonas. I wouldn't want this to come between us in the future. I'd rather not do this if you feel you won't be able to look me in the eye again afterward."

Jonas smiled at her, open and inviting. "If I couldn't look the people I fucked in the eye afterward, I'd have a big problem on my hands."

"Good," she purred, and then she moved to lie down, her long, wavy hair hanging over the foot end of the bed and her endless legs near the headboard. At first the configuration seemed a little strange to Jonas, until he saw Nicky kneel next to her at the foot end. Jonas sat down at the opposite side of where Nicky was, next to Tanna's figure and started stroking her, just like Nicky was doing. It felt very sensual to run his hands over her silky skin, and he had visions of Tanna and Nicky rubbing their equally hairless soft skin against each other. She was kissing Nicky now, more playfully than passionately, and at the same time, pushing her hips in the general direction of Jonas's hand, which was caressing her belly and dipping teasingly underneath the elastic of her panties from time to time. Suddenly, Jonas felt Nicky leading his hand lower, over her pubic hair and down between her legs. As he pushed Jonas's finger against Tanna's clit, she veered up. She was very wet and obviously still a little sensitive, both from when Nicky had made her come earlier and probably a little from the anticipation as well. Despite this, she moved against their entangled hands, pushing up, demanding more friction. They continued rubbing her, and she started moaning softly against Nicky's mouth, turned her head, and kissed Jonas. Her kisses were sloppy and her hands started clawing at his body. "Are you hard enough?" she asked unashamedly. "Because I want you inside me soon."

From the corner of his eye, Jonas saw Nicky leave the bed. When he returned, he walked to Jonas's side. "Don't jump," Nicky whispered, clear amusement in his voice. "I'll get you your condom on." Jonas felt Nicky fist him a few times before rolling on the latex. "Now go for it, she's pretty close to coming already."

Jonas didn't know if that was a good thing, but he pushed his body closer to Tanna's anyway. He tried to make it feel sexy. "Are you ready?"

She nodded and rolled on her back pulling him on top of her as she did. Her legs were spread and her hands ran over Jonas's sides, making him shiver slightly. He leaned on one arm and guided himself into her slowly. She moaned, moving her hands down his back until she could cup his ass to urge him on. "Fuck, you fill me up nicely," she said, quite unladylike. "Now please fuck me harder."

After a few experimental thrusts and quite some urging from Tanna, he started fucking her in short sharp bursts, until she cried out and Jonas felt her flesh starting to throb around him. "Don't stop now!" she shouted. "Please!" Her face contorted as she came, clinging to Jonas. He kept thrusting inside her until she begged him to take it a little easier.

Jonas saw her reach for Nicky. "You were right, he's amazing." She then turned back toward Jonas. "I like sleeping with women," she admitted, "but sometimes there's nothing like coming around a nice big cock."

Jonas felt himself blush, but he knew they'd only just gotten started.

"Can you pull me up until we're sitting?" she asked. "So I can ride you?"

Jonas nodded and put his arm around her. Together with the fact she was wrapped around him with arms and legs, he managed to move around the bed until he was sitting against the headboard, pillows nicely propped up by Nicky, without slipping out of her. The new arrangement gave her quite a lot of freedom and even while they were still finding their respective positions, she was slowly riding Jonas, rubbing her clit against his pubic hair.

She reached for Nicky again, urging him to come closer and asking him to bring the lube. Jonas was growing more excited, knowing Nicky would become a part of their intimacy, and he too stretched out his arm to pull the young man closer. Nicky smiled and pushed Tanna closer to Jonas so he could kiss him. When he pulled away Tanna started to chant, riding the hard cock inside her with more gusto. "Fuck! Yeah! Fuck! Going to come again!"

Nicky put some lube on his fingers and Tanna jumped for a moment, just before she shuddered violently again. Nicky smiled at Jonas and Jonas chuckled. "She's quite multi-orgasmic, isn't she?"

"Mmm," Nicky nodded. "And I'm not even inside her yet. Does make her very relaxed, though."

Jonas cocked his head. "I think three orgasms in quick succession would do that to me too." He saw Nicky fumbling a bit behind Tanna's back. "Need some help there, lover?" he asked.

Nicky shook his head, lower lip seductively tucked between his teeth. Tanna was between them, her head on Jonas's shoulder and still moving up and down, slowly now. Nicky kissed her exposed neck. "Ready, dearest?"

Tanna looked up and smiled at Nicky. She shifted a little, opening her legs even more and leaning on Jonas now, her arms still around his neck. Jonas felt her muscles react as Nicky slowly pushed inside her. "Fuck, she's tight," Nicky murmured. "Oh my God, I can feel you!" he exclaimed, clearly surprised.

"I can feel you too," Jonas acknowledged, reaching out to entangle his hand in Nicky's hair. "Strange, the three of us together like this. Very different from when a man is in the middle."

No sooner had Nicky moved a little, than Tanna was convulsing again. "Oh fuck, I've never—" her words drifted off. Between Jonas and Nicky, Tanna was held upright as they both moved in and out of her, urged on by the pitch of her moans. Despite the great care they took of her, their eyes were on each other, gazing for reactions or signs that their passions were spiraling out of control.

Tanna came twice more, the last time practically crying and shuddering uncontrollably. As she was coming down off the high, both men remaining still to let her recuperate, she suddenly pulled away, making them slip out of her almost simultaneously.

"No more," she said, her arms stretched out to keep both men away from her. "Can't take any more!" She was shaking involuntarily, and Nicky wrapped his arms around her as they both helped her to lie down on the bed. They lay down on either side of her keeping her warm. "God, that was intense, is intense," she corrected herself. "It will take me some time to stop twitching." She smiled at Jonas and then kissed him tenderly. "Do you have some energy left to make love to Nicky now?"

Over Tanna's shoulder, Jonas looked at Nicky, smiled softly, and looked back at Tanna. "Yes, I do."

"Can I watch?"

"Yes," Jonas answered determinedly, remembering his earlier conversation with Nicky.

They both got rid of their condoms. Nicky wrapped the blankets around Tanna so she wouldn't catch cold and then joined Jonas on the bed.

"So how shall we do this?" Jonas asked Nicky, who was lying next to him, their bodies aligned and arms around each other.

"Why don't we ask Tanna what she wants to see?" Nicky offered.

"You're such an exhibitionist," Jonas stated, one eyebrow raised.

"Takes one to know one," Nicky teased as he rolled over Jonas to land on Tanna's side.

Both their eyes turned to Tanna, who had the decency to blush. "This is for you guys, I don't care! I just want to see my two favorite men get it on!"

Nicky looked over his shoulder at Jonas and Jonas gave a bare nod. "Tanna, we don't care what we do. We like it all, so tell me what you want to see."

She blushed even more and Jonas was surprised to see the always confident Tanna turn shy.

"I don't know, guys. I've never seen two guys really, intensely into each other. I mean I know the basics, but here? Right in front of me? I dunno…. Can you make it look like you're really enjoying it? I mean, you made it so amazing for me, you two deserve to get each other off too."

Jonas leaned closer to Nicky and whispered in his ear. "I think we can do better than just get each other off, don't you? Or 'pretend' like we're enjoying it," he chuckled.

Nicky smiled at Tanna and nodded.

"Don't move," Jonas whispered again. Nicky was on his side, facing Tanna, and Jonas moved down his body, kissing the already overheated skin all the way down to his buttocks. Then he pushed Nicky's leg higher up allowing for better access so he could plunge his tongue between the cheeks of his ass. Nicky moaned loudly at the contact of the hot mouth against his sensitive entrance. Jonas didn't waste any time teasing—they were both horny as hell as it was—and the circular muscle gave way easily as he pushed the tip of his tongue inside.

"Fuck, Jonas, just use enough lube and fuck me already before you make me come like this."

Jonas didn't argue. He simply lifted himself and, after massaging the enticing globes of Nicky's nicely shaped ass a few times, got up to get another condom. As he rolled it onto his erection and coated it with plenty of lube, he watched the bed. Tanna was on her side, chastely covered by a blanket tucked tightly around her long, slender form. Out of context, one might think she looked innocent, almost angelic. She was going to watch him fuck Nicky, though; Nicky, who was splayed out on the bed half on his stomach, his left knee pulled up so his entrance was exposed, inviting Jonas to plunge right in.

"How do you want me?" Nicky asked, looking over his shoulder.

"Are you comfortable?" Jonas asked in return. Nicky nodded. "Then I think I have you right where I want you." He grabbed Nicky by the hips, used his thumbs to spread the cheeks, and then moved swiftly over him, one knee on either side of Nicky's hips so he could cover him with his own body. He rubbed his slick erection over the cleft of Nicky's ass as he kissed his neck. "Tell me how you want me. Hard and fast or slow and teasing?"

"Don't care," Nicky groaned. "Just stick it inside me, fill me up."

Jonas rubbed his hard shaft back and forth a few times before pulling back just enough to feel the head find its way toward its destination. In one hard thrust, he pushed inside. Nicky gasped, so he waited for him to adjust. Jonas liked the warm, smooth body underneath him, liked how the young man was a little sweaty from their earlier exercise, tiny beads visible near Nicky's neck and on his shoulders. He rubbed the slightly broader muscles and then moved down Nicky's arms, pulling them back. Would he like being restrained? He couldn't see Nicky's face but felt safe judging from Tanna's expression, which was one of approval. She looked at him with her dark blue eyes and smiled, so he started rocking back and forth, in and out of Nicky's tight little hole, defiantly looking at her. When she noticed him holding her gaze, she looked away as if she suddenly realized what was happening.

Nicky was moaning and Jonas let go of his arms. "Stretch your legs back," he demanded in a soft voice. "Make yourself tight for me." Jonas continued his slow movements, wondering how long it would take the young man to urge him to move faster. Not long, he hoped, since the tightness and the fact Tanna was watching with clear eagerness was making him edge closer to his release despite the teasingly slow rhythm.

Nicky curved his back and turned his neck, silently asking for a kiss. "You feel so good, I'm leaking all over Tanna's bed," Nicky murmured against Jonas's mouth.

"You want to turn over?" Jonas asked.

Nicky nodded and Jonas slowly pulled all the way out of his lover. He watched Nicky turn around, his swollen cock falling heavily along his treasure trail, the head glistening with moisture. Unable to resist, he bent down to take it in his mouth, tasting the precome, and then moved up to kiss Nicky—deeply this time, sharing the taste. He wiped the curls away from the young man's face and felt the knot in his stomach again. So beautiful and, without all the make-up, so pure. Jonas wrapped his arms around him, effectively lifting Nicky's shoulders off the bed as he kissed him again, lovingly, passionately, rubbing their erections together. Jonas's cock found its way to Nicky's still relaxed opening without too much coaxing and soon they were moving together again in their own perfect rhythm, by now totally oblivious to the fact that there was a third person in the room.

Jonas felt Nicky pull his legs up. "Faster... please, Jonas... need to come...."

Knowing he was close as well, he stopped moving just long enough to change their position. Grabbing Nicky's thighs, he folded them back on him, bending him in two, and started thrusting again, this time hard, fast, and accurate. Nicky lifted his hand toward Tanna and she grabbed it.

"Does it feel good, baby?" she asked tenderly. "Are you going to come hard for Jonas?"

Nicky nodded frantically, his eyes squeezed shut and his face contorted, his knuckles white from the force of his grasp.

Jonas thought of helping Nicky along by fisting his cock but then realized it would be too easy. Nicky had come untouched several times before and even being watched by Johnny hadn't made him lose the ability to do it just from being fucked. It made Jonas feel powerful that the young man didn't seem to need more than a good hard pounding. Then he heard him cry out, every muscle in his body spasming, and creamy white fluid was splattering on Nicky's belly, stomach, and chest, all the way to his neck. Just moments later, Jonas felt his balls contract and as he emptied himself into the condom, he saw visions of it overflowing and seeping out of Nicky's tight little hole. He collapsed on top of Nicky, panting hard but still feeling the need to kiss him, affirm their bond, and claim him back from Tanna as if there was something to claim. Nicky's lips tasted salty and the young man kissed him back lazily.

Jonas buried his face against Nicky's neck, when he felt him look away.

"Was it what you wanted to see?" Nicky asked Tanna eagerly.

"I think you're falling in love with him, Nicky," she answered. Jonas expected her to sound sad, wistful even, but she didn't. He looked up at her and saw pride in her face as she slid off the bed and waved at them playfully before walking away.

"I'll move," Jonas said, looking for a sheet to cover them with as they were cooling off quickly.

"We better go back to our room," Nicky agreed. "Although I like the way this feels too."

Nicky was looking away shyly and Jonas wondered if Tanna was right. Was Nicky falling in love with him? The last thing he needed was love. This was all fine and good the way it was. A most pleasurable business arrangement. The last thing he needed was the illusion that his feelings were returned.

CHAPTER 9

THE next morning, Nicky seemed distant somehow, although he wasn't dressed up to his usual peacock level yet. Jonas couldn't blame him. He wasn't the type to prolong the agony with one last hug or kiss either.

"I'll call you when things settle down in Paris," Nicky said while he gathered the last of his things. Then something seemed to occur to him. "Do you like the suit I made you? We're getting new fabrics for the men's line and I could make you another one. I still have your measurements so we can make a mock-up, and then you'll have an excuse to come by the atelier to have it fitted."

Jonas looked at Nicky for a few moments. So he needed an excuse now? What happened to "I need you here, come over?"

"I'd love another suit," Jonas answered, his voice strained. "Call me when you're ready." There wasn't much more to say. Jonas knew he couldn't lay claim to Nicky. He was a client and the client dictated when he wanted to be seen, that's all.

They walked downstairs in silence and said goodbye in the hallway. Tanna kissed Jonas on the cheek and gave him a hug. "I'm sure he'll call you soon," she whispered in his ear. "And if he doesn't, I will."

For a moment Jonas saw the unashamed lust in her eyes again, and then it was gone and replaced by her professional look. He looked over at Nicky and saw him become insecure again, something he hadn't seen a lot of in these past days.

"I'd better go. Hiding away for a week means I have a lot to catch up on," Jonas said in an attempt to rescue Nicky from an overly emotional farewell. He put his hand on the designer's back as he walked past him toward the door and let their eyes meet only for the briefest of moments. His jacket seemed too warm and he felt the sudden need to get out of there as quickly as possible. Handle gripped firmly and one foot out the door, he turned around once more.

"Tanna, thank you for organizing everything. Nicky...." Jonas didn't know what to say. His heart was screaming out to tell Nicky that he hoped he'd call again soon, but the blank expression on the younger man's face left no place for emotions, so he nodded at him, picked up his bag and stepped out into the cool air of the London morning toward his waiting chauffeur-driven car.

"Where can I drop you off, sir?" the driver asked him, holding out his hand to take his bag from him.

Jonas gave him the address to his apartment and got in the back. "On second thought, could you wait for ten minutes when we get there? I won't take long. And then can you drop me at Heathrow?"

"Certainly, sir," the middle-aged man answered, directing the car into the busy morning traffic.

Jonas knew Tanna would have given instructions to take him wherever he desired. The man was probably hired for the entire morning. And he needed to get out anyway. London was becoming way too stuffy already.

IT TOOK a week at his Madrid villa for Jonas to feel like himself again, to start appreciating the freedom of not having to share his bed with anyone, to enjoy his solitude as he had most of his life. Even a month later, he still caught himself checking his cell phone to see if Nicky had called, but it remained silent. In four weeks time, he had an appointment with Christopher in New York, but it wouldn't be a long trip and after that Scott and Ally were coming over to stay for a week of leisure. He resolved to have a good talk with Ally about the recommendations she had given Nicky, but since she could charm her way out of anything, he was sure they'd all end up laughing about it afterward.

Jonas looked up from the book he was reading underneath the magnolia tree in his city garden because he thought he'd heard a door close. Sitting still for a few moments, he tried to hear if there was something else moving in the house, but then concluded it was probably his imagination and continued reading. His gut feeling wouldn't go away, though, so he got up and walked inside, hesitantly climbing the few steps toward his kitchen. Everything was still how he'd left it but he found himself treading cautiously around his own house.

Twice this past week he'd noticed a metallic RAV-4 with darkened windows parked near the corner of his street and that morning he'd seen movement near the shrubs at the back wall. He'd attributed it to the fat tabby his neighbor liked to overfeed. That cat didn't climb walls, though. He shook his head, thinking he was becoming paranoid in his old age. Maybe this was his mind telling him he didn't want to live alone anymore. Or maybe he was enjoying it too much.

He smiled and poured himself a cup of coffee.

"Guero."

Jonas's whole body tensed and his arm jerked up, splashing some drops of coffee out of the cup and onto his wrist. A few expletives later, the cup set down on a safe surface and his mind working again, he stopped resisting the arms wrapped tightly around his middle.

"Uardo, you bastard, I could have burned both of us!"

The soft hair of his ex-lover's beard tickled the back of Jonas's neck as smooth lips kissed the exposed skin. "I learned a long time ago not to do this with you holding a knife, mi amor," the darker man replied in a heavy Spanish accent.

"I'm not your amor any more," Jonas said sternly, extricating himself from the other man's grasp and turning around. "What are you doing here?"

"You know me: I'm like one of those ugly dogs who smell blood. When you arrive here I'm always drawn to this house."

Jonas smiled wistfully. "I thought we'd agreed—"

Eduardo moved back into Jonas's personal space and tried to kiss him but Jonas turned his head at the last moment and his ex-lover's lips landed on his cheek. The body leaning against his felt good, though, and since Eduardo didn't seem eager to pull away either, they stood there, intimately close for a long few moments.

"We agreed to stop living together, Jonas," the Spaniard whispered, pronouncing the older man's first name with a soft Y instead of a hard J. "We never agreed to stop seeing each other."

"Uardo," Jonas pleaded. It would be so easy to give into the familiar touch, spend his passion with a man he knew would make him feel good, at least physically. He contemplated it for a moment and then pushed Eduardo away. "I can't, I'm sorry. We have to stop doing this, Eduardo. This isn't good for either of us."

"I told you I would leave her if you come back, and I will," Eduardo repeated what he'd told Jonas on the phone weeks earlier.

"And you know better than to give me an ultimatum," Jonas replied sternly. "You tried that when we split up and it didn't work then. You're no good for me, Uardo."

The Spaniard's look went cold. "I don't see how bad it is for you if you are begging me to fuck you harder until you come."

Jonas closed his eyes and pinched the bridge of his nose. He couldn't give in now. The incessant phone calls were one thing, but Eduardo showing up at his house all the time had to stop. If he let his body take over, he'd never be able to break it off and now that his resolve was still strong he needed to take a stand. It wasn't like Eduardo was a client, so he could set his conscience at ease.

"No more," Jonas whispered.

Eduardo looked like he hadn't understood him, but then Jonas's cell phone started ringing. "That's right. Let a client fuck you, but oh no, not me." The dark Spaniard threw up his hands and furiously walked out of the kitchen, leaving Jonas standing with the noisy cell in his hands.

"Yes," he said into the handset, a little annoyed at the intrusion.

"Jonas?"

He immediately recognized the voice. "Hi, Tanna, how are you? Life back to normal?"

She giggled. "You could say that. Then again, what is normal around here?"

Jonas waited for a moment. The question didn't need an answer and the one thing he wanted to ask—when Nicky wanted him—felt too presumptuous.

"How fast can you get here?"

Tanna's voice sounded less cheerful all of a sudden, and Jonas had visions of Nicky turning back into the morose, depressed young man he'd met that first time.

"Is he okay?" he asked her, surprised by the worry in his own voice.

"He's okay, busy as usual," she answered. "I believe he promised you a suit, and since a few customers rescheduled their appointments, he has time off tomorrow."

Jonas sighed and hoped Tanna hadn't caught that. So it wasn't that Nicky needed him, he simply wanted to live up to his promise and make him a suit. It didn't take Jonas long to think about it, though. "I can be there tomorrow. Around what time?"

"How does one sound?" Tanna suggested.

"I'll be there."

THE next morning, Jonas was at the airport bright and early. He was happy to be away from Madrid and Eduardo's prowling and on his way to see the man who still made his heart skip a beat. He told himself numerous times that Nicky was a client, a man who paid him for his services and not a lover, but the recollection of the week they'd spent in London kept playing with his imagination.

He'd tried to keep himself occupied until about noontime and then made his way over to Nicky's Paris atelier at Maison Bryant. Just moments after introducing himself to the receptionist, Tanna appeared at one of the doors marked "Private."

"Hey, my beautiful man, come on in."

Jonas smiled at her forwardness but followed her immediately. Once inside the small anteroom, she hugged him tightly, one hand on the back of his head. "Mmm, you smell good and feel even better."

As they parted, Jonas smiled shyly. "You look beautiful as usual, Tanna." Somehow he felt that didn't do her justice. She looked perfect, like she'd walked straight off the pages of Vogue when their models weren't skeletons yet. Jonas knew Nicky cut her dresses extra tight because they made her look amazing, but with her perfect stockings, high heels, hair and makeup, she seemed the consummate professional and a woman to be reckoned with.

"Nicky's still with a client, but he'll be done soon. Care to share some lunch with me? Or did they feed you on the plane?"

Jonas could barely swallow, let alone eat, so he told her a white lie. "They did. Flying business has its perks. So I'm sorry, I couldn't eat another bite, but don't let that stop you."

Tanna shook her head and then gave him a compassionate look as if she knew what was going on in his mind. And maybe she did.

"I'll go see how long he's going to be," Tanna suggested before leaving Jonas to his own devices.

The waiting seemed to take forever until suddenly the door burst open and Nicky appeared. Somehow he looked a little more subdued, less peacock, and for a moment Jonas wondered if that was because Nicky knew that he liked him *au naturel*. With a disarming smile on his face, Nicky grabbed Jonas by the hand and dragged him up out of his chair and into the atelier where about thirty pairs of stunned eyes gazed at them.

"There's someone I want you to meet," Nicky explained. He guided Jonas toward the back, where Tanna was standing next to a rather smaller young woman with a flurry of red hair crowning her rosy and almost make-up free face. They were bent over a wide table covered with an assortment of print fabrics and clearly deep in discussion.

"Jonas, this is Maia," Nicky stated as they reached the table. He moved a little closer and added conspiratorially, "She's Tanna's girlfriend, remember I told you about her?"

Jonas remembered how Nicky had described her as being small and mousy and not at all glamorous, and Jonas had to agree with him, but she had a certain spark. He smiled at her, thinking back at how Nicky had told him she must be at least as insatiable in bed as Tanna if she wanted to keep up with her. At the time, they'd both found that image too disturbing to contemplate, but now it subconsciously bubbled back to the surface of Jonas's mind.

Jonas shook his head, waking himself from the daydream to find Maia holding out her hand to greet him.

"Monsieur Hunter, I've heard a lot about you. Your reputation precedes you." She had a slight accent, not French, but rather more Australian, and Jonas took her hand and lifted it to his mouth, at the same time wondering what exactly Tanna had divulged to her about their three-way encounter. The greeting wasn't awkward, though, despite Maia's clear shyness.

"I've heard a lot about you as well," Jonas admitted. "I believe Nicky would be lost without you. He told me you create his fabrics for him."

Again she gave him that bashful smile. "He designs, and I make sure our spinners make it to his specifications, yes, I'll say that much."

"Show him the new cloth for the men's summer suits!" Nicky demanded, at which Maia turned around and picked up a roll of slightly shiny, expensive looking linen. She unrolled it and draped the fabric so everyone got a good look at how it picked up the bright lights of the studio. "The first suit I'll make from it will be for you, Jonas," Nicky said quietly, as if it was only meant to be heard by the four of them. To Jonas's surprise it was accompanied by a rather intimate touch of Nicky's hands moving from the small of his back toward his ass and resting there possessively. "Let's get you into the mock-up so I can make sure it fits perfectly!"

Nicky's enthusiasm was catching, and Jonas couldn't help thinking back to the first time he'd been to the atelier and the difference in attitude Nicky displayed today. He let himself be led to the front where the fitting rooms were and once behind the curtain of the largest one, found himself being accosted by Nicky, whose hands and mouth seemed to be everywhere at once.

"Fuck, I missed you," Nicky exclaimed, clearly not worried about the fact that only a thin layer of muslin separated them from thirty-some seamstresses, beaders and fabric cutters. Nicky slid down until he was on his knees, and before Jonas could say anything, Nicky had undone the fastenings on his trousers and was taking out his already semi-hard cock.

"Need to taste you," Nicky demanded, and Jonas was grateful that the young man was toning down his voice. The fact that Nicky was also moaning around his erection made him grow hard so fast, his head was spinning. He barely allowed himself to look down at how Nicky was licking and sucking on his cock as if it were a jug of water and Nicky had just walked in from the desert. "Man, I missed your cock," Nicky moaned lustfully after raising himself and pushing his clearly aroused body against Jonas's. "Can't wait for you to fuck me. Will you fuck me, Jonas?"

Jonas cocked his head and tugged at his ear. "Don't you think it will be a bit weird for them to hear their boss being fucked against the mirror?

"Nobody's making them stay. They won't lose their jobs if they go outside for a break," Nicky answered cockily.

"What I mean is, wouldn't it suit a boss more to be the one doing the fucking?"

This time it was Nicky's turn to angle his head. "You mean, me top, you bottom?" Jonas could see the idea racing through Nicky's head. "But I've never topped!"

"You fuck Tanna in the ass—" Jonas tried, speaking a lot more quietly than Nicky.

"But that's different, that's—"

"An ass is an ass, trust me on that one. You fuck her because she likes it, and you don't even like women. At least you like men, so fucking a man's ass should be easier."

Nicky pushed his body closer to Jonas's and rubbed his confined arousal against Jonas's still exposed erection. "And you like it too, don't you?" Nicky asked cheekily.

"You know I do. I told you that I bottom more than I top anyway."

"Okay," Nicky answered, still a little hesitantly and not entirely sure of himself. "What do I do?"

Jonas chuckled. "Do something that makes you nice and hard. It's always easier with a strong erection."

"I think I'm nice and hard already, just from sucking you."

"You're a little pervert, aren't you?" Jonas teased, running his hand down Nicky's stomach and past the band of his trousers. "I think you're right, but we need to free this little bird before it hurts itself." Jonas unzipped Nicky's pants and released the designer's bouncing erection; then he started undoing his shirt and red, lopsided cravat so he could reach the young man's enticing and very sensitive chocolate nipples. After lavishing them with attention and a little bit of teeth, he raised himself again and looked at Nicky. "I think you're about ready. Me, on the other hand…."

"Take your clothes off," Nicky ordered, stepping back a bit and slowly touching himself. "I want to see you."

Jonas, not ashamed to expose himself, took his time taking off his jacket and tie, then his shirt and trousers, socks and underwear, all the while very aware he was being intensely scrutinized by Nicky. The young man moved toward a small shelf with a built-in drawer, never taking his eyes off Jonas, and retrieved a small packet of lube from it.

"You keep that in there?" Jonas queried.

"I knew we'd need it today," Nicky answered shyly.

"You have condoms in there too?"

Nicky looked up with a jerk, as if he'd forgotten something. "Of course!" He went back to the shelf to get the rest of his supplies.

Jonas saw him fumbling and came closer, taking the condom from him. "Relax, it's me, remember? Anything you do is fine by me."

Nicky exhaled loudly and rolled his eyes. "I guess, because I've never done this...."

Jonas kissed him lightly. "But you have and I have too, just not with each other. I know you'll make me feel good and I know I can make you feel good too, so just go for it." He waited for Nicky to look him in the eye. "Stud."

A small giggle escaped Nicky's throat, and then he pulled himself together. "Turn around?" he asked more than demanded of Jonas.

Jonas saw him move behind him and stare at their joint reflection in the mirror. He watched Nicky lift his hands to wrap his arms around his stomach and almost shivered in anticipation. The memories of being fucked in front of this very same mirror by Chris came back to him, but the feeling now was so much better. On a purely physical level, the encounter with Chris had been satisfying, but now here with Nicky, Jonas realized it was going to be a much fuller experience.

Nicky smiled as Jonas's cock flinched up when he touched his belly and the older man pulled him closer.

"Make me ready?"

Jonas braced himself, letting go of Nicky's arms to support himself as he leaned against the mirror. He watched as Nicky squeezed some lube onto his fingers and warmed it, and then the hand disappeared behind him. The feeling of the slippery digits rubbing along his cleft and over his opening made him moan. He held back, still very aware of the fact that they had listeners, but as Nicky's fingers zoned in on the more sensitive places and eventually breached him, he groaned audibly. "That's it, just like I prep you, stretch me, make me ready," he pleaded.

"I'm making you harder and I haven't even touched your cock," Nicky stated in amusement.

Jonas sighed, trying to gather his thoughts as he was being stretched by two fingers slipping in and out of his body. "I can make you come without touching you... so why are you... so surprised?"

Nicky giggled nervously, adding a third finger. "You're very tight."

"But I'm ready," Jonas added, clearly straining to keep a semblance of control. Then he remembered he was still holding the condom, so he quickly extricated himself from Nicky's grasp, turned around, and fell to his knees. He took Nicky's cock in his mouth, returning it to its earlier rigidity, and rolled on the condom. "Lube?" he asked.

Nicky, looking down quite stunned at everything that was happening, chuckled and pointed at the one chair in the cubicle, where Jonas had hung his clothes. The package retrieved, they returned to their earlier positions. It was a little awkward with their usual positions reversed, but Jonas knew he wanted this. He was prepped and ready. To his surprise Nicky's initial thrust was confident, but then he seemed to be holding back, possibly to let him get used to being filled.

"'s okay, Nicky, feels good," he managed to say.

"You look good," the designer whispered in his ear as he slowly pushed in further. "And you're still really tight."

Jonas opened his eyes and looked straight ahead. The image in the mirror was amazing. Himself, stark naked and painfully hard; Nicky behind him, still mostly dressed in tight flare pants, his shirt open and hanging off his shoulders. Nicky's thrusts were becoming quite powerful, and Jonas's body jerked with every one of them, making his cock bounce. The designer was breathing heavily into his ear and he heard moans. His own? He was beyond caring, so mesmerized by the image in front of him and the sensation that he was being royally fucked, a cock grazing over the most sensitive spot in his entire body every time it pumped in and out of him. He didn't know how long he was going to last, but he refused to let his mind wander to more dreary places just to keep from coming. He wanted to savor every movement, every thrust, knowing it would be rare if ever again that Nicky would be fucking him into a state of ecstasy.

"You're close, aren't you?" Nicky asked, surprisingly lucid. "I can tell by the sounds you make. I know those sounds. Tell me you're close."

"Come with me?" Jonas almost begged.

"Touch yourself," Nicky demanded, and almost automatically, Jonas's hand reached for his already copiously leaking erection. He spread the precome around and started fisting himself in time with Nicky's thrusts.

"Oh yeah, like that…. You look so sexy, so sordid… touching yourself like that… while I'm fucking… you," Nicky said in between thrusts, his voice dripping with need.

Jonas felt his own groin move between getting maximum feeling from Nicky's fucking to pushing into his own hand. This is what it must feel like to be the middle of the sandwich. As Nicky's thrusts became more erratic, Jonas looked up one more time and felt his entire body prepare itself for his release. Before he could hold back, he cried out, his seed splattering all over the mirror and his own hand. Nicky wasn't silent either as he delivered a few more powerful thrusts into Jonas's tensed up body and then slumped down, hanging onto the older man. They were both panting hard, and Jonas turned in Nicky's arms. "You okay?"

Nicky nodded. "We better get cleaned up, because I have another client coming in soon."

A little disappointed, Jonas nodded and extricated himself from Nicky's embrace. They took the box of tissues off the small shelf and proceeded to wipe themselves and their surroundings clean of any evidence of their activities.

Jonas knew how to dress quickly, so within no time, he was ready to leave the cubicle with Nicky.

The young man pulled him closer one more time. "I'll ask Tanna to pay you double for today. You did come out at such short notice."

Jonas felt stabbed in the heart. He was no more to Nicky than a hired hand. A paid fuck. Swell.

It took all of his acting skills not to show his pain. He didn't even enjoy the curious looks they got from the women of all ages and the few men who'd stayed at their stations during the audio show.

Any plans for staying the night went out the window and Jonas kicked himself for expecting anything more than what he got today. He couldn't get to the airport fast enough and longed for the solitude of his own house and bed. The evening commuter flight was a late one, though, and Jonas was stuck at the airport with not much more than a book and his own thoughts. It was no surprise that by the time his plane landed in Madrid, his attitude had changed. Anger had replaced the hurt, and instead of going straight home he let the cab driver drop him off a few blocks from his house, in front of an apartment building.

Jonas knew where he wanted to go and despite the fact it was now quite late and dark out, he rang the doorbell incessantly. When no one answered right away, he started knocking, then banging on the door.

When a man finally opened the door, Jonas walked past him into the hallway and waited for him to close the door behind them.

That's when he pushed him to the wall and kissed him possessively.

"She's not here, is she?"

He shook his head. "You know she does not live here."

"Okay, you get your way. But it's sex and nothing more. Don't come around and beg later, because I can't give you anything more than this."

Eduardo nodded. "I know. Come here, mi amor."

CHAPTER 10

THEIR coupling had been rough and needy. After Jonas's initial warning that it would only be sex and nothing more, no more words were exchanged. There was no need. After ten years they knew each other's bodies so well that they easily took their cues off one another.

As they moved into the sitting area of the small bohemian apartment, Jonas still admired the perfectly balanced body of his ex-lover and how well it had matured over the years. He knew they'd never make it to the bedroom, and Jonas was relieved by that. The bedroom was no doubt where she slept when she came over, and he didn't care to catch her scent or any evidence of the presence of a woman in Eduardo's life. All he wanted now was release: release from the tension in his stomach, release from his anger.

Eduardo was quick to get out of his clothes, and Jonas was amused to see he was rock hard already. No amount of posing on a red carpet with his curvy Spanish fury would ever make Jonas believe Eduardo wasn't gay. Maybe she didn't sleep over here at all; maybe it was all just a ruse. Jonas hadn't bothered getting naked himself. It would all be over in a few minutes anyway, and then he'd be out the door as soon as his legs could carry him.

The Spanish actor understood Jonas's mood just as the American had expected. He was on his knees, arms braced against the back of the couch, cock rubbing over the worn out leather seat. Jonas knew the lube and condoms would still be where they'd always been and he only needed to take his erection out of his pants to roll on the latex. He reveled in the fact that Eduardo still opened up to him like a flower to sunshine, and it took only a few quick strokes of a slippery finger to know Eduardo could take him without hurting too much. The younger man groaned when Jonas entered him in one long stroke.

"Tell me you need this," Jonas demanded.

"Lo necesito, Jonas. ¡Lo necesito tanto!"

"Tell me she can't give you everything you need."

"No puede. Sabes que no puede y por eso te necesito a ti."

"Tell me how good this feels."

"Como si hubiera muerto e ido al cielo."

Jonas was desperate for his release, pistoning in and out of the younger man's body with total disregard for his lover's pleasure. Eduardo wasn't a quiet lover either. His Spanish fire came out in groans and moans, and as Jonas pushed him down on the couch more, increasing the friction on the actor's cock, the moans became whimpers and prayers.

"Dios, Jonas. No pares. ¡Joder! Meteme toda la polla. Así. ¡No pares nunca, Dios!"

When Eduardo's climax came even before his own, Jonas was disgustingly happy and he thrust even harder into the tight, contracting sheath until he felt the rush overtake him.

As he pulled out of Eduardo's now-limp form and the dark Spaniard sagged down to the ground, Jonas realized his body might have found temporary release but his heart was still crying out. He ripped off the used condom and looked at with it with distaste before dropping it into the wastepaper basket next to the coffee table. Looking down at his ex-lover, he shook his head as if only just realizing how he'd used him. The understanding and compassion he found in Eduardo's face was Jonas's undoing. With a stifled sob he hastily tucked himself into his trousers and took one more look at Eduardo before rushing out of the apartment.

He ran all the way home and didn't realize how exhausted he was until he collapsed against the smooth wall of his patio at the back of his house. Panting heavily, he dropped his face into his hands and found that he was crying.

HAVING Scott and Ally over at his Madrid house was always nice. It had taken Jonas a few weeks of solitude to get over the turbulent Paris visit and what happened after that, but he had finally understood that life went on. Going back to work in New York with Christopher was the best way of proving that. He had joined the newspaper mogul at the wedding of his ex-wife with the sole purpose of getting caught. Not during sex on the balcony of course, but rather afterward, while they were straightening their clothes. The ex was sufficiently embarrassed without it turning into a scene, and Jonas was on a plane home the next day.

Now they were sitting in Jonas's garden, the leftovers of a scrumptious dinner on the table and enjoying a delicious Rioja. The presence of his friends relaxed Jonas, made him feel human. For a fleeting moment he thought that Nicky would fit right in. He'd joke with Ally about the sexual prowess of their men, and the innuendo would have them in stitches. They were laughing a lot now too, but it was always two against one. Nicky would certainly level the playing field.

Jonas shook his head.

"What no?" Ally asked, shaking Jonas out of his thoughts.

"What was I answering to?" Jonas asked Ally, smiling at her widely.

"Scott was betting you wouldn't be sleeping in your own room tonight," Ally said, her voice low and sultry. "I told him since we'd just arrived, you'd give us the first night to recuperate from the journey, get a good night's sleep, because we know it will be the last good night's sleep before we leave again."

"And then I said you'd been without for so long you'd probably be too randy to let us sleep down the corridor from you."

Jonas smiled at Scott too. "Didn't mean to confuse you. I was miles away."

"Oh, we noticed," Ally answered, leaning over Jonas as she cleared the table.

With Scott still outside enjoying a smoke, Jonas found himself alone in the kitchen with Ally.

"Are you okay, darling?" she asked with clear concern in her voice. "You're worrying us, to be honest."

Jonas shrugged, but he had a hard time hiding what he was feeling. He and Ally had shared a lot more than her husband over the years, and he didn't want to lie to her so he chose to say nothing. It came as no surprise that Ally wouldn't let him stay silent.

"It's Nicky, isn't it?"

Jonas felt his eyes well up with tears but he closed them tightly and held his breath until the feeling subsided.

"You fell in love with him?" Ally paused after her question, looking straight at Jonas with deep worry lines in her face. "And he didn't return the feelings?" She saw Jonas's face change and then seemed to understand. "Oh, I think he did! Jonas!"

Jonas frantically shook his head. "I'm nothing more than a hired hand to him. Someone with the right abilities to make him feel good when he needs it, and he's oh so willing to pay for it!"

"I think you should call him."

Jonas looked up at Ally, trying to see clearly through the haze of tears and anger that was clouding his vision. "I can't call him," he replied quietly, trying hard to keep his anger at bay.

"Why not?" Ally asked, her voice understanding. "Maybe you misunderstood. Wouldn't it be horrible if two people who clearly belong together were kept apart over a misunderstanding? I know him, remember? For a very successful guy, he's still like all the artsy ones, he's a scatterbrain! He says things and then later regrets them, and frankly I'm glad he does, because he's embarrassed himself more than once at our house."

Ally had taken Jonas's hand in hers and was squeezing it in support. At least this gave Jonas something to look at. "Tanna called me to ask me to come over to Paris because Nicky had some free time, so I went straight away. I wasn't there longer than an hour, Ally. He needed a good fuck and then dismissed me. No invitation for dinner, no 'can I see you later?' He knew I flew in. He just dismissed me, threw me away like a used rag." By now Ally had her arm around his shoulder but he still couldn't look at her. "We had a wonderful week together in London, Ally."

"I know," she interrupted. "He told me. Couldn't stop talking about you and how amazing you were. That's why I think it's all a misunderstanding."

"I thought there was something there. I thought we'd connected somehow." He sighed and looked at her. "You know I don't just fall in love with the first cute guy that crosses my path, Ally!"

She rested the side of her head against Jonas's and didn't say anything.

"And on top of everything, I'm seeing things... people. Well, him, actually."

"What do you mean?" she asked, looking at him again with that worried look he so dreaded.

"This past week alone, twice here in the house I looked up and thought I was looking at him. I go into town for groceries and I think I see him, and then when I get closer it's some other guy who doesn't even look like him. It's like I'm slowly going crazy."

"We'll keep yeh sane," Scott replied from the doorway with his heavy Northern English accent. "All that solitude fucks with a bloke's mind. You need to be around people, Joe."

Jonas held out his hand and Scott came closer. He put his hand on Jonas's shoulder, then the back of his head, and then they head butted each other gently. It all felt very familiar. He knew the kind of love he felt from his friends wasn't your traditional love. It was acceptance and gratefulness for the approval they received for their unusual relationship. Scott nuzzled him, fishing for a kiss, and Jonas felt Ally snuggle closer to him as he indulged the fair-haired Northerner. It never ceased to amaze him how easy their relationship had always been. He and Scott went back further than Scott's marriage to Ally. Scott was always the lady's man, never seen without an actress or a model on his arm. Ally was the first one to understand that in bed there was no way Scott could ever choose between a man and a woman. This probably had a lot to do with the fact that she liked to watch. Jonas had thought she'd soon grow tired of them, despite the fact they didn't find the time to indulge each other more than a few times a year. Instead she became a participant, albeit a passive one. She sometimes had requests and suggestions, but never came close to them unless Scott specifically asked her. Scott was also Jonas's guilty little secret. To Eduardo, Scott had always been on Jonas's client list, but money had never been exchanged between them. Scott didn't object to his status either.

"I know you're not in the mood, Joe," Scott whispered as he continued brushing his lips up against Jonas's temple.

"This feels good," Jonas replied, leaning into the touch. "But if you don't want to…." He felt Scott look up at Ally for confirmation.

"We're not going anywhere," Ally said in a low, soothing voice.

"MMM, I better leave," Jonas murmured, his lips against Scott's jaw and his now limp body fitting perfectly against the fair man's frame.

"You know you're always welcome to stay, darling," Ally whispered. She'd been on the chair while Jonas and Scott had made love, watching them. In retrospect it had been more of a cuddle session, something he'd never expected from Scott, who was usually explosive and hungry when he had man-flesh under his hands. This time, the Northerner's touches had been soothing and caring, so much so that Jonas had come first, also an unusual thing for the always-in-control American. They had continued kissing while they came down from the high of their orgasms until Scott had turned away slightly to kiss Ally, who had joined them on the bed afterward.

Jonas knew he was welcome to stay and sleep together with them. There wasn't a jealous bone in Ally's body where Jonas was concerned—although Scott once told him he didn't dare let his eyes wander to other women or men. Still, this time Jonas felt compelled to leave the two to their privacy and go back to his own bedroom.

When he got up from the bed and passed the window, he noticed it was raining rather heavily. "Shall I open the doors to the terrace for a little while? The rain'll cool down the room, and it might be nice to sleep in here when it's not so hot and balmy."

Suddenly a dark figure passed in front of Jonas and then scurried off. "What the...." Jonas shook his head and opened the large French doors even more.

"You're not seeing things now, Joe, I saw him too!" Scott shouted behind him as both men stepped out into the torrential rain in their birthday suits. The intruder had jumped over the banister, and they heard whimpering loud enough not to be drowned out by the noise of the downpour. As they leaned over the railing, they saw a dark clad figure lying on the lawn, clutching his ankle.

Without thinking about it, Jonas pushed Scott aside and ran inside, closely followed by the other man. Their wet feet made it precarious to run over the hardwood floors but they made it downstairs without injuring themselves, and after some fiddling with the lock they both ran toward the injured intruder.

"Que pasa, cabrón?" Jonas asked harshly while he pushed the dark stranger's shoulders down on the water-soaked grass. The man was dressed lightly in a T-shirt and dark cotton trousers which were now clinging to his thin frame. Jonas saw him wipe the strands of long hair away from his face, his eyes screwed up as he squinted at the two men with the rain falling in his face.

"Oh my God," Jonas exclaimed. "Nicky, what are you doing here?"

The young man scrambled away from Jonas and tried to get up. The slippery grass and the fact he was clearly hurting made his getaway impossible, and Jonas caught him as he fell back down. Without thinking twice, Jonas scooped him up in his arms.

Nicky wouldn't have it, though. "Get your hands off me!"

Jonas, slowly losing his patience, hitched him up higher and pulled him closer so as not to drop him. Scott came to the rescue, and this seemed to calm Nicky down enough so they could carry him inside.

Ally was standing in the living room in her undies with her hands on her hips. "You two are a sight! And what did you scavengers bring in?"

"Nicky," Scott answered with a deep sigh.

"Nicky?" Ally asked, her light mood suddenly gone now. "What...?" She looked at the two very wet and naked men, but when she got little response, she turned her attention to the dark, bundled up figure they were still carrying. Quickly she spread some of the towels she'd taken out onto a worn leather couch and gestured for the men to drop him there.

Nicky made himself even smaller, if that was at all possible. He was clutching his right arm and held his right leg rather strangely as well.

"Come on you two, get dry and put on some clothes. I'll take care of him."

Jonas and Scott each took a towel from the stack and retreated upstairs to the bathroom.

"I CAN'T believe he was stalking me," Jonas sighed, breaking an unusual and rather uncomfortable silence between him and Scott. They were both getting dressed after drying themselves off.

"Don't know if it was stalking," Scott soothed him, sensing Jonas was quite angry with the young man.

"Well, what do you call following someone to another country and climbing onto his balcony, then?"

"Jonas, calm down." Scott put his hand on the other man's shoulder. "He didn't call you, send you threatening e-mails, didn't try to hurt you in any way."

"He made me feel like I was losing it, Scott!" Jonas threw down the sweater he'd taken out of his closet, deciding it was too hot to wear it anyway and not having the patience to fold it again. "This isn't the first time, either. The other times I put it down to the wind or my imagination. And he did call."

Scott's eyebrows rose.

"It wasn't his number and I didn't immediately connect the dots." Jonas squared his jaw. "I'm going to give him a good piece of my mind, though! Who does he think he is?"

"Jonas!" Scott tried to hold him back, but he was out the door and down the stairs in no time.

Ally was closing the door to the living room behind her when she saw Jonas approaching. She'd known the American long enough to see he was mad as hell. "Oh, no, you're not going in there!"

"And why not? This is my house and I go where I please."

"Jonas." Ally held him back by softly putting her delicate hand on his chest. "He's upset, tired, and in pain."

"And how do you think I feel?"

"You didn't fall off a balcony," Ally answered sternly.

Jonas looked at her. Usually he admired her coolness, how she could hide her emotions so well when he knew there was a bubbling volcano underneath those icy features. Today she was standing in his way, though, and because of his own emotions, he couldn't quite understand her lack of them.

"I won't let you go in there if you're that explosive," she told him determinedly. "Why don't you run back upstairs and find him some dry clothes? He's soaked and not feeling too proud of himself right now. The least we can do is make him a little more comfortable before we interrogate him."

"Right," Jonas answered arrogantly.

"I'll get the clothes," Scott offered, not waiting for an answer before making his way back upstairs.

As soon as Scott was out of earshot, Ally grabbed Jonas by the shoulders. "Listen, buster, as soon as we get him into dry clothes you can go talk to him, but you two really need to sort this out together. Alone. And right now, I'm afraid to leave you alone with him! What's got into you, Jonas?"

"I'm no more than a paid fuck to Nicky. He made that abundantly clear last time I was in Paris." Jonas was straining to keep his voice down.

"Your clients don't usually show up on your balcony, do they? The only people who know about this house are Eduardo, Scott, and I."

Jonas nodded. "He had me followed. The week I arrived here, there was a car with darkened windows parked at the corner. My first impression was that it was paparazzi. Eduardo was hanging around here, and they're always trying to snap his picture these days, but no photos showed up anywhere, so now I'm thinking it was something else."

"Now that doesn't sound like just a client, Jonas," Ally tried. "That sounds like a jilted lover. Did you push him away?"

Jonas shook his head. "He pushed me away."

"Does he know how you feel about him?"

Jonas shrugged.

"Did you tell him you love him?"

For a moment Jonas looked like he got caught; then he composed himself and looked away from her. "It's not that simple. He paid me to have sex with him, Ally."

"And as usual he got more than he bargained for," Scott interrupted. "I think you should tell him."

"Strange that, coming from a man I just made love to," Jonas said, trying to make light of the situation.

"Ah, but you see, Joe. I don't love you. I've known you for so long, I'm immune to your charms."

Jonas saw the smugness in Scott's face and the way he was looking at Ally and realized something about his friends. "You set us up, didn't you?"

"Set up?" Scott replied, trying too hard to look innocent.

"You know," Ally intervened, "I think I'll go help Nicky get dry. You two fight among yourselves." She teasingly stuck out her tongue at Jonas and weaved around him to enter the living room carrying the clothes Scott had brought down.

"Yes, set up," Jonas continued after watching Ally leave. "Nicky and I? You introduced us and figured we'd like each other."

"Can't take the blame for that, I'm afraid, Joe. Was Ally's idea that you two deserved each other."

"Would you hate me if I said she's probably right?"

Scott took Jonas's head in a vice grip and rubbed his knuckles over the top of his skull. When he let go, he looked at the startled American with a smug look. "Just don't tell her that. I'd never hear the end of it! Seriously Joe, you know I lied when I said I didn't love yeh, but you deserve someone of your own."

"That's not easy in my line of work, and he's...." Jonas pointed at the door. "I don't know if he's strong enough to deal with that."

"Only one way to find out," Scott smiled broadly. "And pushing him away every time is not the way to go about it. Trust me."

Jonas raised an eyebrow.

"Do you know how many great women I lost by telling them I liked blokes too and wasn't about to give them up? Not that I blame them, of course, and it did bring me to Ally, but you gotta go for it, Joe. As it stands now, you don't have him anyway, right?"

Jonas chuckled. "So what did Ally say when you told her?"

Scott's eyes shone. "She said, 'Okay, fine, but pick one guy and stick with him, wear a condom, and you're letting me watch!' I swear she didn't even blink!"

They were both laughing hard when Ally reappeared. "Think you can go in there now and not bite his head off?" she asked Jonas.

Jonas nodded, but she held him back before he entered. "He's vulnerable, Jonas. Don't make any big decisions in there, just talk to him, okay? And I'd like to get him to a hospital so they can check him over but he doesn't want to go. I'm worried he's got some broken bones, but he says no."

"I'll see what I can do," Jonas said, calmer now, before opening the door hesitantly and walking into his living room.

Ally had lit some lamps and it felt cozy, the rain still pounding incessantly against the large windows. Nicky was on the couch, legs up, and adjusting the draping of the large towel covering them. Jonas could tell he was only using his left hand, leaving his right one in his lap.

"Need any help with that?" he asked gently.

"No thank you," Nicky answered, nose up in the air, but his lips thin from pinching them.

"Ally says you hurt yourself."

"I'll be fine by the morning, and then I'll get out of your hair."

The rehearsed arrogance of Nicky's expression and his own nervousness made it hard for Jonas to keep a straight face. Every time Nicky felt out of sorts, insecure, he returned to his "Prima Donna" persona as Jonas liked to call it, regarding everything with disdain and turning up his nose as if he was smelling something foul. This time was no different. Jonas had caught him in the act of doing something that was frankly not very friendly, he was in an environment he had not been in before, and he was alone. He had no allies here, at least not in his mind.

"You can stay as long as you need to," Jonas stated. "Ally thinks you should see a doctor."

"I'm fine," Nicky repeated.

"Okay," Jonas acknowledged. "Then can you explain to me what you were doing?"

Nicky gave him a questioning look, without actually making eye contact.

"Were you stalking me?"

"I was doing no such thing!" Nicky answered with great indignation. When Jonas didn't immediately respond, he added. "I simply came to pay you a visit."

"Visitors usually come through the front door, after ringing the doorbell. Some even call beforehand to ask whether it's appropriate to drop by." Jonas tried not to sound condescending but he realized it was a close call. "They don't climb onto a balcony to spy on the people they're going to 'visit'."

"It was late, I didn't—"

"Nicky!" Jonas interrupted him. He was startled by the loudness of his outburst and momentarily looked at the door, hoping Scott or Ally wouldn't barge in. "Stop lying to me," he continued, much softer now.

"You're one to demand that," Nicky murmured.

Jonas sighed. He knew Nicky was right. "Touché." He walked over to where Nicky was and pulled up a chair so he could sit close to him. "I didn't know how to act around you, Nicky," Jonas said, pausing to think about how he was going to formulate his concerns. "You come across as this strong person, but I know how vulnerable you are, deep inside… especially when it comes to personal relationships."

Nicky's face became tense again, his lips thin and pursed.

"The reason I know that is because I'm just like you. I can't give myself completely either; for fear that I might lose myself. I can't show my true self, because it leaves me wide open. It's much easier, in my profession, to come across as this guy who loves his job, but doesn't have a life of his own."

"But you have a lover. And Scott of course, but I knew that." Nicky was calmer now too, but still a little edgy.

"I *had* a lover. Past tense. Yes, we were together for eight years. We haven't been together for almost two years now." Jonas didn't mind confessing this to Nicky.

"But you still sleep with him?"

"You were watching then too?" Jonas asked, feeling his walls come up again. How dare he follow him around.

Nicky shook his head. "I had a private eye follow you. He took pictures through the window of the kitchen here when you and he were kissing, and then you entering his house and leaving in a hurry fifteen minutes later."

Jonas inhaled deeply, trying not to feel the bile rise. "Pictures don't always tell the truth, Nicky. You, being in the public eye, should know that! It's the story you tell that goes with the pictures!"

"So tell me the story," Nicky asked calmly.

Jonas closed his eyes and sighed. What did he have to lose by telling the truth? It wasn't as if Nicky had ever really been his.

"Eduardo comes to see me whenever I'm here. He always says it's on his jogging route. We used to still have sex, despite the fact we weren't together anymore. He was here one day in between our week in London and my visit to Paris. We didn't sleep together then, but he wanted to. He tried very hard to seduce me, but I wouldn't bite that time. Then you called and I came to Paris." Jonas paused, wondering if Nicky would supply his own version of what happened in Paris, but he didn't. "I felt so cheap, so dirty when you dismissed me at your atelier."

"I'm sorry," Nicky said, barely audibly.

Jonas could tell he had a hard time keeping his face neutral. The emotions trying to find their way to the surface were all too clear. "I felt like a fifty dollar whore, Nicky. Like a guy you pick up off the street to fuck and then send on his way." He heard Nicky apologize again, saw him wanting to say more, but he stopped him by raising his hand. "I flew back here and went to Eduardo's apartment to release the tension. I thought by giving him what he wanted from me, I could shake this feeling of worthlessness. He needed me and I wanted to give him what he needed. When all the while I just wanted you to need me for more than sex."

Nicky looked up at him with tear-filled eyes. "I thought I was just a client to you. I thought you making me feel loved was just your talent, what made you so highly regarded by your clients. I never realized...."

Jonas moved closer to Nicky, cupping his head with his hands and then wrapping his arms around the thin frame, holding the young man's head against his chest. He loosened his grip slightly when he felt Nicky wince in pain, but he didn't let go completely. "I'm still a bit upset about you stalking me."

"I'm upset about you having a lover I didn't know about."

"Ex-lover," Jonas corrected.

"Yeah, yeah, half ex," Nicky said, trying to joke. "And how miserable were you, shagging Scott like that?"

"Well, if you hadn't been there watching, you wouldn't have known that, but then you knew! I told you about Scott and Ally."

Nicky nodded against Jonas's shoulder.

"Sleeping with men is still my job, Nicky, that hasn't changed."

"But Scott and Ally don't pay you," Nicky said, looking up at Jonas.

Jonas cocked his head. "True."

"I think I'm jealous," Nicky said, only half-joking.

"I won't be a kept man, Nicky. I want to have my own money and my independence and that means I still see my clients."

"And Eduardo knew about this too?"

Jonas nodded. "Yes, he did."

"I don't know if I can deal with that," Nicky stated blankly.

Jonas pulled away from him and went back to sit on his chair.

"Then I guess we're through."

Nicky didn't answer.

"I'll ask Ally to get you something to drink and make you comfortable for the night. Then tomorrow you either go to the hospital to get your injuries looked at or you go home to Paris. It's up to you; I won't interfere anymore."

He took one more look at Nicky and then walked out and upstairs to his bedroom.

 HAPTER 11

THE voicemail message he got a few weeks later was both very straightforward and a little cryptic.

In any case, it made Jonas uneasy.

> Hi Jonas, it's me, Nicky.
>
> I'm probably the last person you want to talk to right now, but I want to be that selfish prick one more time and ask you to meet me at *Les petits parapluies* in the Quartier Latin in Paris. It's a small restaurant that will look closed on Monday, but you can come in through the garden gate and there will be a table set for you in the Jardin Secret.
>
> I want to explain a few things to you and I can't do it over the phone. Please at least give me the chance. One evening. Next Monday at nine p.m. It's the only restaurant by that name in Paris so it should be easy to find.

Nicky's voice sounded hesitant, almost shy, but above all, terribly insecure. Jonas had promised himself he would forget all about the eccentric fashion designer, but since he hadn't even come close to succeeding he decided that the least he could do was talk things over with Nicky. Maybe that way they could both find closure. *Or something more*, his heart told him.

No, Nicky wasn't even his type. Oh, who was he kidding? Even thinking about Nicky made lust boil up inside him. He just didn't know whether his heart could take much more. Besides, how many more ways could the young man tell him that he wasn't interested? On the other hand, Nicky was reaching out to him now.

And what did Nicky need to explain to him? That he had been jealous of Eduardo? That was plain as daylight. Nicky had been right to be, too.

Letting go of Eduardo had been the hardest thing he'd ever done in his life, simply because he hadn't been able to make a clean break. They had continued to see each other despite their break-up and Eduardo moving out of Jonas's Madrid house.

It wasn't until Nicky had stolen Jonas's heart that Jonas had been able to tell Eduardo to leave him alone, but even that hadn't gone smoothly.

Maybe Nicky wanted to explain about himself, about his dual personality, the over-the-top, spoiled rotten child of a fashion designer and quiet, shy, hesitant private persona, but Jonas knew there was no need. After all, who knew more about not showing your true colors in public than he did?

Did he want to try to persuade Jonas to give up his clients? Maybe, but if he didn't give the young man a chance he'd never know.

MONDAY night in Paris in September was a typically balmy night, and Jonas had worn a jacket over a light shirt and thin cotton pants. He had no qualms about choosing comfort over style, even while on a date—no, a *meeting*—with a renowned fashion designer.

He was uncharacteristically nervous, though, as he approached the restaurant. Yes, Nicky had made the first move, but he had just as much to apologize for as Nicky did.

Like the voicemail message had said, the restaurant was dark inside. There was a narrow passage next to the quaint house that Jonas hoped would lead to the secret garden. When he opened the creaking wooden door, small candles placed at regular intervals on the floor lit the way.

Yes, this had to be it. The passage opened up into a courtyard, cordoned off by bushes and trees. There were potted plants all over, and Jonas counted about five tables for two, all of them a nice distance from each other to secure privacy. One of the tables was in a corner and was set for one. His heart sank. He'd hoped that Nicky would join him, but this evidently wasn't the case.

"Monsieur Hunter?" a man with a strong French accent asked.

Jonas nodded.

"Asseyez-vous, s'il vous plait." He pointed at the corner table and bowed slightly.

"Merci," Jonas answered, wondering what the idea was as he sat down and waited.

The man returned with a bottle of white wine and a basket of bread. "Monsieur Bryant a choisi le vin, j'espère que ça n'est pas un problème?"

"J'espère que ce sera parfait," Jonas answered, as always glad for his language skills. The wine was cool and tasted nice, but Jonas couldn't help thinking it would taste nicer if Monsieur Bryant was there as well.

He appeared just moments later in a waiter's costume, his long hair cut a lot shorter than before and with a starched napkin over his left arm and a plate of escargots in his right. He placed the dish in front of Jonas and retreated without saying a word.

Jonas, a little startled by what had just happened, took a few moments to react, but then he got up and followed Nicky inside, where he stopped him by placing his hand on the young man's shoulder.

"You don't like snails?" Nicky asked, turning around.

"Oh, I do," Jonas responded. "But I would enjoy them more if I could share them with you."

Jonas saw the self-confidence drain out of Nicky in front of his eyes. "I came here to talk to you, Nicky, not to have dinner. Combining the two would be wonderful, but you said you wanted to talk, so here I am."

Nicky sighed and looked away, so Jonas lifted his hand and wiped a stray strand of hair away from Nicky's forehead. He realized it was a very intimate gesture but was happy to see Nicky didn't pull away.

"Are you sure?"

Jonas nodded. "Three hundred percent."

A shy smile appeared on Nicky's face. "I organized this whole evening, you know, like a date. Something we've never done. And then I chickened out. I thought, what if he doesn't want that? What if after all we've said and after my behavior last time, he doesn't want to go out on a date with a spoiled brat?"

Jonas smiled. "I'll admit that you hurt me in Paris, and the last time we saw each other... well, that was almost scary."

"See! I knew it—"

"Nicky?" Jonas stopped him from turning away completely. "I'd love to go out on a date with you."

"Really?"

Jonas nodded. "It was a great start. The wine was delicious but the snails are getting cold, so we better go back outside and eat them quickly." He held out his hand and Nicky took it, albeit a little hesitantly.

Hand in hand, they walked back outside. It was a little darker now and the stars were coming out. They sat down together on the curved bench. "This is a very romantic place."

Nicky smiled shyly. "Jacques, the chef, is a friend of mine. He's the guy who posed as the maître d'. He's the only one here and will stay in the kitchen from now on. I said I'd serve dinner, so...." Nicky stopped and looked up at Jonas as the older man offered him a piece of bread soaked in garlic butter.

"I better feed you, because you're not going to eat otherwise, are you?" Jonas teased.

"I'm too nervous to eat," Nicky admitted.

"Don't be. Everything that could possibly go wrong between us already has, so it can't get any worse." Jonas's hand covered Nicky's, and he could feel Nicky's doubt, could feel the young man almost pulling away but then giving in to the touch.

"That's what you think," Nicky said, smiling though as he bit into the bread. A small drop of melted garlic butter trickled down his chin, and Jonas caught it with his finger and Nicky licked it off.

"We have a lot to talk about," Jonas acknowledged, fishing one of the snails out of its shell and ignoring the intimacy of what had just transpired. "I have a few things to apologize for."

"No!" Nicky almost shouted. "No, you don't. I was jealous. Seeing the pictures of you with your lover, the obvious intimacy you shared and then later with Scott, when I saw it with my own two eyes... I wanted it to be me and—"

Jonas silenced him by feeding him a snail. "Eduardo and I broke up way before you came along, Nicky," Jonas admitted, dipping some of the bread in the butter and eating it. "I just couldn't let him go. I was holding on to a man I loved so many years ago, but he had changed and I hadn't changed with him. I still wanted that out-of-work actor who hated to be typecast as the gorgeous piece of meat, the struggling man who had ideals and wouldn't compromise them for anything. We broke up because he wasn't that man any more. We broke up when he got a girlfriend because it was better for his career."

"I'm sorry, Jonas."

Jonas shook his head and pursed his lips. "Every time I'd come to my house in Spain, the one I used to share with him, he'd show up. He'd tell me how much he missed me and how he needed a man from time to time and couldn't think of anyone else to turn to, and I was weak. I let him into my house and my bed every single time, but we never managed to capture the magic we had when we were still together. I've since explained to him I can't do it anymore and that I had to put him behind me."

"And he accepted that?"

Jonas nodded. "He's not a bad guy. He knew that one day someone would walk into my life who did make the magic happen for me and he'd lose me. Now help me eat this amazing dish!" He pushed a piece of bread into Nicky's hand and dipped his own crust in the leftover melted garlic butter.

"But we weren't even together," Nicky mumbled, trying to chew the bread and talk at the same time.

"Yes, but the feelings I had for you made me understand that I had to do it. Now eat!"

Nicky dipped his bread into the garlic butter, a little hesitantly at first, but with growing confidence, and soon the plate was wiped clean.

"I like your hair this way," Jonas remarked. "It looks nice shorter."

"Long story," Nicky admitted, rolling his eyes.

"We have all night," Jonas tried.

Just as Nicky took in a deep breath to start speaking, a little bell sounded.

"That will be the main course," Nicky said, clearly relieved.

"Saved by the bell!" Jonas laughed.

Just moments later, Nicky reappeared with two plates. "Salmon or Filet Pure?"

"Ooh, tough choice," Jonas said, knotting his eyebrows. "You're eating with me, I hope?"

Nicky nodded, still standing there with the clearly hot plates.

"What's your favorite?"

Nicky shrugged. "I like both, they're the signature dishes of this restaurant...."

"In that case, why don't you give me one, you start with the other and we can switch half way?"

It seemed to take Nicky a few moments to contemplate this strange idea but he eventually conceded, and Jonas actually saw a smile appear on the young man's face as he put the salmon down in front of Jonas and the steak next to it before sitting down. "Hang on," he said casually, for the briefest of moments touching Jonas's arm with his hand and then getting up again to return almost immediately with a glass, a handful of cutlery and a napkin.

"Good," Jonas smiled. "Now I don't feel so lonely anymore."

There was still some tension in the air as they dug into their plates. Not as much as when the evening started but it could definitely improve, Jonas thought, so he wanted to try and make Nicky feel a bit more at ease.

"This salmon is out of this world!" he exclaimed as he put a piece on his fork, covered it with a small amount of sauce and presented it to Nicky. Just like with the garlic butter and bread, Nicky looked at it and then at Jonas. When he opened his mouth to accept it, his look was a lot more seductive than the first time.

"Mmm, I agree," Nicky replied even before he'd swallowed most of it. "Want to try the filet?"

Jonas nodded. "I want to know why you felt you owed me an apology, though. Besides the fact you stalked me and trespassed on my property to see me."

The smile left Nicky's face immediately and he put his fork and knife down on his plate.

"Don't stop eating, it'll get cold and that would be a shame," Jonas added, trying to keep the conversation light despite knowing it wouldn't be an easy discussion.

Nicky cut off a piece of the meat and let Jonas take it with his own fork. "I don't know where to start," Nicky whispered.

"Anywhere will do. Just tell me what you need to tell me. You organized all this, don't back out now, Nicky." Jonas could tell it was hard on the young man, but he knew that if he didn't push through now, the designer would stop showing him the real Nicky because that was what Jonas thought he was seeing now.

"I'm just a horrible person, Jonas."

"No you're not, you're—"

"Just hear me out please?" Nicky interrupted.

"... human," Jonas continued. "Okay, so tell me," he conceded, trying not to sound impatient.

"I started building this shield, way back in design college. On the one hand it paid to be gay, flamboyant, in-your-face, outrageous even. The wilder the better. On the other hand you had to be mysterious. They told me so many times that I was shallow, that my pretty face wasn't going to help me with my career because that was all people were going to see."

It wasn't lost on Jonas that Nicky wasn't looking him in the eye. Did that mean he still wasn't being entirely truthful? He decided to give Nicky the benefit of the doubt and simply let him finish what he needed to say. He hoped he'd get a chance to ask his questions later.

"Going away to college was an eye opener. I'd had girlfriends before, nothing serious, but there I discovered that what really turned me on were guys, men. Not the dolled up kids who thought they were designers from the moment they stepped into the college; no, real men, with calluses on their hands and sweaty armpits and—" He chuckled. "And then there was Tanna." Nicky paused for a moment, picking up his fork to push the food around the plate a bit, but he didn't eat.

Jonas offered him a bite of his *pomme dauphinois*, and to his surprise, Nicky accepted.

"I love women, Jonas." This time Nicky did look at his table companion. "I adore them, worship them. They are the most exquisite creatures to roam this earth. This is what confused me for the longest time. How could I love them so, how could I love Tanna that much, but not be turned on by them?"

Jonas raised an eyebrow, not sure if this was meant to be a rhetorical question or whether Nicky really expected him to answer it.

"Tanna made her own way through scores of men and probably just as many women. She just had this voracious appetite for sex. Still has, actually. She once told me a day wasn't complete unless she'd had at least one orgasm. By whose hand really wasn't very important to her as long as her lover was competent and exciting; she'd try anything at least once, and I'm sure she has! Poor Maia knows she can't give Tanna everything she needs." Nicky picked at his food again and even stuck a piece in his mouth. "Damn, this is cold now." He started to get up but Jonas stopped him by taking hold of his wrist.

"We'll warm it up later. Now tell me about *you*, Nicky. You've told me about Tanna, and it's all good information, but I'm here for you and nobody else."

Nicky averted his eyes again, but sat down nevertheless. He seemed to struggle to find the right words.

Jonas decided to help him along. "Why don't you start by telling me why you didn't call me again after our encounter at the atelier?"

"It felt wrong," Nicky answered quietly.

"Why?" Jonas asked, almost afraid of the answer.

"Because I wanted more; I wanted more than a fuck. I wanted you, Jonas, us, like that week in London." He was looking straight at Jonas now, and Jonas was crushed by the hurt in the younger man's eyes.

"But then I realized: this is why you're so good at your job. You make it real for people. You make them feel good and that's why you're so expensive, but oh so worth every penny."

"Nicky, I—"

"It was meant to feel this good, because it's your job."

"Can I defend myself, please?" Jonas asked.

Nicky gave him a faint "I guess" gesture, so Jonas continued.

"My clients don't usually put those demands on me. Christopher hires me to have sex with him in public places. And believe me, we've had sex in much more public places than your atelier. He's a friend and I trust him, but we're nowhere near as close as you and I were in London."

"Clay?" Nicky asked, slightly fearful.

"A very intense week, two, three time a year." Jonas saw Nicky almost cringe. "Intense physically. Emotionally... draining, I suppose, because of the lack of emotions." Jonas took Nicky's hand. "He's... we're friends, sort of. He takes me to sports games and we do other fun stuff together too, but he's closed off so completely. He doesn't let anyone near, not even me."

"You said that of me once, too." Nicky didn't grip Jonas's hand or look him in the eye. He didn't pull away either, and that gave Jonas hope.

Jonas sighed. "When I met you, you were, well frankly, difficult to be in the same room with."

Nicky's head hunched down even more between his shoulders.

"You were so used to getting your way, so spoiled you never gave anyone a kind word. You just expected people to jump even before you issued your commands."

Nicky looked deadly ashamed, becoming so small he almost disappeared. Jonas lifted the younger man's head by putting his finger underneath his chin, making him look at him. He had only moderate success.

"That first time, I saw you change. I saw you allowing yourself to actually enjoy what we did."

"I did. I enjoyed it a lot." Nicky paused, seemingly thinking hard about what to say next, and Jonas gave him the time. "I couldn't believe you stayed after what I did to you. And you were kind and patient and gentle too!"

"I've been treated worse," Jonas admitted. "You intrigued me. On the one hand you were so full of confidence, to the point of arrogance, but underneath that thin layer of veneer, I felt there was something else and I wanted to scratch the surface and see what that was."

"I suppose you got more than you bargained for," Nicky said, smiling but not directly at Jonas, whose eye contact he was still shunning.

"You could say that. For one, I never expected to fall in love." Now it was Jonas's turn to look away, but he felt Nicky's eyes burn into his skin.

"You...."

"When Tanna told you that you were falling in love with me, my heart jumped. And then when I saw your face and hers, I knew you weren't denying it. I almost panicked, Nicky, because of what it entailed and because of what it would mean for you and me."

"Of what it would change between us?" Nicky asked.

"My feelings were a little more selfish, I'm afraid," Jonas confessed.

"You would have to tell your lover you fell in love with a client...."

"Eduardo lost the right to that a long time ago, Nicky," Jonas said quietly, looking at Nicky's hand inside his own. "But yes, I fell in love with a client, only you never felt like one. I never felt like I was making love to you for the money."

Suddenly Nicky's face was inside Jonas's personal space and Jonas could smell him, could feel the heat radiating off his skin. He raised his head slightly, allowing Nicky to kiss him, ever so gently. Jonas closed his eyes and moved his lips just a fraction of an inch. The kiss was the most tender they'd ever shared and Jonas tensed up, afraid to take it further although he wanted to. He wanted this moment to last forever, didn't want this soft, almost chaste kiss to end.

Nicky pulled back, but he didn't move away completely. The young man leaned against him and gently settled his head on Jonas's shoulder.

Jonas felt the tension drain away. "That was nice," he said, licking his bottom lip in the hope he could taste some remnant of Nicky. "But what about what you said when we parted the last time? About wanting me to give up my job?"

"I've had time to think," Nicky admitted. "You told me Eduardo was fine with it, and I thought about it and figured I could be too. Oh, and I talked to Ally about what it was like to share a husband."

Jonas raised an eyebrow.

"She said she wasn't always there when you and Scott, you know…."

Jonas nodded, trying to keep a smile at bay.

"She told me she wasn't jealous and she didn't see it as being unfaithful on Scott's part. It was just something he needed and she said she had a dream of a husband because she let him. I just have a few questions."

"Shoot," Jonas said, tugging his ear.

"No more secrets. You told me about most of your clients, right? Anyone you haven't told me about?"

Jonas tried to recall. "Christopher, Clay, Scott and Ally, Johnny, I told you about them, didn't I?"

Nicky chuckled. "In delightful detail, yes."

"There's a movie director called David, but I haven't heard from him for a while now. He's an older guy, married of course. Not much to tell I'm afraid, except that he has a thing for blood. Luckily it's fake blood or paint, sometimes gravy. He likes smearing things all over me."

Nicky shuddered. "Okay, I can deal with that." Nicky took a deep breath in. "If we're together I want to know where you're going, when you need to leave. I don't need details, but I don't want any tension between us about this, and if I know where you are I'll be fine."

"I can do that," Jonas acknowledged.

"Safe sex always? I don't want to second guess you about this, Jonas; it's too important."

"Always," Jonas nodded decidedly. "Even between us, no matter how hurried or in what weird place we had sex it was always safe, wasn't it?"

"Good," Nicky smiled. "Now, are you still hungry? We could heat the plates up again. Jacques has a microwave but he'd probably throw a hissy fit if he found out we nuked his food."

"Maybe we shouldn't then. It's nice here, and we might want to come back someday."

"Jacques has gone home. He trusts me with dessert, though," Nicky said, and Jonas was sure he could hear some pride in the words.

"Dessert sounds good. What are we having?"

Nicky got up from the cast iron bench and pulled Jonas to his feet. "Come, I'll show you."

Jonas followed Nicky into kitchen where the designer took two square plates out of the refrigerator and put them on the counter. Watching from the entrance he couldn't quite make out what Nicky was doing, so he moved closer and gently curved his arms around the younger man's waist.

"Oooh," Nicky exclaimed. "Never seduce a man holding a blowtorch!"

They both laughed.

"I'm surprised Jacques trusts you to play with fire in his kitchen, Nicky." The smell of caramelized sugar started filling the air. "But crème brûlée is definitely one of my favorites."

"You trust me to use sharp pins around your groin area when I measure your suit," Nicky quipped.

"True," Jonas had to admit. "But this could burn the house down."

"Unlike when I have my hands all over your most intimate body parts and you just make me burn for you." Nicky flicked off the torch and set it on the counter before being turned around by Jonas and mercilessly kissed.

Jonas felt his body react, his heart overjoyed with having the object of his affection melting in his arms again. His hands were in Nicky's now shorter curls, keeping the young man's face close to his, but there was no need as Nicky was kissing him back with abandon. They eventually broke for air, moving apart only as much as they needed to catch their breath, leaving their foreheads touching.

"You want some dessert now?" Nicky asked, trying not to look cross-eyed as he gazed at Jonas from this close position.

"You've never cooked for me before, so I'm not about to say no."

Nicky nuzzled him some more before reluctantly breaking apart to pick up the dessert dishes. "Spoons are on the countertop there."

As Nicky was making his way through the narrow corridor toward the secret garden, Jonas couldn't help wrapping his arms around him and pulling him closer, kissing the designer on the neck. The feeling of Nicky melting into his touch was intoxicating, and he was anticipating how the rest of the evening would play out, hoping he'd be invited to Nicky's house later.

"We'll never make it outside this way," Nicky whispered.

"Do you want me to let you go?" Jonas asked, still holding his soon-to-be-lover-again tightly.

"God, no, but this isn't very practical!"

Jonas loosened his grip and they made their way toward the bench in the corner somewhat clumsily. As Jonas sat down, Nicky ended next to him, his leg hooked over Jonas's knee possessively.

"I want you to try this," Nicky suggested, digging into the pudding and breaking the caramelized layer on top. He fed a spoonful of it to Jonas, who moaned when the sensation hit his taste buds.

"This is truly exceptional," Jonas said, licking his lips. "And I've had quite a few crème brulée before."

Nicky used the same spoon and the same dish to take a bite for himself and then offered another one to Jonas. "You've had quite a few lovers too, yet you came back for me."

"I know a good thing when I see it," Jonas replied, wanting to strengthen this sudden confidence he saw in Nicky, but it didn't work. The designer looked away, his shoulders sagging again. Jonas gently stroked the side of Nicky's face and made him look up. "It took a lot of courage to call me back, Nicky. I desperately wanted you to, but I couldn't make the first move."

"Why not? We're equals now," Nicky asked, fear still in his eyes.

Jonas sighed and looked straight at the younger man. "You were so angry with me, and I was scared that you would scream and shout at me again if I called too soon."

"I wasn't angry with you; I was jealous. I saw you with him and you so obviously shared this intimacy, this physical closeness that only lovers have with each other, and I wanted it to be me, not him. I know that makes me sound like a child, but I missed you so much, Jonas, and I was miserable. I knew the only person who could make me feel better was you."

Nicky stopped and for the first time didn't look away after revealing his innermost feelings. The look he gave Jonas was still hesitant, but it showed hope, expectancy.

Jonas smiled somewhat. "I told Eduardo that I'd met you and then lost you again."

"How did he take that news?"

Jonas shrugged. "I don't think he believed me."

Nicky's eyebrows climbed toward his hairline.

"He knows I don't fall head over heels in love and certainly not with someone who's supposed to be paying me."

"Did you convince him?"

Jonas didn't answer right away. Instead he looked at the half eaten dessert dish and then at the spoon in Nicky's hand.

"Oh," Nicky uttered. "You want more of this?"

Jonas nodded. "It's very good." He turned a little toward Nicky and put his hand on the designer's thigh as he was presented with a spoon full of pudding.

"You're avoiding the subject here," Nicky said, looking mischievous but obviously only half joking.

Jonas swallowed and gestured that Nicky eat some too. "It's a non-subject. Eduardo has no say over who I date, sleep with, fall in love with or marry for that matter. He likes to think he's still a part of my life, but he's not and I think he knows that too. And to the other men, I'm a distraction, even for Scott." He sighed deeply and then smiled as he saw Nicky looking at him expectantly, while almost unconsciously spooning the rest of the dessert into his mouth. Jonas bit his lower lip and, in a lightning fast move, snatched the other spoon from the table and scooped up the last of the dessert left on the plate.

Nicky did a double take and then started chuckling. "We have another...."

"I know," Jonas answered in a teasing tone, while he grabbed the second dish. As Nicky reached out with his spoon, he pulled it away. "Uh-uh!"

Nicky mimicked an annoyed look and attempted to scoop some up again, but Jonas pulled away even further, this time taking a bite himself. That's when Nicky resorted to pouting.

"You know I can't resist that face, Nicky."

Lip wobble and puppy dog eyes reproached him.

"Okay, you win," Jonas admitted, narrowing his eyes. He offered Nicky a spoonful, but intentionally let the crème dribble down Nicky's chin, so he could lean forward and kiss the young man, licking off the excess. Unlike the kiss in the kitchen, this time their mouths moved more gently, unhurried. The dish was soon abandoned, and before long, Nicky was almost on Jonas's lap, their kisses intensifying rapidly until they needed to break for air.

"I suppose we should tidy up around here before we leave?" Jonas asked.

Nicky nodded. "A bit. Just get everything back to the kitchen. Someone will do the dishes in the morning."

"Okay," Jonas acknowledged. He couldn't keep from running his fingers through the designer's shorter curls. "I really like your hair this way."

"I was sick and tired of the pirate look."

They both got up and carried plates and glasses to the kitchen, and then Nicky turned off all the lights and closed up the restaurant.

Jonas waited for him outside in the passageway, which was still lit by the low candles. As Nicky rounded the corner, Jonas saw him hesitate. He was looking straight at him, but it was too dark to read the expression on his face. "Everything okay?"

Nicky nodded. "I was just thinking how fortunate I was and how I don't deserve you."

Jonas held out his hand toward Nicky. "Let's walk. It's a nice night out, and I think there are things we need to talk about that work better when we're not looking each other in the eye."

Nicky chuckled. "Good thing the streets are pretty much deserted. We wouldn't want to create a scene." He bent down to extinguish each candle and then took Jonas's hand.

Jonas peered out of the garden gate. "No paparazzi, coast is clear."

"Think they'd notice us if we sort of casually walked hand in hand?"

"Naah, happens all the time in Paris."

CHAPTER 12

THEY walked through Paris for a long time unhindered, never bothered by anyone; in fact, it felt like the city was deserted. They talked a lot about their families and about growing up different from everyone around them. About what they needed in a relationship and about what they didn't want.

Eventually they ended up overlooking the Seine as the sun started creeping over the horizon. Nicky was cold and had almost crawled entirely into Jonas's arms and the jacket he'd been wearing. Right now there was silence only broken by the pigeons checking them out as a potential source of food. Throughout the night the moments they weren't talking had become less and less tense, and Jonas started to feel very comfortable holding the young man in his arms like that.

Nicky yawned demonstratively. "I think we'd better head home, unless you want to carry me."

"I think you'd better walk. You're not as light as you look, you know," Jonas answered, hinting at the night when Nicky fell off his balcony and Jonas carried him inside.

"Okay," Nicky admitted with a theatrical sigh. "I was thinking how nice it was. Home in Paris is my house, in London we can take turns, in Madrid it's your house, and in Milan it's me again."

"New York?"

"Penthouse," Nicky admitted proudly.

"Tokyo?"

"Penthouse," he repeated.

"Nice!" Jonas chuckled. "But you have a lot more houses than me!"

"Well, you can always work harder," Nicky teased, tickling his lover's sides.

Jonas knew Nicky was exhausted. He flagged down a taxi and gave the address to the driver. It was no surprised that he had to wake the designer up by the time they made it to the house.

"Want to fuck you," Nicky drawled against Jonas's neck after the two of them made it inside.

Jonas chuckled. "It'll be a miracle if you make it upstairs, let alone get it up, dear."

Nicky fumbled between them. "Look, he's been wanting to say hi since that kiss in the kitchen."

Jonas looked down and saw Nicky's erection sticking out of his opened trousers. "That's an awful long time to be sporting wood."

"I know," Nicky moaned, "but you wanted to take a walk, and I figured we had all the time in the world." He stretched and yawned languidly, and then he lazily took Jonas's hand and pulled him up the stairs, stopping along the way for more kissing and groping. By the time they made it to the bedroom, Jonas was rock hard as well despite his tiredness. The fact that somewhere halfway up the stairs Nicky had stuck his hand down the front of his light linen pants probably had a lot to do with it. Jonas was still trying to get out of as many clothes as possible when he was pushed down on the bed.

"Want to taste you," Nicky said hurriedly. "Want your cock in my mouth. You know how much I like to suck your cock, don't you, Jonas?" Feeling the young man settle himself between his legs, arms resting on his thighs and deliciously hot mouth and tongue on and around his already leaking erection, was making him dizzy, so flat on his back was indeed the safest position.

"God, yeah," Jonas exclaimed, feeling his legendary restraint slip with every lick of the tongue and squeeze of the balls. Watching the designer deep throat him, solely focused on the large member, was almost too much.

"Close, Nicky," Jonas warned him huskily.

"Oh yeah," Nicky answered taking his mouth off for just a moment. "Want it all!"

Jonas didn't want it to end this quickly, but then again, being sucked to completion wasn't something he'd experienced often lately so he tried not to resist. He wanted to fully enjoy the tightening of his balls and involuntary contractions of his groin. Watching Nicky lap up every bit of seed that spurted out of him with such hunger was in itself incredibly arousing.

Seeing the beautiful, supple body crawl onto the bed and over him wasn't bad either. Tasting himself in Nicky's lazy but intense kiss was something else he enjoyed tremendously. In fact, the idea that this was something with the potential to become permanent was nestling itself into his stomach and creating a warm, fuzzy feeling there.

"Let me make it good for you too," Jonas murmured against Nicky's swollen lips. "So you can sleep, my love."

Nicky ground his groin against Jonas's now softening cock. "Touch me," he whispered in Jonas's ear, his voice dripping with need. Nicky raised himself slightly, rolling his hips so his heavy cock flopped onto the older man's taut belly. Jonas took the rigid shaft in his hand and spread the precome from the moist head to the rest of the shaft; then he cupped the young man's balls with his other hand and pushed his fingers into the sensitive skin just behind them. Leaning on his outstretched arms, Nicky involuntarily thrust into Jonas's strong hand. "Fuck yeah, that's it!"

"Go on," Jonas urged him, and Nicky stopped holding back.

"Gonna come... Jonas... come all... over you!"

Jonas squeezed just a little tighter, making the foreskin slide forward a little more as Nicky pulled back. With the next strong thrust, Nicky came, shooting thick strands of semen onto Jonas's chest and shoulder. The young designer pushed a few more times, convulsively, before sagging down into Jonas's inviting arms.

Jonas smiled as he squeezed him tight, taking in the feel of the young man's satin smooth skin, the smell of his hair, now short but still all over the place, the heaviness of his deceptively thin frame. He felt extremely content as the body relaxed even more, breathing becoming shallow and relaxed. He cupped Nicky's head and slowly rolled to his side, carefully placing it on the pillow beside him. When he pulled away, Nicky protested mildly and incoherently. When he stood up, the complaints were rather more vocal. Jonas laughed as he made his way around the bed in search of the packet of wet wipes that had become synonymous to sex with Nicky. He was beyond tired but he knew Nicky would be grateful later when they woke and he was spared feeling the flaky stickiness of dried come all over their bodies.

Not finding what he needed on Nicky's side of the bed, he moved to the bathroom. When he returned to the dimly lit bedroom, Nicky had fallen asleep mid-stretch, half on his back, half on his side, his arms over his head and his mouth slightly open. Jonas brushed away the satin sheets to reveal the body he looked forward to worshipping for the rest of his life and carefully started wiping the long sides and flat abdomen.

"Mmm, 's cold!" Nicky whined.

"Just using a few wipes to get us clean," Jonas replied softly as he wiped himself as well.

"Fuck the wipes," Nicky answered. "Need you here right now or you'll ruin my sleep."

Jonas threw the baby wipes in the wastepaper basket and crawled back under the covers.

"Diva," he muttered under his breath, while Nicky snuggled closer in his arms.

"Yeah, but I'm your diva," Nicky replied with a chuckle.

Jonas put his hand over Nicky's face and pushed him away, just for fun. He felt content to lie there with his arms full of Nicky any night, though, so feeling the young man snuggle closer again made him fall asleep with a smile on his face.

THE next morning Jonas woke up alone. He turned over and felt that Nicky's side of the bed was still warm, so he couldn't have left that long ago. He inhaled his lover's scent from his pillow and felt it harden his morning erection. A drawn-out yawn made him open his eyes. The curtains and the French doors to the balcony were open. For a moment he blinked to adjust to the bright light streaming in from outside, but then the long form came into focus.

Nicky was standing on his balcony stark naked, having himself a languid stretch.

"Come back to bed, you moron," Jonas joked. "You'll scare the neighbors."

"They should be used to it by now," Nicky answered without turning around. "I've been doing this for as long as I can remember. In this house, that is."

Jonas raised an eyebrow, remembering the time he spent in this bedroom and never saw daylight, but he didn't say anything. Instead he got up and wrapped the sheet around himself before venturing out onto the balcony. There were no apartments at the other side of the street, just a park which slowly sloped down. To one side the road curved down as well, so unless a neighbor hung himself out of his window to look onto the terrace, there was no way anyone could see them. When Jonas turned to the other side, he saw the balcony was lined with neatly manicured shrubs about as tall as they were, and he needed to lean over the railing to see the people walking on the street below them.

"You can spread the shrubs a bit if you want to catch Tanna and Maia snogging *al fresco*," Nicky whispered, suddenly closer to Jonas. "They sometimes sleep on their terrace."

"No thank you," Jonas answered, walking around Nicky to sit down on the cast iron garden bench near the back of the balcony. "It is nice out though; lots of oxygen in the air."

"Mmm," Nicky nodded, throwing a pillow on the floor and kneeling on it. He tried to find his way through the sheet covering his lover. "You've hidden my favorite toy, Jonas; that's not fair." He pressed between Jonas's legs and made the older man jump.

"I better go pee before I make a big stain on the stones here."

"I don't mind," Nicky replied cheekily.

"But I do," Jonas teased, getting up after bundling the satin around him.

"Can I hold it?" Nicky asked innocently, or at least pretending to be.

"Hold it?" Jonas stood in the middle of the bedroom, not quite sure what he'd just heard.

"You know," Nicky teased, all innocence lost. "Instead of you holding your penis while you pee, I do."

"Perv," Jonas shot at him, feeling strangely fascinated. It was one of those intimate things and he'd never been that intimate with anyone, not even Eduardo. He slowly walked toward the bathroom feeling more and more turned on as Nicky followed him with a wicked gleam in his eye. He stood in front of the toilet, still hugging his sheet, while Nicky moved behind him. "You know what it's like to pee with an erection, Nicky, don't make this any harder!"

"You hard, then?" Nicky asked him innocently. "Let me relieve you of your sheet," he teasingly suggested, but instead of grabbing the cloth, Nicky put his hands flat on Jonas's stomach and dipped them underneath the fabric. He moved down just a bit, but stopped way short of his target. "You really need to go badly, don't you?"

Jonas sighed. "Yes, Nicky." He closed his eyes and nodded. Nicky's hands on his belly and the feel of the designer's erection against his ass only made him harder, so the longer he waited, the more difficult it would become to actually relieve himself. He started to extricate himself from the sheet as Nicky pulled their bodies even tighter together. It still felt slightly strange that they were this free with each other now, even though that's what he had wanted all along. He swallowed when Nicky's slender hand wrapped around his erection, and tried to relax. It wasn't easy to forget whose hand was holding him, and even though he wasn't the type of man who couldn't pee with anyone else in the room, nothing happened. He groaned in frustration and placed his hands on the cool tile above the toilet, making him lean slightly forward.

"Relax, Jonas, it's me," Nicky whispered. "Trust me."

Maybe that was it; maybe subconsciously, he didn't trust his lover enough yet. The flat hand on his belly pressed onto his full bladder, making it slightly painful, and he decided then and there to follow Nicky's lead. The sudden release of pressure felt amazing, especially because it was accompanied by a kiss to his neck and a nick of teeth over his earlobe.

"Thank you, lover," Nicky murmured, rubbing his arousal against Jonas's ass. He moved his hand back and forth over Jonas's erection, sliding the skin around and making it more and more difficult for Jonas.

The older man twisted his head so he could nuzzle Nicky. "Hold off for a moment, Nicky. Let me finish first."

Nicky smiled against Jonas's mouth. "I want you to fuck me as soon as you're finished, and for that I need you nice and hard."

"Oh, I will be, don't worry," Jonas assured him, squeezing out the last droplets. "Done," he announced.

Nicky giggled and then shook Jonas's cock before letting go of it and grabbed the sheet still between them to wrap his lover into and hug him tight. "I love you," he said quietly.

Jonas managed to free his hands and placed them over Nicky's. "I love you too."

They stood there for a while, hugging in the cold bathroom, until suddenly Nicky let go and pulled the sheet to make Jonas follow him. As soon as they entered the bedroom, Nicky ran to the balcony. "Fuck me here, Jonas! I've always wanted to get fucked here!"

Jonas chuckled at Nicky's abandon and at the loudness of his voice. For a moment he thought that if anyone within a mile radius spoke English, they'd have heard him. Then again, Jonas didn't care. He'd been fucked in parks and squares and on plenty of balconies before and certainly appreciated sex *al fresco*, so he abandoned his sheet and brought lube and condoms to where Nicky was leaning on the stone balustrade. He couldn't help admiring the firm ass cheeks, the long legs and back, the unadulterated sexuality Nicky was displaying by standing there, legs slightly spread, watching his own erection proudly bouncing as he moved his hips. Jonas wanted it to last, their first coupling after the fight, their first as real lovers, but he knew Nicky was too horny for that; he'd never have the patience. The fact that he easily opened up to Jonas's strong slippery fingers was further evidence of that.

"Fuck, Jonas, stop!" Nicky yelled suddenly.

"What's wrong?"

"You're making me come and I only want to come with you inside me," Nicky panted, clearly trying to hold it together. "Just do it, I can't wait any longer."

Jonas knew Nicky wasn't completely ready yet but he slowly withdrew his fingers, wiped them on the discarded sheet, and rolled a condom onto his own straining shaft. He would simply use enough lube and take it slow. Nicky pushed his ass against Jonas's groin as soon as Jonas came a little closer.

"Need you," he almost begged. "Need you so much."

Jonas lined up his slicked cock and slowly pushed inside the pliable body. He wanted to thrust inside the tight heat but he didn't want to hurt his lover, didn't want a repeat of the very first time they were this intimate. This time, Nicky's reaction was very different. They were both standing, Jonas's arms around Nicky's chest, holding him up. The young man's back was bent to maximize the contact with Jonas's hairy chest and his head was thrown back. As

Jonas started moving slowly, the strained look on Nicky's face was replaced by blissful abandon.

"Oh God, yes, Jonas... feels so good... too good."

Jonas's range of movement was limited but clearly it was enough for the young man as he thrust shallowly. The ease of their movements together and the fact Nicky had turned his head, wordlessly begging for a kiss, was making the older man's passion rise. They didn't quite make it all the way to the kissing stage though, Nicky's seemingly unstoppable flood of words becoming more and more incoherent.

"Harder... please harder, make me... come," he murmured against Jonas's mouth. "You... come too... please...."

Jonas's hands roamed over Nicky's smooth chest, rubbing over a nipple, down his sides, over his belly button and toward the bouncing shaft. He cupped both Nicky's cock and sac in one hand and pulled him closer, pushing himself deeper into the gorgeous body. That started Nicky's convulsions, accompanied by groans that started low but increased in pitch. Jonas moved his hand into the stickiness of Nicky's release as the young man lost his balance and slumped onto the balcony balustrade. Jonas's upper body followed, and it took only two more thrusts into the tight, convulsing sheath for him to see stars as well.

Jonas clung to Nicky as they both panted hard.

"Don't move yet," Nicky pleaded. "You feel so good inside me; I'm not ready to let you go yet."

"I'm not going anywhere," Jonas assured him. "Not for as long as you'll have me."

They eventually disentangled and shared a shower, their lips never far from each other and their hands running over each other's bodies, using the excuse of washing one another to reacquaint themselves with each other's most intimate body parts. Every sense of rushing seemed to have left them, and they passed the time having a lazy breakfast of croissants and baguettes with cheese, drinking coffee out on the terrace in their bathrobes only to end up in bed again.

They talked a lot, at first mostly about their pasts, but as the shadows lengthened and the bright sunshine was replaced by the more subdued colors of dusk, they tentatively started discussing a future together.

Some of the old topics cropped up: about how Jonas wanted his independence and therefore his own money, and about how Nicky worked so hard there really wasn't any time for him to have a partner. No harsh words were exchanged this time, though, the commitment to find a way to build a life together much stronger than their respective egos. The fact that they were both naked and fairly aroused by hours of kissing and touching probably helped in that respect.

"You have no idea how much I love this body of yours, Jonas," Nicky murmured in between his slow licking of Jonas's nipples until they were both reddened and hard.

"Yes, I do," Jonas answered, after which he realized the humor in his answer. He laughed when he saw Nicky look at him with an interested face. "I mean I'm flattered, because I know how much I like yours and mine has so much more wear."

Nicky smiled too now. "Old clothes become softer with age. If you take good care of them, they become very comfortable and easy to wear. You feel loved and cared for when you wear old clothes."

"Nice analogy," Jonas admitted. "I like fairly new clothes. The fabric isn't frayed at the edges, the seams are still intact. It feels like it's been worn before but it's not old yet."

"Guess it's good we don't both like the same things, hey?" Nicky mused, before stretching up to kiss Jonas again. "I've decided to delegate more of the day to day work of Maison Bryant," Nicky added, suddenly changing the subject right after he stopped kissing.

Jonas wondered when he'd decided that, before his little stalking excursion, or after it? Or was this a spur of the moment thing?

"Tanna has the same training as me, and I know Maia's been wanting to do more than create fabrics for years."

Jonas hugged Nicky closer. "I thought Tanna was the business wizard. I didn't think she made the creative decisions."

Nicky looked up at him. "That's by choice. She graduated just like me, but only barely. She isn't as creative with fabrics as she is with marketing, media exposure, and paperwork. She's the one who books the fashion shows and the models as you know, and she makes sure that everyone does their job. I'd be totally lost without her, because I hate all that. And Maia does have the creativity, but I'm such a control freak I never let her take any responsibilities until now. Jonas?" Nicky's voice changed all of a sudden, from rambling about his job to the very curious way he spoke his lover's name. "Does talking about Tanna turn you on?"

Jonas knew exactly where Nicky's hand was and what he'd discovered under the sheets that were wrapped around them in the cooling evening. He turned both of them around until Nicky was flat on his back with Jonas full length on top of him. "*You* turn me on, Nicky."

Nicky giggled as much as he could with the weight of Jonas's body on top of him. He spread his legs wantonly and let Jonas grip his forearms and move them until they were above his head.

"Now I have you right where I want you," Jonas groaned. He started playfully biting at Nicky's lips. "You don't have to go anywhere, do you? This week?"

He saw Nicky's face turn from playful to being more cautious. "No, nothing special going on. There's a party somewhere that I would have gone to if we hadn't... but no, I had nothing planned."

"Good," Jonas replied good-humored, "because I want to mark you."

"Mark me?"

Nicky tensed up, so Jonas smiled. "Trust me? You know I won't hurt you, right?"

Nicky smiled back and Jonas started kissing him, still holding his arms over his head. Near his jaw Jonas nicked him slightly with his teeth, not biting with any sort of force, but his lover seemed to respond to it nevertheless. Or maybe it was the grinding of his hips against Nicky's groin that was making the younger man moan. Jonas continued his exploration of Nicky's neck, let his tongue roam over the large artery pulsing underneath the skin. He reveled in the fact that Nicky stretched his neck to accommodate him, and stopped for a moment to chuckle.

"What?" Nicky asked, looking more amused than annoyed.

"I was thinking of biting you, like on the cover of those cheesy vampire romance novels."

A broad smile appeared around Nicky's mouth. "To suck my blood?"

"Mmm, maybe not," Jonas conceded. "But I still want to make love to you."

"Yeah, fuck me," Nicky chuckled.

"No," Jonas said softly as he rubbed his forehead against Nicky's eyebrows. "Make love, not fuck," he said softly. "What we did out there earlier was fucking. I want to worship you."

"What if I don't want to be worshipped?" Nicky asked, repeating a conversation they'd had much earlier in their relationship.

"Everyone wants to be worshipped by someone who loves them," Jonas continued, still placing small kisses all over Nicky's face. "I love you, and I want to make you feel good."

"You mean take it slow?"

Jonas looked up. "Yes, slow and good for both of us, like equals. You can worship me right back if it makes you feel better," he added a little sheepishly.

"Okay," Nicky conceded, kissing Jonas back.

Jonas ground his hardening cock against Nicky's groin and felt the pure enjoyment of rubbing their skins together, of the feeling of Nicky's soft, peachy flesh against his coarser, more hairy body. He wondered how long it would take his lover to lose his patience and take command of what they were doing. For now, the younger man clearly let Jonas take the lead.

"I like that," Nicky whispered, when they came up for air "You holding my hands like that."

"You like being restrained?"

Before Jonas knew what was happening, Nicky had turned them around and was lifting himself up until he was straddling Jonas's hips. Despite a small struggle, he couldn't get Jonas to let go of his wrists. His arousal was unmistakable, though, in the redness of his chest and the rigidness of his cock. For a moment Jonas feared the fierceness he saw in Nicky's expression and almost let go of his charge when a smile spread cross the beautiful face.

"I don't know, but I'd like to try it."

"You have handcuffs?" Jonas asked, testing the waters.

"No handcuffs," Nicky replied firmly. "Just your hands holding mine while I ride you. Slowly, like you asked."

"I'll need to let go to prep you," Jonas said.

"Okay." Nicky shook his hands free and reached behind Jonas for the supplies. He crawled down a bit so his face was just above Jonas's cock. "Let me prep you first?"

Jonas nodded, and Nicky took the head of the semi-rigid cock in his mouth, looking up at Jonas to gauge his reaction. All Jonas could do was close his eyes and throw back his head because the rush of blood and the speed with which his erection swelled overwhelmed him. There was very little else that was more of a turn on than Nicky giving him a blow job, simply because the designer loved doing it so much. Reflexively, Jonas spread his legs, and Nicky's hands cupped his balls. He was the one who had asked to take it slow, but there was no way he could comply with his own request.

"Nicky, stop." Then a little louder, "Please stop, you'll make me come."

The ministrations stopped, and when he opened his eyes, he saw Nicky leaning over him, looking at him intently.

"I could taste how close you were." Nicky let his finger stroke the line of Jonas's jaw. "I love to taste your seed, but I want to ride you more."

Nicky kissed him with abandon, sorely neglecting the rest of his body, then just as abruptly moved again. The next thing he knew, Nicky had turned around and all Jonas could see was that perfect little ass sticking up in the air. He raised himself until he was sitting and put his hands on Nicky's hips. The way Nicky was leaning forward, Jonas had a perfect view of the little rosy button of scrunched skin between the globes. Nicky swatted Jonas's hands away and wet his finger in his mouth, before slowly inserting it in his puckered opening. Jonas couldn't resist. The position was slightly awkward, but he desperately wanted to aid in his lover's preparation, so he took Nicky's hips in his hands again and pulled him closer. "Don't take your finger out," he commanded.

Jonas let his tongue circle around the finger and heard Nicky moan, then whimper. He moved away a little to allow Nicky to insert another finger, then again proceeded to ease the burn with his tongue. Soon Nicky was begging for more, stretching himself while leaking copiously. The older man inserted a finger of his own and sought out Nicky's prostate. A single swipe over the slightly raised area made Nicky's entire body tremble, and for a moment, Jonas feared he'd made him come. Nicky recovered, though, pushing himself up until he was on all fours and sporting a predatory look as he turned around to face Jonas.

"You better still be hard, because I can't wait any longer."

Without losing eye contact, Jonas found the condoms and lube. He plumped up the pillows so he could sit up comfortably and prepared himself to be mounted.

It almost seemed like a release for Nicky to finally sink down over the now purple, distended member. In one slow movement, Nicky reached between his crouched legs to hold it up and sat down on it, sighing deeply as he reached the bottom. Jonas knew he needed a little time to adjust despite the long preparation, so he slowly stroked the long thighs at either side of his hips until Nicky took his hands and entangled their fingers.

"Support me," he asked hoarsely. He slowly started rolling his hips and began to move up and down, slowly at first. Soon he was getting up almost all the way and sinking down again, varying the angle little by little until the pitch of his moans told Jonas he had found the right spot. Their hands still entangled, Jonas felt Nicky use the leverage it gave him but also the restraint. Nicky's cock was hitting Jonas's belly with every thrust down and was popping up again when Nicky raised himself up. It was offering him just shy of enough stimulation, and from Nicky's expression, he desperately wanted more friction. Resisting the temptation to let go of Nicky's hands so the younger man could wank himself to completion, he ordered him to wrap them around his neck. As soon as Nicky complied, Jonas hooked his arms underneath Nicky's knees and pulled him to his chest, trapping his cock between them. Moving his hands to cup Nicky's ass, he pulled the younger man up and then let him sink back down.

"Fuck yeah," Nicky sighed. "Faster."

"I thought we agreed we'd take it slow?"

"Fuck slow... we can... take it... slow... any time... you like." He quickly kissed Jonas. "Now... I need to... come!"

Actively helping the movement along, Nicky ground his leaking erection against Jonas's belly. It was all becoming too much as Jonas felt his groin tighten. "Fuck!"

"Are you coming?" Nicky asked as Jonas gave up his grip on his ass and legs. He started to ride the cock in earnest now. "Oh yes, Jonas... coming... too... yes!"

Thick strands of seed splattered between their bellies as Nicky rode out his orgasm. He didn't stop, just slowed down, as their racing heartbeats calmed in their chests.

"If you don't stop, I'll slip out of you," Jonas croaked, slowly opening his eyes to gaze at his lover.

Nicky immediately stopped. "Don't want that."

"I don't either," Jonas admitted. He suddenly shivered, and they looked at the open French doors and how dark it was outside. "Guess not all September evenings are as warm as last night's."

Nicky snuggled closer until Jonas wrapped his arms around him. "But it sure was a hot day!"

CHAPTER 13

JONAS never looked back.

Becoming lovers was both an easy and a difficult transition. They slipped into each other's lives almost seamlessly but it did mean Jonas spent more time than ever on airplanes. It seemed they were always jetting off somewhere, and Jonas was grateful that in most of their regular places they didn't need to live in a hotel room, but on the whole, he missed simply being home. The alternative—letting Nicky do the jetting around alone—was something he wouldn't even consider. It was hard enough being apart whenever one of Jonas's clients wanted him for longer than a few days.

Jonas had ceaseless admiration for Nicky, who didn't seem to understand the concept of jetlag and was always bubbling with excitement. His lover's tireless energy didn't always extend into their bedroom, though.

Somewhere after their first anniversary, Jonas's clients all seemed to want him at the same time, and he found himself taking on three appointments in a row. When he came home after not seeing Nicky for two weeks, he found his lover asleep in their bed and there was no welcome home sex.

At first it didn't really bother Jonas that much. Their first full year together had been quite prolific, and Jonas had to admit that after two sex-filled weeks at the hands of others, he didn't mind taking it a bit easier. Only when, after three weeks of being home almost twenty-four/seven with Nicky, they hadn't done more than kiss and cuddle, Jonas started to worry. Was Nicky growing tired of him? Was there someone else in Nicky's life?

Jonas pretty much discarded the second idea right away. Nicky was carefully shielded from the outside world since there were a lot of whackos around who weren't to be trusted around someone as famous as him, but there was nobody in Nicky's extensive entourage that Jonas was particularly worried about. Of course Nicky still had an almost symbiotic relationship with Tanna, and Jonas was aware that whenever Maia wasn't enough for Tanna Nicky was her easy second choice, but that was nothing new and had never interfered with their love life before. They were clearly going through a lull, and Jonas made a mental note to talk to Nicky about it as soon as the designer slowed down enough to actually listen.

"Nicky, we need to get away, just the two of us," Jonas told Nicky one morning after his lover had kissed him awake only to leave him alone in bed sporting morning wood.

"I can't," Nicky answered resolutely. "We're drawing up plans to open a store, and Tanna will kill me if I take off now. This is the only time we have a few weeks without traveling and Tanna thinks she's found the perfect location and—"

Jonas interrupted Nicky's rambling by pulling him into his arms and kissing his neck. Although Nicky was fully clothed, Jonas was sure he could feel just how turned on he was.

"Mmm, that feels nice." Nicky reacted by closing his eyes and molding into Jonas's embrace until he seemed to realize he had other plans and pulled away. "I don't have time for this, Jonas."

"No, you never do anymore," Jonas murmured quietly, more to himself than to Nicky as he moved back into the bedroom. He expected Nicky to leave but when he turned around, Nicky was watching him intently.

"I'm sorry," Nicky said, his face serious, just before he turned around.

Jonas couldn't help but feel that the words and the body language didn't go together. Was Nicky tired of him? Or was he just stressed out? Confronting his lover when he was about to run out the door meant setting himself up for yet another disappointment, so he stood down.

"You could come with me to look at the location," Nicky suddenly suggested, his back still toward Jonas and his hand already on the door handle.

"You don't need me there," Jonas replied, still feeling angry about Nicky's constant rejection.

"No, I don't, but I still value your opinion."

Resisting Nicky when he gave him one of his pleading looks was hard enough on a good day, and this wasn't a good day. "Okay," Jonas conceded. "Give me five minutes to get ready."

THE site where the new store was going to be was a mess, but the location was perfect. The Rue Saint Honoré was the place to be if you were a name in fashion, and a small storefront had just become available. With her finger on the pulse of Paris *haute couture*, Tanna had taken an option on it right away, and now they had twenty-four hours to decide whether Nicky wanted to open his very first store there.

It was a big step and Jonas knew it. Up to now, Nicky had sold his prêt-a-porter line in joint stores that carried several big name designers, but this store meant having his own name on the marquee and therefore increasing his exposure, not to mention the fact that Nicky would be able to have a say in everything from the store's decorations to what the shop girls would be wearing and how they would approach the clientele. Having a successful flag store was the one thing missing in Nicky's career, and Jonas could understand this made his lover nervous.

Jonas watched Nicky and Tanna walk among the rubble the last owner had left on the premises and saw how differently they approached this project. Nicky couldn't stop talking about how dark it was and how they'd have to find an interior decorator who could bring some light into the place, and Tanna was already calculating the cost of Nicky's dreams in her head. Jonas of course, stayed in the background. He would give his opinion if Nicky asked him, but other than that, he remained silent. He enjoyed watching the two of them, though. Nicky was darting in and out of every nook and cranny like a puppy while Tanna was trying not to damage her delicate Armani Privé shoes on the exposed concrete floor.

"I think we should do it, Tan," Nicky shouted at Tanna from a small platform running up to a walkway that circled about half of the store. "What do you think, Jonas? Can you see us doing a runway show here? For the opening of the store?" He walked ostentatiously back and forth.

Jonas chuckled. "Yes, I can see you prancing around."

Nicky walked down the steps and joined Tanna downstairs. "Let's do it," he announced triumphantly.

"Are you sure?" Tanna checked. "You thought it was too dark? And too small?"

"Oh come on, we'll never get a location like this again. All the stores around here are big names. Dolce & Gabbana are across the street, Prada, Gucci! Chanel is just around the corner!"

Tanna threw Jonas a pleading look, but Jonas just shrugged, while Nicky ran outside to look at the dilapidated marquee.

"He's going to nag and curse all the while we're redecorating this," Tanna sighed.

Jonas couldn't help but smile. "You don't know that. He seems happy now, and it looks like a dump. Just wait until it starts to take shape."

Tanna shook her head. "You weren't around when we did the house. I almost shipped him off to Timbuktu with a big stamp on his belly, only he wouldn't leave."

Jonas chuckled. "I'll be around to get him out of your hair," he soothed her.

"If you can stand it. It's one thing when he has a design deadline, but when he's got an interior designer working for him, he has to relinquish control and he becomes intolerable. Mark my words!"

"Have you called the realtor yet?" Nicky asked Tanna after running back inside.

Tanna took out her cell phone. "Last chance to back out?" She looked at Nicky and then at Jonas. When neither man seemed willing to stop her, she dialed the number.

LATER that night, Jonas still had the feeling Nicky was avoiding him. Nicky was spending much more time than usual at the studio during the day, and he'd barely made it home when he announced that he was expected at a party in the city. Jonas rarely joined him at those functions because it was just not Jonas's thing, but also because there was too much chance to bump into people who knew Jonas's clients. Being at a fashion show or an official representation with Nicky wasn't a problem. In Jonas's professional life, he often accompanied one of his clients to an official function and then stayed discreetly in the background. The kind of parties Nicky went to also classified in that category, but Jonas disliked them immensely because it felt like work and he didn't want anything connected with Nicky to feel like that.

So Jonas stayed at home and waited for Nicky to return.

It was well past three a.m. when Jonas woke up hearing Nicky creep into their rooms. He'd gone to bed after midnight and probably wouldn't have woken up if it hadn't been for the racket Nicky made while traversing the living room toward the bedroom.

"Oops!" Jonas heard Nicky utter, followed by a loud curse. Sounds of pain coming from the next room made Jonas get up out of bed to see what was going on.

Nicky was half lying on the sofa, clutching his shin and muttering expletives.

"Everything okay?"

Nicky looked at Jonas, and a dippy smile appeared on his face. "Knocked my leg on the coffee table."

Jonas could tell Nicky was drunk, which was no surprise, but Jonas also knew that Nicky wasn't adverse to some chemical abuse as well, only it was too dark to see just how unfocused Nicky's eyes were. He decided it didn't matter for now and simply sat down next to his lover, taking Nicky's leg and placing it on his knees.

"Let me look at this."

"Ouch!" Nicky shouted when Jonas hitched up Nicky's pants to survey the damage.

"You broke skin, baby. Let me take care of this first. I'll go get something to clean it up. Why don't you get out of your pants?"

Jonas retrieved a washcloth and some antiseptic from the bathroom and returned to find Nicky butt naked from the waist down and negotiating his release from his rather flamboyant shirt.

"Come here," Jonas soothed, helping Nicky out. He'd done this more than once. Nicky wasn't too bad with drinking when there wasn't much going on. At catered receptions he rarely got more than slightly buzzed, but when he went out to parties, he invariably came home either blind drunk, or high, or both. "Relax," Jonas said softly when Nicky wouldn't stop moving. "Let me clean this up and you'll feel better, trust me."

"I'm sorry, *mon amour*," Nicky eventually sighed after protesting loudly to Jonas's attempts to get the superficial gash on Nicky's leg bandaged.

"Talk to me, Nicky," Jonas pleaded, taking Nicky's hand in his and rubbing his finger over the back.

Nicky moaned softly. "Can't talk. Can't think right now." He let his head fall back on the couch and closed his eyes.

"Then let me take you to bed so you can sleep it off." Jonas got up and held out his hand to Nicky.

"Why?" Nicky suddenly asked, sitting up and stopping midway to steady himself as if he needed to swallow away a bout of nausea. He ignored Jonas's offer, though.

"Why what?"

"Why are you so nice to me?"

"For starters, you're my lover and that's what lovers do for each other." Jonas knew that if Nicky wasn't happy when he was drunk, he could get mighty melancholy, so he tried to play nice for now, knowing they could always have a serious discussion in the morning, or at least after Nicky's hangover disappeared.

"I don't deserve it."

"Probably not," Jonas chuckled, beckoning toward Nicky with his outstretched hand. "I don't even want to know what you've been up to," he added casually, bending down to take Nicky's hand in an attempt to get him off the couch and onto his feet.

"I slept around on you when you were gone."

Jonas let go of Nicky's hand. He didn't know how to respond to what his lover had just confessed to and tried to gauge the purpose of the admission. He knew Nicky hadn't been unfaithful to him before, but they'd discussed that physically they couldn't be faithful because of Jonas's work. Emotionally they were monogamous. That was what they'd agreed on many times, so if Nicky told him he'd slept around, it must mean he'd fallen in love with someone else. It would explain his standoffishness and the fact that Nicky was avoiding being alone with him.

Jonas sat down in the chair next to the sofa, resting his elbows on his knees and letting his head fall between his shoulders. "We discussed before that physically—"

"Yeah, I know," Nicky interrupted, purposely avoiding crossing eyes with Jonas.

"So you fell in love with someone else?" Jonas continued quietly. Hearing himself say the words hurt, but he wanted to be sure. Mentally he was already packing his bags and moving back to his house in Spain.

"No!" Nicky said. "It didn't mean anything. I was drunk and I knew him from before... before you."

"Was it Josh?" Jonas asked blandly.

"No. It's nobody you know and it didn't mean anything."

Nicky's words mellowed Jonas somewhat. He couldn't hold it against Nicky if there weren't any feelings involved. He slept with his clients and he had at least some sort of friendship with them, so in all honesty, Nicky had more reason to be jealous than Jonas did.

Jonas moved to sit closer to Nicky again, sensing that his lover's unease hadn't abated. If it wasn't feelings, there had to be something else. Then it dawned on him.

"Was it safe?"

Nicky closed his eyes, and tears rolled down his face.

"Oh, man." Jonas pulled Nicky into his arms and squeezed him tightly as Nicky sobbed.

"I don't know, Jonas," Nicky managed to squeeze out of his heaving chest. For a moment he buried himself deep into Jonas's caress, but then he pulled away and got up to put as much space between them as possible.

"Nicky? Nick?" Jonas called after him and lit one of the small lights to get a better look. "You'll have to get tested, but I'm sure it'll be okay."

It took Jonas some time to get Nicky to calm down and allow him closer again. He knew that Nicky's emotions were augmented by whatever he'd taken or drunk at the party and that if he gave his lover some time, he'd see sense.

Eventually they settled against the far wall of the living room and Jonas managed to put his arm around Nicky without his lover feeling the need to pull away.

"What if he gave me something, Jonas?"

"It's always possible, I suppose," Jonas answered truthfully, tenderly caressing Nicky's curly hair. "That's why we get tested."

"It's not that simple when you're famous. It'll be all over the tabloids in no time."

Jonas sighed. "I can recommend a doctor in London. He's very discreet. He's tested me numerous times since the big scare in the eighties and it never went outside of his practice. He even lets you come in after hours so there are no secretaries to worry about, and he uses an alias to send the tests through."

Nicky didn't answer right away. It gave Jonas some time to think. All this time since he'd returned from work, Nicky had made him worry that he no longer loved him when the opposite was true. Nicky had stayed away from him because he didn't want to infect him with something and he didn't know how to tell him they needed to use condoms again for a while. However awkward, Nicky did it to protect him. It only made Jonas love Nicky more.

Suddenly Nicky shivered. Jonas had slowly managed to get Nicky to relax, and the effects of the alcohol were wearing off. "Let's get you to bed, hey?" Jonas suggested.

"I…." Nicky sighed as if he needed time to find the right words. "Sleeping next to you is torture right now, Jonas."

Jonas raised an eyebrow.

"I want you so much, and it gets worse with every passing day. I used to go without sex for weeks sometimes and it never bothered me, but after we got together, we—" Nicky's voice faltered and he sniffed.

"We were pretty active," Jonas chuckled. "But we can use condoms for a while, can't we?"

"I hate having anything between us."

Jonas pulled Nicky closer again. "I know, baby, but we'll just have to be careful for a while. It's okay, we'll make it through. It'll be just like in the beginning."

Nicky nodded, and Jonas felt some of the tension leave his lover's body. Nicky was still cold, and Jonas managed to persuade him to crawl into bed with him. They kissed and cuddled a bit, but didn't make love. When Nicky finally fell asleep, Jonas got up again and saw that it was almost dawn. He wrote a note for Tanna, letting her know not to expect Nicky for work that morning, and then got back into bed, cradling Nicky in his arms.

Although it felt good to hold Nicky close again, sleep evaded Jonas. He realized he was jealous, although he had no right to be. He had the best of both worlds: a lover who adored him and couldn't keep his hands off him at home, and a job that allowed him to work only a few weeks a year where he got to bed a whole array of men. Men who not only looked and felt different, but who liked to indulge their sexual fantasies with him, and Jonas had to admit, some of those fantasies he enjoyed very much.

Nicky, on the other hand, worked incessantly and had one lover: Jonas.

So why was Jonas jealous? Why did the idea that another man touched his lover send shivers down his spine? They'd discussed letting Nicky "share" some of Jonas's experiences, especially after Nicky had shown some interest in Clay and Clay, quite separately, had admitted he wanted a threesome. Jonas's first thought was that he wouldn't mind suggesting to Nicky that he be the third man. In fact, the idea had excited him. He'd come close to sharing Nicky with Scott, though Ally had vetoed the idea; yet Jonas wouldn't have minded that either.

Jonas realized that he was okay with "sharing" Nicky while he was there, but that what Nicky had done felt like betrayal. Nicky had betrayed the trust they had between them by sleeping with another man on a whim.

Jonas shook the demons out of his head. It was abundantly clear that Nicky felt remorse, and that it probably wouldn't happen again. Why would he let something like this spoil what they had together? His relationship with Nicky was the most amazing thing he'd ever experienced and he didn't want to lose it. Jonas looked at his sleeping lover, the love that had always been between them as strong as ever. It let him relax enough to slowly drift off to sleep.

THE following weeks were hectic ones. Right after signing the deal to acquire the store, Jonas and Nicky nipped over to London for the medical tests. Jonas got tested along with Nicky, just to help Nicky get over his fear of needles. It hadn't worked but that hadn't stopped Jonas.

Back in Paris, neither of them had time to stress over the test results. Nicky had hired a renowned interior designer for the store and had thrown a major tantrum when the man hadn't immediately jumped on a plane, so they'd taken a business flight to Milan to meet with him. Jonas, as usual, stayed in the background and amused himself by watching the two men interact. Nicky played the part of the spoiled rotten wild child perfectly and demanded everything be bigger and better than any other store. Andrea Moretti, a short, stocky man who looked like he didn't have a hairless inch on his entire body, was more subdued but couldn't hide his Italian temperament. The more Nicky exasperated him, the more he started to resemble a kettle about to boil over. He kept his cool, although Jonas saw him vent toward his assistant a few times. Jonas instantly felt sorry for the young man running back and forth with coffee and biscotti.

The test results came back negative, as predicted, but the doctor told Nicky that he'd have to be retested in three months' time, so sex was still on a slow burn. Nicky detested going back to using condoms, so their contact was limited to lots of kissing and cuddling and the occasional hand job. Jonas had to admit he didn't mind too much. They were together pretty much twenty-four/seven, and if anything, it allowed them more intimacy and more time to talk.

The closer it came to the opening of the store, the more impossible Nicky became. As Tanna had predicted, Nicky was driving himself crazy with wanting the store to be perfect. Jonas understood that there was only one chance to make a first impression, but he had his work cut out trying to keep Nicky sane.

"You said it would be here, so I want it here. Now!" Nicky shouted at the uncomfortably fidgety design assistant. When she tried to protest, Nicky gave her an arrogant look. "I don't care how you do it. I always keep my promises; I suggest you do the same." And with that, Nicky turned around and grabbed some of the design sketches for the back of the shop and determinedly paced away.

Jonas was on the phone with Ally immediately after the exchange. "He's driving me crazy, Al. I'd like to get him away from here for a few days, but he seems to think he's indispensable."

"Just wait until the shop opens; he'll be fine then," Ally tried to soothe him.

"That's another three weeks, Al."

"I don't suppose you have a client who wants to see you?"

Jonas shook his head. "I turned down Christopher already. I can't leave now."

"Guess someone else feels indispensable," Ally chuckled.

Jonas smiled. Ally clearly caught him. "Maybe I am."

"Maybe you like feeling he needs you," Ally suggested in her mock arrogant voice. She didn't wait for an answer, though. "Why don't you arrange for some time off after the shop opens, and maybe we can all go to the island?"

Jonas remembered the last time they were there. It was idyllic and very restful. Maybe Ally was right. "I'll ask him. Better yet, I'll arrange the time with Tanna and then simply tell him he's got a vacation planned."

"That's my boy," Ally laughed. "One day, you'll learn to be a good wife, darling."

Jonas chuckled as he put down the phone. He was going to have to do something, give himself something to look forward to in order to get through the coming weeks.

From where he was sitting, Jonas surveyed the store. Although a lot had been done already, it still looked like a war zone. A rough, temporary wooden floor was laid down and carpenters were building shelves over at one end while plasterers were still working on the opposite wall. One corner of the shop was occupied by furniture that had been delivered early and was still tightly packed in crates.

Builders were everywhere, and in a former life, Jonas would have
certainly let his eyes wander over their butch frames and visible
muscles, but he wasn't interested in that now. His mind was
occupied by trying to figure out ways to make life palatable for the
coming weeks.

"I don't want to hear your excuses. I'm paying you a lot of
money to get this done, but it's starting to look like I should have
just done it myself!"

Jonas smiled, more to keep his own spirits up than for any
other reason, and decided to go rescue the poor designer's assistant
from Nicky's wrath.

He found them face to face, Nicky with his hands on his hips
and the girl standing tall with a determined look on her face. Jonas
couldn't tell who was winning the battle of wills but he knew it
wasn't a very constructive way to do business, so he walked up to
them and put his hand lightly on Nicky's waist.

"Why don't we leave these people to work and get some fresh
air?" Jonas suggested.

Nicky gave him a steely look. "Because—" But then his face
softened and his voice lowered. "Because I want them to do their
job."

"It's not your job to make them do theirs," Jonas tried, pulling
Nicky closer.

"No, but if this doesn't work," he gestured toward the shop,
"then it's my head on the chopping block."

"And that would be a pity. Now let's go grab some lunch."

For a moment, Nicky intensely scrutinized Jonas, as if he
wanted to determine Jonas's true agenda, but he mellowed again.
"Okay. On one condition."

Jonas nodded.

Nicky moved closer to him and whispered in his ear. "I want
you for lunch."

Jonas didn't need to be told twice. He called the car, and luckily their driver responded quickly. Nicky was all over him as soon as the partition between them and the driver closed, and Jonas couldn't be happier to feel Nicky's arousal. The drive would be a short one, and Jonas was glad of that too, until Nicky gave him a predatory look and sank down between Jonas's legs to the floor of the vehicle, his hands hastily opening Jonas's trousers. Before Jonas could react, Nicky's mouth was all over his groin, and he wasn't taking no for an answer.

"Nick... Nicky, could you please wait for five minutes?"

Nicky shook his head, smiling around Jonas's substantial erection but not missing a beat. The deprivation Jonas had suffered the last weeks made the heat in him rise much faster than he wanted, but he seemed unable to push Nicky away, right up to when the limousine came to a carefully controlled stop in front of their house.

"Let's go inside," Jonas croaked, pushing Nicky away and tucking himself into his fine dress pants before opening the door. He was happy that they'd agreed with their driver it was unnecessary to open the door for them, knowing how "hungry" Nicky got sometimes. This time was no different.

They barely made it inside when Nicky attacked him again. Neither could wait long enough to make it up to the bedroom, but everywhere they went they encountered people, from the housekeeper to one of the cleaning ladies to Laurent, Nicky's assistant who, to Jonas's puzzlement, was rearranging furniture in the lounge downstairs. There was nowhere to hide, so they settled on the very public space of the hallway, hoping the rest of the household would make themselves scarce.

"Wanted somewhere more private, but I guess this will do," Nicky murmured in between devouring his lover's mouth. He went right for the kill and unzipped Jonas's trousers and sank to his knees. "God, I missed this."

Jonas sought and found a solid surface to lean against as he looked down at Nicky hungrily taking him in his mouth again. Ever since their first "date" when Nicky treated him to this for the first time, Jonas had thoroughly enjoyed his lover's extremely talented mouth, and these months of abstinence had only made him long for it more. As Nicky's lips and tongue roamed all over his distended member, he was quickly losing his notorious cool.

"Nicky, stop," he croaked without too much conviction. "Nicky, you'll make me come if—"

Nicky let Jonas's cock plop out of his mouth and looked up with his most innocent expression in his eyes. "Maybe I want you to come," he teased.

"You said you wanted me for lunch?"

Nicky nodded. "Which means I need to ingest something nutritious," he replied, delving in and hungrily sucking and licking the erection in front of him.

Jonas thought about it for a split second and pulled away, leaning down to grab Nicky off the floor and into his arms. "Pervert."

Nicky giggled, but he didn't put up much of a struggle when Jonas turned him around until he was leaning against the wall and started kissing his neck and brushing aside his shirt to lick his collar bone.

"God, I need you to fuck me. Right now," Nicky crooned as he started taking his clothes off right there in the hallway.

Jonas certainly wanted to. He was hard and aroused, and since it'd been so long since they'd actually gone this far, he was eager enough to not mind the public space, but there was also a nagging doubt in the back of his mind. After all these weeks, what had made Nicky change his mind? Why hadn't he been able to wait another week, since they were going to be retested then?

"Did you bring condoms? Otherwise we'll have to run upstairs...." Jonas stopped talking when Nicky's face changed from pure, unadulterated lust to intense hurt. His lip started quivering, and then he turned around and ran up the stairs. For a moment Jonas thought Nicky would be coming back with a handful of rubbers, but then it dawned on him that he must have said something wrong. A little hesitantly, Jonas followed Nicky's trail and walked upstairs only find their bedroom door locked.

"Nicky, open the door."

"Go away."

Jonas could tell Nicky was just inside in the door. "Let's talk about this, baby?"

"Go. Away." This time Nicky's voice was more insistent.

Jonas was used to Nicky's tantrums, but they were rarely, if ever, directed at him. Jonas placed his hand against the door and listened for anything going on inside. It was eerily quiet, and that worried Jonas more than a noisy tantrum would have. He had to stand face to face with Nicky and judge his expression. Only then could he leave him alone; not like this when there were numerous sharp objects inside the room and Jonas had no idea what Nicky was capable of. Jonas tried to listen some more, and when it stayed quiet, he took a few steps back and pushed his shoulder into the door. It took another attempt before it gave way. Once Jonas was inside Nicky's rooms, the blunt pain in his upper arm made itself apparent. Rubbing his shoulder, he turned on the light in the darkened room and realized Nicky wasn't there.

"Nick? Baby, where are you?"

No answer. All sorts of doom scenarios were running through Jonas's head, from Nicky jumping out the window to Nicky hanging himself in his closet. Jonas ran into the bathroom first, since it was the place Nicky always retreated to when he ran away. This time it was empty. Back inside the room, Jonas saw the windows were shut, so he briskly walked into the bedroom and could only just make out a lump on the bed.

"What part of 'Go away' don't you understand?" the lump said.

Although Nicky was still cross, Jonas was happy to see he seemed all right. He knew he had to tread lightly since he was still at risk of being thrown out again and wanted to get to the bottom of this before that happened. "I'll leave if you tell me what's wrong."

Nicky didn't answer.

"I need to know if you just need some time alone, and that you won't hurt yourself in some fit of—" Jonas stopped himself from saying what he thought. He knew it wouldn't get them anywhere if he lost his temper.

"What could possibly be wrong?" Nicky said in the high-and-mighty tone of voice Jonas hadn't heard much of since they first got together. "I haven't had a holiday in months. I barely sleep. I have a bunch of morons working for me who can't even get a tiny shop ready on time, and the fashion press is having me for breakfast, lunch and dinner and I don't mean they're feasting on my new line. They are tearing it to pieces on their ridiculously glossy pages and telling me I've lost my touch!"

Jonas couldn't help but smile. It wasn't that he was happy his lover was cracking under the pressure, but he was happy it was just that: pressure and stress, not something more substantial like "I've fallen out of love with you" or "I have a horribly disfiguring disease." At least the darkness of the room hid his expression.

"Oh, and I have a lover who can't stand me touching him."

There it was.

"It's not that, Nicky."

"You mean there's more?" Nicky sounded calmer now, as if he would listen to reason.

Jonas sat down on the bed next to the lump of duvet where he knew Nicky was hiding. "Despite all your tantrums and antics, I love you. And I know that when you get horny and hungry, you don't care about precautions. I also know that you would regret not taking care later, so I thought I'd do it for you. Because I care for you and I figured I'd spare you the feelings of guilt afterward."

"So you still love me?" Nicky asked with the tiniest of voices.

"Of course I do."

A hand crawled from underneath the duvet toward him, and a little later, Nicky's head appeared as well. "I'm such a—"

"Moron?" Jonas suggested, using one of Nicky's words of the moment.

"No," Nicky answered, sounding slightly hurt, but not much. "I was thinking about 'loser'."

Jonas took Nicky's hand in his. "You're not a loser."

"But I could have lost you. I behaved like a spoiled brat and I know how much you loathe me acting out like that."

Jonas cocked his head. "Yeah, because I think you're so much better than that. You're a grown-up. You shouldn't have to resort to throwing tantrums like the average three-year-old. Especially not at me."

"I know," Nicky sighed.

"So how are we going to resolve this?"

"Will you crawl under here with me? Please?" Nicky asked softly.

Jonas didn't need to hear that twice. He pulled the duvet aside and crawled in, searching for Nicky's slight form along the way and pulling him close once he'd found him.

Nicky chuckled. "I was hoping you'd take your clothes off first!"

"You're still dressed too!" Jonas protested.

"I guess this is good," Nicky conceded, snaking his arms underneath Jonas's and pushing his hands into Jonas's trousers once he'd made it round the back.

They continued to cuddle and kiss, and it dawned on Jonas it was still the middle of the day, and he couldn't remember the last time he was in bed with his lover while the sun was still shining outside. It made him long for some time off too. Then he remembered the phone conversation with Ally.

"Ally's invited us to the island. Let's go?" Jonas pleaded.

"Mmm, that depends," Nicky answered.

"On what?"

"On whether she'll let me have a taste of her husband's cock."

"You have a one track mind, Nicky. She and Scott agreed that he could have one man in his life, and that she'd get to watch. That's all."

Jonas's eyes were well enough adjusted to the sparse light to see Nicky's pout. "I don't see why you should get all the good stuff," Nicky said.

"I have a better idea," Jonas continued. "But you'll have to play my client again."

"Oh?" Nicky asked, his interest clearly sparked.

"Clay wants a piece of you. He wants a threesome, and I think he'll like the third man to be you. At least, I think I can twist his arm."

"Clay with the huge cock and enough talent to use it wisely? Clay who does boobies all day long and wants nothing but cock once the door of his practice closes? Hell, yeah!"

Jonas chuckled. "The very same."

Nicky snuggled closer and started unzipping Jonas. "You better give me a good pounding then, because with the lack of practice I've had lately, I won't be able to take him."

Jonas tried to stay calm, although he was almost shaking with anticipation on the inside. "Let alone both of us."

"He wants me to take both of you?"

Jonas nodded. He knew this was the one fantasy he hadn't fulfilled for Nicky yet.

"Oh shit!" Nicky giggled.

Jonas crawled on top of Nicky and started kissing him slowly, taking his time to let the kisses deepen until Nicky was almost begging. By the time Nicky was whimpering, Jonas was rock hard. They undressed each other and then made love so slowly that Nicky lost his patience more than once, but Jonas brought him back again every time. Nicky came as soon as Jonas entered him from behind, with Nicky holding on to the headboard.

Despite Jonas's hunger for his lover, he stopped thrusting and started kissing and touching Nicky again, making him feel loved, making him feel wanted, until Nicky was ready for round two. Again, Nicky came first, this time from the friction between their bellies as Jonas fucked him teasingly, slowly, while they were looking at each other.

They made love again later that night when the stars were out, *al fresco* on their terrace; and when they made their way to their warm bed again, Nicky shivering violently with cold, Jonas knew they'd definitely made up.

"The shop will be fine, Nick," Jonas soothed his lover, running his hand through Nicky's unruly curls. "And next season the fashion journalists will realize that whatever new flavor they found this season can't live up to their expectations and hit the jackpot twice in a row, and they'll come flocking back to you. And Lagerfeld and D & G and Armani and Versace."

"Oh, I can take them," Nicky sighed. "It's the ones I don't know that I worry about."

"I know, baby," Jonas replied, kissing Nicky's forehead. "But I think you'll find you have nothing to worry about."

"I think I'll need that vacation. We both do," Nicky whispered as he snuggled closer to find that crook in Jonas's arms that fit him perfectly.

"I'll arrange it all for you," Jonas said, equally quiet as he felt himself relax for what seemed like the first time in weeks.

THE opening day for the store approaching rapidly, Nicky still threw tantrums left and right. Only this time, they seemed to hit home with the interior designer and the builders. This was mostly thanks to the fact that Tanna and Jonas were there to pick up the pieces and calm the people down enough that work could get done.

Tanna had a flirty, yet professional way about her that seemed
to charm Andrea to no end—and he needed charming, because
Nicky didn't seem satisfied with anything.

"Now, Mister Moretti," she told him in her velvet voice. "You
know Nicky is an artist, just like you. And just like you, he's
temperamental. He wants things to be just right. I'm sure you want
things to be just right as well, since you will share the spotlight
when this store opens next week. You have a reputation to uphold,
just like Nicky."

Tanna moved closer to Andrea and Jonas had to stifle a shiver
when she touched the collar on the designer's shirt, a gesture Jonas
found intensely intimate.

"You look stern, Mr. Moretti, but I know that underneath that
shield you put up, you're just a big teddy bear."

Jonas cocked his head, trying to stay focused on the magazine
he was reading instead of on the spectacle Tanna was making of
herself. She seemed to be getting somewhere though, since Andrea
Moretti colored a nice shade of crimson.

"Mizz Taylor," Andrea crooned with a heavy Italian accent.
"How could I resist such a fine woman like you? I understand what
you are trying to say, you suffer from Nicky too, but he is a famous
designer—"

"As are you, Mr. Moretti," Tanna intervened, using her most
seductive voice.

"Yes, I am," Andrea agreed.

"So please give Nicky that curved wall, like you agreed
beforehand."

"I will do my best," the designer conceded.

Tanna smiled at him warmly and then turned around.

Jonas had to keep a straight face when she rolled her eyes at
him. She waited for him to get up so she could hook her arm in his.

"Please get me out of here!" she hissed. "Where's Nicky? I
want to have dinner somewhere nice." Tanna lowered her voice so

only Jonas could hear her. "That man gives me the creeps. Even talking to him is enough to put me in the mood for a nice, long, hot shower."

Jonas chuckled as he walked her out to the car. He knew he'd have to go inside again to fetch Nicky, but he also knew that Tanna wanted to put as much space between her and Andrea now, so he didn't mind. Being the quiet man in the background did have its perks sometimes.

CHAPTER 14

JONAS had never counted the days until a certain event. He'd always lived in the moment and felt that looking forward too much meant he'd age that much faster, so he simply didn't. His resolve was tested in the days leading up to the store opening, though.

During that last week the inevitable fires arose—from a wall that was curved differently than had been interpreted by the carpenters who'd made the shelf it was going to adorn, to a couch that was too large for the alcove it was supposed to stand in—but Andrea and Tanna settled every matter. Jonas was in awe of the way Tanna could make snap decisions and how she put Nicky in his place every time he lost it. That was usually Jonas's cue to intervene and pull Nicky into a quiet place to feed him some tea or just to talk to him. Nicky was nothing if not high maintenance, but Jonas didn't mind being the maintenance man.

Although they were very much a couple again, anywhere outside of their bedroom Nicky was simply intolerable. Even Tanna would run away from him from time to time, and she was usually the epitome of patience and grace; but like she'd predicted, Nicky's frayed nerves were making their impact on everyone and everything.

Three days before the gala opening, after all the plastering and painting was over, they'd taken the temporary protective wood covering off the floor only to discover that the glossy black resin surface that had been laid in there before most of the work had started was scratched in more than a few places. The firm that had laid the floor was called in, since it was their work schedule that had made it necessary to put the floor down before all the construction was finished. They were told there was no other option than to lay the floor again, which, given the time it needed to dry, would take three days, leaving no time to decorate the store, let alone put up all the shelves and hang out the clothes.

As Nicky threw a hissy fit, Tanna took over, persuading the flooring boss that since it was their suggestion that nothing would happen to the floor if they put the wood over it, it was also their job to work through the night to get the new floor ready. Workmen were booked for the last twenty-four hours so the shelving would be in place in time to put out the merchandise, and Jonas was enlisted to drag Nicky practically kicking and screaming from the shop to the atelier where Maia would be waiting for him to pick out the clothes that would be displayed in the store for opening night. It took both of them to calm Nicky down enough for him to make any sense, and Jonas was happily amused, taking mental notes of how exactly Maia managed to make the decisions but still give Nicky the feeling that he'd had a say in all of it.

The evening before the opening, they were finally allowed in the store again and Jonas had no idea how they were going to get it up and running in less than twenty-four hours. He knew that Nicky had picked out tons of decorations—all very stylish and *en vogue* of course—but the walls were still bare. The carpenters were hanging up the shelving, and a clearly overworked Andrea was directing his minions to all places at once. Of course, Nicky saw fit to give them contradictory orders, which resulted in Andrea turning beet red with anger and Nicky throwing him looks of disdain, but Jonas felt sorry for the minions, who were caught between a rock and a hard place.

Although Jonas was very much used to being the observer, the one sitting in a chair with a magazine patiently waiting, he now had to become a reluctant handy man, unpacking furniture and unwrapping the strange chrome handlebars that were supposed to be the clothes hangers. He didn't mind doing a bit of manual labor. In his house in Spain getting his hands dirty was the ultimate way to relax, but here the tension in the air was making it hard to breathe, and the fact that fashion groupies were already camping out in front of the large shuttered storefront meant they couldn't even open a door or a window.

Jonas silently endured, and for the first time in his adult life, he was counting the hours until the store opened and he could whisk Nicky away with him to their holiday hideaway.

"This is never going to be ready in time," Nicky sighed, standing next to Jonas in a ruffled shirt and skinny black pants and looking a lot more disheveled than Jonas had ever seen him. Jonas too had exchanged his usual dress code of stylish suits for jeans and a T-shirt, which had gotten him a few admiring looks from some of the minions, and one of the carpenters had definitely checked out his ass.

"Everything will work out," Jonas told Nicky calmly.

"Oh, what do you know," Nicky replied gruffly. Jonas didn't answer. Above all, he knew when to shut up.

At 11 a.m. and after working through the night, the shop was mostly ready, with the exception of the clothes that were not yet hanging.

"Go home, people," Tanna shouted over the ruckus of nervous chatter. "Get a few hours of sleep. The shop girls will hang up the clothes, and Maia will make sure that Nicky's decisions have been met."

"I can't leave," Nicky protested. "This is nowhere near ready!"

"Darling," Tanna preached. "You of all people need to look rested and relaxed."

"How can I be relaxed when this looks like a shambles, Tan? We can't open this store. We'll have to postpone it!"

"Nonsense," Tanna replied. "We're expecting three hundred invited guests, and there are already about sixty or seventy girls standing outside hoping to catch a glimpse of some celebrity or other. We'll do fine; we always do!"

"She's right," Jonas said, coming to Tanna's aid. "Let me take you home and get some sleep, even if it's just for an hour or two.

Then we can come back, and you can survey the work they've done. The girls are going to manage this store anyway after the opening."

"But it needs to be perfect tonight!"

Jonas gave him a cautioning look, and Nicky tried to protest one more time but then gave in. "Okay, but I need to be back here at least three hours before the opening. What if I think they did a lousy job and I want everything changed?"

"Then I'm sure you'll tell them exactly that," Tanna replied, resolutely pushing Nicky in Jonas's direction.

"But who's going to dress the models and supervise the make-up and…?"

"Maia's here, Nicky," Tanna answered resolutely. "You told her everything that needs to be done, right?"

Nicky nodded.

"Let's go home, okay?" Jonas pulled Nicky closer and kissed his temple. "Let me make sure you can sleep," he whispered, and Nicky giggled. Jonas was on to something and had an envelope with the results of Nicky's second batch of blood tests in his pocket to aid in the celebration. He had meant to save them for after the opening, but maybe they could start a little early.

Their ever-reliable driver picked them up, and Nicky started their lovemaking in the limo, like he always did. Only this time he felt heavy in Jonas's arms, and soon his actions went from sluggish to non-existent. Jonas could hardly believe how effortless it was. Now all he had to do was stay awake himself until they got home.

Jonas startled when their driver discreetly woke him up.

"We're here, angel," Jonas said, gently shaking Nicky. Nicky barely opened his eyes and let himself be led into the house and up the stairs.

Once they were inside their bedroom, Nicky turned around and flopped himself into Jonas's arms. "Fuck, I want to make love to you so badly,"

"Later," Jonas soothed him. He started undressing Nicky, and Nicky took this as a sign that Jonas wanted more than sleep.

"Fuck me, fuck me now."

Nicky's voice was lazy and sleepy, so Jonas didn't argue. He simply took his own clothes off and directed Nicky into bed with the sole objective of getting them both horizontal before Nicky collapsed. Nicky's hands found their prize object, though, and started stroking Jonas's cock. Just as Jonas was getting quite turned on, the stroking stopped, and Jonas sighed in frustration. Nicky was sound asleep in his arms. The celebration was going to have to wait.

BY THE time the shop was ready to open its doors, there were so many people standing in the street they were blocking the entire road. Tanna calmly called the police to inform them of the problem and let them take over, instead focusing on the goings-on inside the shop. Nicky was dead nervous, but after his afternoon nap, clearly ready to rock 'n' roll. The shop girls were fully made up and individually checked by Nicky to make sure they had the perfect look, and the models were wearing parts of Nicky's new *haute couture* collection to showcase for the opening.

They actually managed to be ready ahead of time.

"What do you think?" Tanna asked. "Shall we let them in?"

"That depends," Nicky answered with a smile. "Is Karl Lagerfeld here already?"

"Of course not," Maia answered. "Mr. Lagerfeld will be fashionably late."

"Then I think we should open fashionably late as well," Nicky replied.

"You're not going to wait for him, I hope?" Maia laughed, her arm wrapped around Tanna's minute waist.

"Oh, no, but there aren't quite enough people waiting outside yet," Nicky giggled. "After all, we only get to make a splash once!

Let's have our own celebration before we let everyone else in."
Nicky looked at Jonas, gesturing in the direction of a small bottle of
excellent champagne. The larger bottles would be used for the
official opening, but for now, the four of them were going to share a
glass of bubbly for their own private little shindig.

Jonas opened the bottle as if he was a professional sommelier.
After all, he was a well trained professional, and there were only so
many ways to impress prospective clients. Opening expensive
champagne to preserve as much of the flavor as possible, in other
words, without popping the cork, was something Jonas had learned
early on in his career. He filled the four glasses and handed the
ladies one each before giving the last one to Nicky.

"To a successful flag store," Jonas said quietly so only the four
of them could hear. He raised his glass before taking Nicky in his
arms and kissing his neck, careful not to muss Nicky's discreet but
flawless make-up. He let go almost immediately, not wanting to
rumple Nicky's avant-garde suit. "You look amazing, angel," he
whispered into Nicky's ear. Nicky stayed close to him, clearly
enjoying the proximity.

"Do you like what Maia made for me?" Nicky asked,
unusually coy.

"I do. It doesn't look like a costume for once. No ruffles and
no excess. Very stylish, but still very Nicky Bryant."

"Did you hear that, Maia?" Nicky asked, raising his voice to
draw the women's attention. "Jonas likes my suit."

Jonas thought he looked like a ten-year old boy for a moment.

"Of course he does," Maia answered. "You're wearing it, and
he loves everything you design or wear." She threw Jonas a proud
look anyway.

"I think you should say something to the girls, and then it's
about time we let the public in," Tanna announced as she let go of
Maia.

"So, you think I look presentable?" Nicky asked, taking a deep
breath in.

Jonas wiped a speck of dust off Nicky's chest where, on a traditional suit, there would be a lapel. "Knock 'em dead."

Nicky winked at Jonas and turned around, walking determinedly in the direction of the front counter. In those few steps, Jonas saw Nicky transform from his lover into the eccentric and over-the-top fashion designer the outside world knew and expected to see. The shop girls were suitably impressed and probably more than a little nervous.

"My darlings," Nicky announced. "Clients are a necessary evil. They usually fall into one of two categories. Either they are demanding and difficult because they expect to pay a lot of money and so want an equivalent standard of service, or they are totally in awe of me and will do anything and pay anything to be allowed to wear my creations. In either case, we need to treat them with respect. You are my minions, and your behavior reflects directly on me, so treat my clients well and show them how Nicky Bryant does business, and you'll have a long and fruitful career in my shop."

He turned around and faced Tanna. "What do you think? Ready to rock'n'roll?"

Nicky walked outside, flanked by Tanna and Maia. Through the open door, Jonas could see the flash of light bulbs and heard the noise level rise instantly, but he remained inside, discreetly in the shadows as always. He would avoid the public eye, ever present when Nicky needed him but otherwise invisible. He liked it that way, preferring to be Nicky's refuge rather than his partner in crime. He didn't want to share Nicky's spotlight, although Nicky had offered to walk out together. This was Nicky's night, and he knew Nicky would enjoy every minute of it.

The large sheet that covered the shop front came down after a small tug of Nicky's hand, revealing the inside of the shop to the outside world for the first time. Nicky spoke to the journalists in English, French, and Italian and introduced interior designer Andrea Moretti as if they were best friends, conveniently forgetting the many conflicts that had arisen while the shop was being conceived.

All the screaming young girls standing outside in the street got what they came for as many famous names, including a handful of older and younger socialites, and many a big name in fashion made an appearance. They were closely followed by several rock stars and a few world famous actors. Nicky greeted them all as if they were long lost friends rather than just there to grab the exposure; all for appearances' sake, of course. Although it didn't surprise Jonas, he was still in awe of Nicky's stamina and acting talent.

The party lasted long into the night, but as people drifted back to the other side of town to continue their partying in the night clubs, Nicky pulled Jonas into the small room at the back that served as the coffee room for the shop girls.

"I missed you, missed touching you," Nicky said as he pulled Jonas closer. "You know these public appearances make me randy as hell."

"Oh, I know," Jonas replied calmly. "As soon as we're somewhere private, I'll help you out with that."

"Want it now," Nicky demanded.

"Patience, angel."

Nicky raised an eyebrow. "Did you forget who you're talking to?" He tried to look stern and serious, but failed, at least in Jonas's eyes, since Jonas knew Nicky all too well.

Jonas leaned closer so he could whisper in Nicky's ear. "In an hour or two, I'll take you home and I'll fuck you so hard you'll be sore for days."

Nicky licked his lower lip.

"We have something to celebrate," Jonas continued, taking the envelope from the doctor's office from the inside pocket of his suit jacket.

"My results?"

Jonas nodded.

"All good?"

"I didn't open the envelope yet, but the doc called to say everything was the same as last time," Jonas answered, trying to contain his excitement.

Nicky didn't filter his emotions. "Then I really need you right now. Without a condom. Just you. Right this instant."

Nicky was already unbuttoning Jonas's trousers when the door opened and two girls walked in with a tray of dirty glasses. They were already halfway inside when they realized they weren't alone, but by then Nicky had pulled Jonas up the back stairs to the fire escape and out on the roof.

"Wow, it's gorgeous here. What a view," Jonas said, in awe of the lights of the city around them as they exited onto a small flat terrace. The view was that of the other rooftops in the vicinity, but all the visible windows were dark, since none of the adjacent shops were open. Most of the apartments were quite a distance away, so Jonas felt fairly safe.

"I didn't come up here for the view, love," Nicky said. "Please tell me you brought lube?"

"Sorry," Jonas apologized. "I wasn't planning on us celebrating anywhere but at home."

Nicky kissed him violently. "Mmm, rim me for all I care, but I want you now." Nicky hastily unzipped his pants and started pulling them down as he turned around so he could grab the railing and bend forward.

Although Jonas didn't mind Nicky being demanding, he wasn't entirely happy about the situation. He knew Nicky was beyond reasoning, though. Nicky wanted satisfaction now, and Jonas knew which battles to pick. This was one he'd lost from the start.

Nicky was loud and extremely vocal in his appreciation of Jonas's rimming talents and even louder when Jonas pushed into him. Their coupling was violent and fast, and both men were totally oblivious to their immediate surroundings. They didn't see the curtain being pulled aside as someone wondered who was making all that racket, and they totally missed the long telephoto lens that appeared at the open window of one of the adjacent shops.

THE following morning, Jonas was awakened by Tanna. He could never get used to opening his eyes and seeing her standing next to their bed, although he'd long since accepted that this could happen.

"What the matter?" Jonas asked, yawning sleepily as he crawled carefully from under Nicky's outstretched body.

"Trouble," Tanna answered with a deadly serious face.

"Bad reviews for the shop?"

Tanna shook her head but didn't answer. Instead she opened the laptop she was carrying and showed Jonas a webpage of picture thumbnails.

Jonas started to feel uneasy, but he clicked one of the pictures anyway. There was no mistaking it for anything else. Pictures of him and Nicky on that rooftop were all over the Internet, and you had to be blind as a bat to not see what they were doing. There was even a piece of video from earlier that night, in the shop, with Nicky explaining things about his designs and greeting a fellow designer. Jonas was visible in the background and his face was encircled. The subtitle read "Nicky Bryant's lover Jonas Hunter." There was only one thing Jonas was grateful for. It didn't say "Jonas Hunter, male escort."

"We can't tell Nicky," Jonas told Tanna. "He doesn't deserve this. He's had enough stress these past weeks. I'll take him away to Spain for a week or two. He can work from there, but he'll be away from the city and we can wait out the storm there."

Tanna shook her head. "I agree we shouldn't issue any sort of statement and it's better to ignore these tabloid photos and just go on with our lives, but Nicky deserves to know. We can shelter him, but we can't keep him in the dark."

Jonas sighed. "I'll tell him."

Tanna nodded and got up, leaving the laptop on the table. At the last moment, Jonas held her back. "What if they dig deeper and find out what I do for a living? It'll reflect badly on Nicky. Would it be better if I leave for a bit?"

"Who's leaving?"

Both Tanna and Jonas looked up to see Nicky walking closer. He was hugging the bed sheet, but his hair was sticking to all sides and only one eye was open.

"Nobody," Tanna was quick to answer. She looked intently at Jonas, though. "Tell him, Jonas. Tell Nicky where you're taking him and tell him why."

"We going on a trip?" Nicky asked, still looking distracted and possibly slightly buzzed.

"Sit, angel," Jonas asked softly.

Nicky sat down and nestled himself close to Jonas, guiding his arm around his shoulders.

"I don't care," Nicky replied to Jonas's explanation of what was put on the Internet. He was a lot more awake now.

"There's no mistaking the fact we're having sex on a rooftop in Paris. If you zoom in you can even see the dangly and not so dangly bits. It's going to come back and bite you in the ass, Nicky." As soon as the words left Jonas's mouth he wished he could take them back. The more he thought about them, the funnier they became, until he was giggling like a girl.

Nicky at first didn't quite get it, and then it suddenly hit him. "It poked me in the ass, that's plenty!" Then he turned serious. "You suggested to Tanna you could leave so I could cover this up, right?"

Jonas stopped laughing as well. "You're not exactly out, Nicky."

"No," Nicky agreed. "But I never said I was straight. People know nothing about my private life."

"Well, they do now."

Nicky looked Jonas in the eye. "I don't care."

"What if they find out what I do for a living?"

"Are you ashamed of what you do?" Nicky asked.

Jonas shook his head. "You know I'm not."

"Neither am I," Nicky replied determinedly.

"But it could reflect on you."

"It could cost you clients," Nicky was quick to counter. "I can imagine Clay wouldn't feel too comfortable taking you to basketball games if it was universally known that you were an ass for hire."

Jonas winced. "Don't call it that."

Nicky crawled back into Jonas's arms. "Just saying, it's as bad for you as it is for me. All we can do is wait it out and hope it goes away. I never spoke about my private life with journalists, and I'm not about to start now."

"That's what Tanna said too," Jonas agreed.

"I don't want this to come between us, Jonas," Nicky said determinedly. "I love you and this doesn't change that. Even if they nail me to the stake for this, I won't give you up."

"I'm glad to hear that. The feeling is mutual," Jonas replied with a relieved sigh.

"Good, that's settled, then. So where are you taking me?"

"How does Spain sound? My villa?" Jonas suggested.

"God, I hope it doesn't rain this time."

CHAPTER 15

JONAS was quite used to the hustle and bustle and excitement of fashion shows by now. After all, he'd seen enough of them in the last two years to understand that an enormous amount of work went into getting all that glamour and glitter to come across from that narrow strip of a runway.

Following Nicky all over the world had been a real rollercoaster, but one he wouldn't have wanted to miss for anything. They'd both stuck to their initial promises. Nicky did delegate more of the work, and subsequently, Maia had blossomed from a shy mousy girl to a strong, confident woman. She was in charge of the day to day running of the atelier and used her considerable talent with fabrics to make Nicky's designs come to life. Nicky still did the runway shows, of course, and the private clients, since it was his face and image that represented Maison Bryant, but other than that, the only time he spent long days in the atelier was when Jonas was gone, which was every few weeks or so.

Jonas's clients probably didn't notice the change in his personal life. At least that's what he told himself. He knew it wasn't just vanity that made him look in the mirror and see that he looked relaxed and happy. He felt it too, and even spending time with the men who'd been hiring him for years seemed easier because he knew Nicky was okay with it.

During one of his appointments with Clay, he'd managed to plant a suggestion in the surgeon's mind. Clay had caught him leafing through a men's fashion magazine and reading an article on Nicky, complete with glossy photos.

"Now there's a guy I'd like to do," the plastic surgeon had told him, eyes dark with lust. "He used to be this prissy, girly kid, but these past few years he's become a lot more masculine, laying off the make-up and showing off that delightful body of his on the catwalk. I must admit whenever I see something about him on TV or in magazines, my hands tingle to touch that soft skin of his."

"How do you know it's soft?" Jonas had asked, trying to feign innocence. He hid his glee at how easy it had been.

"I'm a plastics man, I know about skin," Clay had answered matter-of-factly. "He's one of those men with a woman's skin. Soft, satiny, and hairless. I bet he gets hard when you touch his nipples and has a small, tight ass."

Jonas had swallowed, equally turned on and creeped out by how closely Clay had described his lover. "Who says he's even gay? All those fashion designers are flamboyant."

"Oh, this guy is gay, definitely. He's queerer than you and I together, trust me," Clay had quipped.

"I heard he had a wife," Jonas had chuckled along, silently glad the tabloid pictures had obviously eluded Clay.

"No bloody way! That guy likes it up the ass, I tell you."

Jonas hadn't reacted to Clay's insolence.

Clay's sexual fantasy regarding Nicky was a simple one. Clay had whispered it in Jonas's ear while he was fucking the older man in the shower. He wanted to share the designer with Jonas, the two of them fucking the young man together until he begged for release. Jonas had smiled. He was more than aware of what Nicky's fantasies were and saw a curious match in the two men's desires. He'd have to ask his lover first, though.

Nicky had been as eager as a puppy and that hadn't surprised Jonas. Clay's reputation preceded him, after all. Getting the two men on the same continent was another matter, though. Eventually it was Tanna who'd succeeded. She had booked Nicky a runway show in

Buenos Aires during the same week that there was a World Conference on Plastic Surgery in the Argentinean city.

Jonas had briefed Nicky carefully. "As far as he's concerned, you are one of my clients."

"Does this mean he's going to shag you before you bring him to the show?" Nicky had asked that morning. His face displayed an amused smirk.

"If he wants to, tough luck. I'll tell him he has to save his strength for you."

"Will he listen?" Nicky had clearly been amused by the idea of the insatiable Clay.

Jonas had kissed him firmly. "He better, if he wants a piece of your ass!"

"So I'm your client?"

"Yes, you are. And what we're about to do to you is your biggest fantasy as well as Clay's," Jonas had answered.

"Biggest? You can say that again!" Nicky had snorted. He moved closer to his lover and nudged him. "I'm going to enjoy both of you."

"I'll make sure he doesn't hurt you," Jonas whispered tenderly.

"I'll make sure he doesn't hurt you either," Nicky replied, but Jonas could tell his lover wasn't nearly as serious about it as he was. "I bet you'll make a bundle from this little three-way. Not to mention, I'm sure you'll enjoy it too. Now I need to go, fame in Argentina awaits me!"

Jonas smiled widely as he watched Nicky flounce his way out the door.

CLAY and Jonas had only ever gone to sporting events together, so Jonas was pleasantly surprised at seeing Clay's wide grin when they walked into the room where the fashion show was going to be held.

The large room was decorated with browns and black, shiny surfaces interweaving with matte rawhides, and the lighting was subdued. Most of the other visitors were already seated, and the men squeezed their way through elegant society ladies and their well-to-do spouses toward their front row seats.

The show started with the women in frilly skirts, checkered shirts, body warmers, and cowboy boots. The girls in the first group were riding wooden stick horses, but the second group were riding butch, bare-chested men in tight jeans and wearing bridles.

As usual, the whole show was meticulously choreographed. Jonas had seen Craig, Nicky's choreographer, ordering the models around earlier and many times before. Despite the fact Craig was the original screaming queen, Jonas had yet to meet a model who messed with him. For a moment, he wanted to share this with Clay and then remembered he wasn't supposed to know things like that. Seeing Clay's enthralled look and wide smile told him small talk wasn't really necessary. The man was as captivated by the models showing a variety of day and evening suits and leisure wear as he was at a Lakers game, only without the cheering.

The finale was spectacular as usual. The women walked out slowly in long, straight evening gowns made of smooth black leather. The skirts were all virtually the same but the tops were all different, from tight and form-fitting to mere strips of leather covering only the necessary areas. As they spread out over the catwalk, intermittently facing one way or the other, the men came from behind the curtain skipping. They were wearing tight little leather hot pants and chaps and horse's heads. As they came to stand next to the women, they visibly butched up and hooked their thumbs around the belts of their chaps and paraded around as if they lived with a horse between their legs, bumping into the aloof females.

Suddenly they halted and started taking off their horse's heads, one after another. Just as Jonas was thinking the model in front of them looked curiously familiar, he took off his mask and Nicky's seductive eyes were checking Clay out.

The surgeon looked at Jonas momentarily and then back at Nicky when the rest of the crowd caught on and the roar of applause broke out all around them. People were standing up, and Nicky graciously accepted the accolades from all around, his eyes barely leaving the tall, dark haired man next to Jonas.

Jonas had to shake Clay out of his reverie as the hall started emptying. "There's a limo waiting for us. His limo. He'll join us in there."

"And then what?"

"Hotel suite." *Luckily not ours,* Jonas thought. "And then hopefully I can make two of my clients' dreams come true. Don't I just have the most amazing job," Jonas added under his breath, but loud enough for Clay to hear. Judging from the surgeon's smile, he had sounded enthusiastic enough.

The driver guarding the back door to the parking lot had obviously received his instructions; he asked Jonas for identification and then opened the door to let them through. The limousine was comfortable as usual, but Jonas still hoped they wouldn't have to wait too long. He knew Clay would like Nicky, especially the clearly confident Nicky, but he had never thought that Clay would be so mesmerized by his lover. For a moment he felt jealousy creeping in, and then he remembered Nicky's words: "I'll make sure he doesn't hurt you." Jonas realized that Nicky hadn't meant hurt in a physical way. He was going to make sure Clay didn't hurt them, their relationship, their connection. They were going to live out one of Nicky's fantasies, but Nicky was going to make sure Jonas's feelings wouldn't get hurt. Jonas smiled inwardly as he remembered why he loved this man.

Putting it all right in his head, Jonas felt the jealousy wane. After all, on a purely physical level, he wasn't faithful to Nicky. He still slept with Ally and Scott, still went on outings with Christopher and spent the occasional week with Clay. They had returned to Johnny's a few times where the old rocker had watched them fuck while drooling over Nicky's young, supple body, but this was different. This time Clay was actually going to fuck Nicky, and he knew both of them were going to enjoy it. He just wasn't sure how much he was going to be able to fake enjoying it too.

At that moment, the limo door opened and Nicky stepped in looking every bit like the star he was in tight leather trousers, braces over bare skin and a white unbuttoned shirt offering a glimpse of the olive chest underneath. Both to Jonas's surprise and happiness, Nicky took the long seat near the side as opposed to squeezing between them in the back seat. After sitting down, he put his long legs up and stretched out like a cat in heat. Jonas almost wanted to tease Clay by telling him to stop drooling as he saw how turned on he was.

"So, Doctor," Nicky drawled, seductively looking at Clay. "Did you like the foreplay?"

Clay shifted and Jonas guessed it was to accommodate some quickly tightening trousers. "You put on quite a show," Clay answered. Jonas knew that the cool Clay exuded was practiced and that underneath that calm exterior there was a raging fire. He couldn't wait to see what Nicky, his own private thunderbolt, was going to do about that. Jonas predicted fireworks and hoped that the hotel room walls were of a sufficient thickness to muffle most of the noise.

Despite the heavy Buenos Aires traffic, their driver quickly found his way toward the back entrance of the hotel, and Jonas was happy to see that even here, Tanna had arranged everything meticulously. This included a young man waiting to hold an elevator for them, taking them straight to the penthouse suite. As they strode into the lift, they looked like three ordinary men, their facial expressions neutral, looking straight ahead, but as soon as the doors closed, Nicky turned around and placed his arm around Jonas's shoulder.

"Why don't you introduce Clay to me properly, because I believe I'm going to get to know him rather intimately."

"If this is what you want," Jonas answered, like they'd rehearsed beforehand. "You said you wanted to meet him first, before deciding whether you wanted to go through with it."

Nicky pretended to check Clay out. "If everything you say about him is true—" he turned toward Jonas and let his finger ghost along Jonas's jaw, "—and you haven't been exaggerating, I don't see why I wouldn't agree to the three of us becoming... better acquainted." He turned away from Jonas toward Clay and started quite insolently pulling at the waistband of the taller man's trousers. "So is it true what Jonas's told me?"

Clay was clearly on his guard. "That depends on what he's told you."

"He tells me you're not only huge, but that you know how to handle your equipment as well."

Clay swallowed, but quickly regained his self-assuredness.

"That has been said about me, yes," Clay replied.

Jonas couldn't see what Nicky was doing because Nicky was blocking his view, but he could see Clay's face and he heard the taller man take a shuddering breath after straightening his back.

"Nice," Nicky remarked casually, and then the elevator pinged, announcing they had reached their destination. As they turned to walk out, Jonas saw Nicky withdraw his hand from Clay's pants, and he stifled a chuckle. Nicky had certainly become a lot more confident in these past years, and Jonas couldn't be happier with that.

Once inside the penthouse, it didn't take them long to get their bearings. The suite was large and airy with a sitting and a dining area, a bedroom with a luxurious bathroom to one side and large windows on the other.

"Give me a minute to freshen up, boys, and when I get back I want you naked and ready," Nicky instructed with a teasing smile on his face as he made his way to the right.

Jonas gestured indicating that Clay should proceed into the bedroom.

"Is he always this pushy?" Clay asked Jonas, unusually insecure.

"Wait until he has you right where he wants you," Jonas said, smiling. "He's used to giving orders. At least now he doesn't throw a tantrum when you refuse."

"You've known him that long, then?" Clay asked as he was getting out of his clothes.

Jonas nodded, stealing a look at Clay's tall, lean physique and his flawless California tan. "I've seen the transition. You know what I mean? He used to be prissy like you said, but that's all gone now. Doesn't mean he isn't one hell of a bottom." Jonas had agreed with Nicky that they'd stay as close to the truth as possible. They'd just casually omit that Nicky wasn't actually paying Jonas anymore and that they were each other's significant other. Jonas's eyes dropped to Clay's groin, his attention drawn to the prominent erection freed from the confines of Clay's clothes as Clay pulled his pants down. "You seem ready for action, just like he likes it."

"I've been hard since I saw him stare at me from the catwalk," Clay admitted freely, unconsciously rubbing his hand over his six-pack abs.

"Oh, yes, he does that to you, doesn't he?" Jonas was about to move closer to Clay now that he was naked as well when Nicky walked confidently back into the bedroom.

"I like it when you boys know how to follow orders," he chuckled. "Now how shall we do this?" he mused. He didn't wait for an answer. "Why don't you two get started and let me watch for a bit? You're obviously a lot more ready than I am." His eyes dropped to their groins and then back up, a smirk hovering around his mouth.

"No way," Clay replied. "I came here for you. I can have him any time I want," he added, casually gesturing at Jonas.

Jonas raised an eyebrow at Nicky and then shrugged slightly. "He's right, Nicky. Come here and we'll have you begging for it in no time."

Nicky slowly strode over and moved to stand between them. "That's a big promise there, Jonas."

"One I'm sure we can make good on," Clay answered as he pulled Nicky closer and let his hand travel down the younger man's back to his ass.

"You don't waste any time, do you?" Nicky stated more than asked as he let himself be pulled against Clay's nicely developed frame. He leaned back inside Clay's sculpted arms and held out his hand to silently ask Jonas to join them.

From Nicky's expression, Jonas knew he was seeing his Nicky as opposed to the Nicky his lover was showing Clay. For Clay he performed, ever the peacock, but his face was softer when the taller man wasn't looking. "Come here," Nicky soundlessly mouthed to Jonas, and Jonas quickly complied.

In no time Nicky was breathing heavily. He'd turned around and now had Clay against his back, the taller man's hands all over him and his mouth against Nicky's neck. Jonas was in front of him, and Nicky was being thoroughly kissed by his lover while his hand was wrapped tightly around Jonas's cock, and his own erection was grinding against Jonas's hip. Then he pushed Jonas away. "Too quick," he panted. "We'll never last."

Jonas moved away and retrieved some supplies from the night stand. "Who do you want first?" he asked Nicky.

Nicky turned away from Jonas and let his eyes rake down Clay's body. "I want to taste that cock of yours," he told the taller man. "Jonas can prep me."

They'd agreed that Nicky trusted Jonas more than Clay when it came to being prepared for fucking, so like everything else, they'd talked about this scenario beforehand. Jonas was definitely happy that Clay was just unsure enough to go along with a rather persuasive Nicky for now.

Nicky pushed Clay down on the bed and got to his knees between the doctor's long legs. He then reached behind him to draw Jonas closer, turning quickly so that his face was hidden from the surgeon. "Prep me and fuck me," he whispered. Jonas could read the unsaid "I love you" in Nicky's expression before the young man turned back toward the heavy cock lying on Clay's taut belly.

"Jonas certainly didn't exaggerate," Nicky said admiringly, looking straight into Clay's darkening hazel eyes. "If anything, he underestimated you."

Clay's mouth opened to speak, but his words were lost and he couldn't reply as he watched his erection disappear almost completely into Nicky's mouth.

Jonas rolled a condom over his own straining erection. It was going to be strange to fuck Nicky with a condom again, but he knew this was the only way. Besides being safer, it would also be a dead giveaway if he didn't. He couldn't wait to plunge into the waiting body, though. He knew Nicky wouldn't need much preparation. Their bodies were so in synch that Jonas knew exactly how far he could push him. After rubbing two lubed up fingers over Nicky's clenching hole he added some lube over the condom and slowly breached the circular muscle. He stopped pushing in when he heard a low moan escape from Nicky's mouth, closely followed by a muttered curse from Clay.

Nicky's mouth was still working on Clay's cock, now running up and down the side. Jonas tried not to think of what he was doing, knowing all too well how skilled his lover's mouth was. Luckily his attention was drawn to the movements Nicky was making, pushing his hips back wantonly so that he could impale himself. Seeing Nicky fuck himself on his cock cemented his resolve to just enjoy the sexual act and treat it like any other encounter with a client. After all, he still enjoyed his job and having Nicky there made him enjoy it even more.

Nicky grabbed another condom, telling Jonas that they were moving to the next phase. "Are you ready for me, big boy?" Nicky asked in a teasing tone, waving the condom packet around. "Because thanks to Jonas here, I'm ready for you."

Clay smiled widely and nodded. "Since you're in charge, how do you want me?"

Nicky pretended to think about it, but Jonas knew he'd done his thinking beforehand. They had talked about all the possible positions, and he was sure Nicky had made up his mind long before they entered the room today.

"Why don't you get comfortable against the headboard? Roll on the condom and make yourself nice and hard and slippery for me," he told Clay. While he was saying this, his hand reaching back to touch Jonas was enough of a gesture to tell Jonas he didn't want him to withdraw just yet. Pushing his torso up from the bed, Nicky let his head drop back on Jonas's shoulder and whispered, "Fuck me some more first, please."

Jonas eagerly complied, feeling a rush of emotion he could only show by thrusting hard into Nicky's tight channel a few times until they were both moaning softly. Almost out of habit, Jonas's hands had drifted to Nicky's nipples, teasing them until they peaked; he knew his lover enjoyed that almost as much as having his cock touched. He could feel Nicky's reluctance to move away when he finally shifted forward after Clay had settled down between the two pillows of the bed.

Nicky took the lube and made a show out of swirling some on Clay's cock, making the surgeon hiss at the coldness of the gel.

"I'm going to need a lot," Nicky whispered to Clay but loud enough for Jonas to hear too. "Because you're really pretty impressive, you know."

Clay smiled, slightly unsure because of the compliment. "Are you sure you'll be able to take both of us then? Jonas isn't small...."

Nicky cut Clay off with a quick kiss. "I guess you'll just have to make it so good for me that I don't care about a little stretch." Nicky turned around, rubbing his ass wantonly against Clay's belly and then straddled him, his hands resting on Clay's firm thighs. "Go on," he said over his shoulder. "You know you want to put it inside me."

While he was slowly sinking down on the enormous cock, Jonas could see Nicky's face contort, so he quickly crawled onto the bed and kissed his lover deeply.

"Fuck, he really is big," Nicky murmured against Jonas's mouth.

"I know," Jonas said reassuringly. He'd warned Nicky about this, but he knew his lover would relax enough eventually to even take him along with Clay. He'd just have to get him turned on enough to want it.

When Nicky started to move, Clay placed his hands on the designer's slender hips, supporting his movements. Nicky's face was becoming more relaxed now, showing that he was enjoying it more. Now that Clay couldn't see Nicky's expression, Jonas knew that his lover was no longer pretending. True proof came in the fact that Nicky's erection, which had waned a little right after the change of position, was now standing proudly again. When Jonas touched it, Nicky hissed, so Jonas settled on his stomach between Clay's legs and took Nicky into his mouth.

"Oh fuck!" Nicky reacted. "Too close!"

Jonas pushed his finger against the underside of Nicky's cock and prevented his lover from coming. Nicky was rambling incoherently now, moving rhythmically between the huge cock inside him and the hot mouth in front of him.

As Jonas tried to look up, he saw that Clay had hooked one of Nicky's arms over his shoulders and was looking down at the view. "Fuck, that's hot," he heard the surgeon say. "Are you gonna make him come like that?"

Jonas pushed himself away. "Not yet. At least not unless I have to."

"He's still pretty tight," Clay panted, trying at the same time to control his own reactions and keep Nicky steady during his undulating.

"We'll just have to do something about that then." Jonas smiled and coated his hand with more lube. With his clean hand he lifted Nicky's chin and kissed him lightly. "You okay, kid?"

Nicky murmured something incoherent and then winked at Jonas. The show was clearly still on.

Jonas had a hard time trying not to acknowledge it so he turned his gaze to Clay. "Don't jump, okay?" he warned Clay. "Lube may be a bit cold." He snaked an arm underneath Nicky's unsupported side and inserted his other hand between his lover's legs, cupping Nicky's balls before going in search of his already well-stretched passage.

"Oh yeah, feels good," Nicky whimpered as Jonas's slippery fingers massaged the muscle.

Jonas didn't leave it at that. "Lean back a bit?" he suggested.

Both Clay and Nicky shifted a little, and Nicky hooked his legs behind Clay's spread knees, opening himself up widely. This way Jonas had an easier time inserting a finger alongside Clay's swollen cock. He could tell from the way Nicky was trying to hold off Clay and the way he was clinging to Jonas's shoulder that it wasn't entirely comfortable yet, but he knew his lover well enough to understand some of the otherwise incoherent stream of mumblings escaping Nicky's mouth, giving him some indication that Nicky was teetering on the edge.

"It's up to you, kid, you tell us whether you want it or not," Jonas whispered, and he immediately got confirmation from Clay, who nodded his head at Jonas.

"Maybe... I should come first?" Nicky panted.

"It would help you relax, yes," Jonas confirmed. "I'd help you out but my hands are rather busy." With one hand leaning against the headboard and the other trying to relax Nicky's entrance, his hands were indeed otherwise occupied. Clay came to the rescue, moving his hand from Nicky's hip to his glistening cock and fisting it rapidly.

"Fuck!" Nicky shouted in frustration. "I can't—"

Jonas knew drastic measures were necessary so he kissed Nicky violently, nipping at his lips with his teeth. For the moment he didn't care how it looked to Clay, he just wanted Nicky to let go of his inhibitions and drop his guard. Slowly he felt his lover give in, and the body under his hands relaxed.

Nicky was breathing heavily. "Do it now, before I lose my nerve."

"Only if you really want to," Jonas replied tenderly.

Nicky smiled softly. "It's my buck, Jonas, so do it."

Jonas knew that if Nicky could stay in character and remember that he was supposed to be a client, he understood what he was doing.

Clay by now had slumped down enough to let Nicky lie back and give Jonas more access to gently find a way to push into the incredibly tight space between Nicky's muscular ring and Clay's now almost purple cock. It was a very intimate and also rather sweaty affair. The combination of the tightness, the throbbing of Clay's erection against his own, and the sounds all three of them were making, from clenched shouts, to profanity, to deep moans, was going to make it all over too soon. It took them a while to find a rhythm they all liked, but as soon as they did, Jonas realized Nicky could take it easily. To his more considerable surprise, it also dawned on him that the connection between him and Nicky was still there too. It didn't matter that there was a third man in the room, in bed with them; but it helped that Clay's eyes were closed, his head leaning back against the headboard in sheer ecstasy. It helped because it gave Nicky the chance to show Jonas how good it felt and how much he appreciated being stretched to the limit with two cocks sliding in and out of his tight body.

"Fuck, I'm bloody close," Nicky groaned.

This time Jonas did have a free hand and he wrapped it around Nicky's leaking erection. He looked over at Clay, who was staring at him intently, but not really seeing; his eyes almost completely black now.

"Oh yeah, like that," Nicky moaned.

"Show me how good it feels," Jonas teased. He knew exactly what would send Nicky over and let his thumb rub across the sensitive slit. Nicky jumped slightly, so Jonas ran his thumb across the edge of the swollen head.

"Oh fuck, yeah!" Nicky's breathing became ragged and then stalled completely as he thrust up in spasm, squeezing both Clay's and Jonas's cocks in the process as copious amounts of thick, clear seed splattered across Nicky's belly. Jonas thrust in powerfully, knowing how it prolonged his lover's orgasm, but he felt Clay slip out as Nicky's body started to relax and fall sideways. He barely remembered to hold the condom as he pulled back so he could let Nicky slide to the mattress.

Clay was quick to react though, pulling off the condom and fisting himself over Nicky's stomach.

"Yeah, that it's, big boy. Come like a porn star, all over me."

Nicky's wickedly seductive look and dirty mouth clearly did it for Clay as he thrust his formidable member into his fist and shot his load all over Nicky, his head thrown back and his eyes squeezed shut.

"Two down, one to go," Nicky concluded, reaching for Jonas. Determined to not fall behind, Jonas came closer, kneeling on the bed next to Nicky. They didn't need words. Nicky knew that Jonas would prefer his lover's hand rather than his own, so Nicky fisted Jonas a few times until he came, grunting softly and painting his own juices across Nicky's chest.

The three of them, with Nicky in the middle, stayed on the bed for a while catching their breath.

"Jonas tells me you top as well," Clay remarked at Nicky. "Maybe next time we should share him, what do you think?"

"Oh, I think we pretty much shared him now too," Nicky rebutted, looking at Jonas. Then he turned back toward Clay. "But Jonas tells me you like to bottom from time to time? How about we share you one day?"

Clay was quick to get up from the bed. "Maybe I better take a shower!"

THEY'D all enjoyed a quick shower at the penthouse, and then Nicky told Clay he had Jonas booked for the rest of the week and that he was welcome to the room they were in.

The second penthouse of the hotel had a separate lift, so they needed to travel down to the ground floor and then take the other lift up again.

Nicky wrapped his arms around Jonas from behind and pulled him closer. "Thank you," he said softly.

Jonas smiled and shrugged.

"I'm serious," Nicky continued. "But will you let me make you mine again?"

"I've always been yours, Nicky," Jonas answered gently. "Ever since that first time I met you, I've been yours."

Nicky gently kissed his neck. "I want to make love to you, just you and me and to hell with the rest of the world."

Jonas leaned back into Nicky's arms. "It's always just you and me. Even in there with Clay. And I think he noticed, too. He let us go way too easily."

They made their way over to the penthouse door and entered, giggling like teenagers because they refused to let go of each other. It was three in the morning by then, which would make it seven in the morning in Paris, and they were both exhausted.

"At least sleep in my arms?" Nicky asked.

Jonas nodded. It was his favorite way to sleep anyway.

JONAS woke up a few hours later. Nicky was behind him and clearly awake. Or at least parts of him were.

"I thought I'd never get you to wake up," a more than slightly amused voice whispered in his ear. "I figured we'd worn you out last night."

Jonas shook his head. "Well, we clearly didn't wear you out. Aren't you sore?"

"A little," Nicky admitted. "Probably too sore to bottom, yes. But we can do other things." He was leisurely stroking Jonas's downy chest hair.

"Like what?" Jonas teased, although he knew all too well what Nicky was getting at.

"Pass me the lube and I'll show you," Nicky answered. "I'll make you mine again, and it'll be just you and me and no latex separating us. That's what it means to me, Jonas, that when it's just the two of us, we don't need the condoms. We know that with other people we take precautions, so that together we don't have to."

Jonas leaned back in an attempt to get even closer to Nicky and then slowly felt the blunt head of Nicky's slicked up erection nudge his entrance until it slipped in almost without effort. They made love for what seemed like minutes, but was in reality several hours.

Jonas knew that no matter what happened, he'd never get enough of this incredible young man. And all because he'd managed to pierce his armor, see behind the façade to reveal the real Nicky.

 PILOGUE

NICKY languidly stretched himself on the incredibly comfortable four poster bed. He was slightly sore in the best possible way, but then again, this island always brought out the best in his lover. A warm breeze wafted across his naked body, and he pulled the white satin sheet over his shoulder, more for comfort than because he was cold.

Eventually he got up, pulling on loose fitting cotton Bermuda shorts and stepping into his flip-flops. Hands in pockets, he strolled across the living room toward Ally and Scott's part of the house. He slowed without stopping to disturb the perfect alignment of the balls on the pool table and then resumed his lazy stroll toward the balcony with the best view.

They had rented the most secluded part of the private island and had requested minimal staff. This meant that four or five people would come by boat to the small jetty around five every afternoon to drop off food and do only the most basic maintenance. An hour later they would all be gone, beds made, bathrooms and kitchens cleaned, and the guests would be left to their own devices. Which was just as well, since the four of them had christened a lot more than their respective bedrooms, and they hadn't restricted themselves to the house either.

Nicky walked onto the deck and saw Ally sitting on the balustrade. She was wearing a white caftan and drinking orange juice. Her eyes lit up as she noticed him, and she pressed her index finger to her lips, making Nicky approach her with a questioning look on his face.

The view from the balcony where they always shared breakfast was spectacular. Azure blue water and white beaches, trees and shrubs, uninhabited islands in the distance, but that was not why Ally had beckoned him. She pointed down toward the balcony of the floor below.

Like the balcony she was sitting on, it was cordoned off by a wide stone wall. The corner of the balustrade was covered by one of the plush bath towels, and sitting on top of it was Jonas, legs spread wide with Scott between them.

"Oh fuck," Nicky sighed, quickly turning his back toward the wall. Ally threw him a questioning look. "I'm never quite prepared for the image of the two of them fucking," he explained.

She smiled understandingly and let her eyes wander over Nicky's frame toward his crotch. "I can see that."

Nicky turned around and pressed himself against the banister, feeling rather embarrassed about his obvious arousal. "They just look so amazing together."

"Why don't you ask Jonas if you can join them next time? I'm sure Scott won't mind."

Nicky was a little baffled by Ally's suggestion. "I thought your agreement with Scott was that he got one man, and we both know that man is Jonas."

Ally smiled enigmatically. "Yes, that is the agreement, but I know Scott wants to, and a little bird told me you wanted it, too. Besides, you and Jonas are joined at the hip anyway, right?"

Nicky nodded. He wasn't sure if this suggestion came from Ally's perverted mind or whether she really wanted to do Scott a favor, so he decided to decline for now. "I'm a perv like you, Ally," he chuckled. "I like to watch!" Smiling shyly he continued. "When Jonas is away, I wank in the shower to images of the two of them!"

"I'd think you'd get off on images of Jonas fucking you?" Ally replied teasingly.

A strangled, "Harder, Scott! Fuck, you're making me come!" made them both look down.

"Seems like we're missing all the good bits," Ally giggled.

Scott was thrusting hard into Jonas's body and at the same time, kissing him almost violently. "Fuck yeah! Love to feel you come!"

Jonas groaned loudly as he was overtaken by his orgasm. At first his face was buried against Scott's shoulder, but then he threw back his head, opened his eyes, and looked straight into Nicky's face.

Nicky pulled back, moving out of Jonas's range of vision. "He saw me!" he whispered at Ally, a mix of amusement and insecurity on his face. Watching them was one thing. He'd done it more than once, following Ally's flawless radar for finding the places they sought out. Or maybe Scott tipped her off. But now Jonas had seen him watching them.

Ally kissed him on the cheek. "Go find him, talk to him."

"It's not that I'm jealous or anything…."

Ally smiled. "I know you're not, but you might want him to take care of that." She pointed down.

Nicky sighed and hurried inside. He didn't get far. The first corner he turned, he bumped into Jonas.

"Did you like it?" Jonas asked, his voice low and seductive.

Nicky nodded.

"You're hard."

Nicky cocked his head and took a deep breath in. "How long before you can… do it again?"

Jonas narrowed his eyes. "Get the sun block and the lube. I'm taking you out into the bay in a dingy."

"A dingy?"

"You don't mind if Ally and Scott watch us, do you?"

"Through the spyglass? From the balcony?" Nicky asked eagerly, his breathing already accelerating.

Jonas nodded and softly kissed his lover, pulling the young man's aroused body against his and running a finger lightly over his long back muscles. "Can you wait that long?"

Don't miss this exciting title from

Zahra Owens

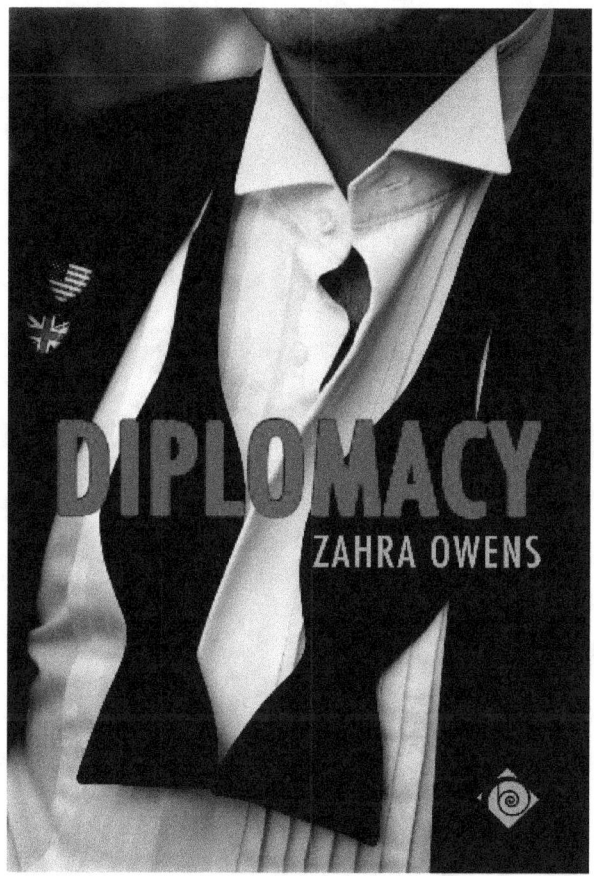

Rising star Jack Christensen is the youngest man ever appointed a U.S. ambassador. A career diplomat just assigned to a European embassy, he has the perfect wife and all the right credentials. But despite having his dream job, something is missing, and he doesn't know what.

Then Lucas Carlton arrives at a reception with his American fiancée, and from the first handshake, he makes an impression that Jack can't dismiss. Lucas's position as the British liaison to the American embassy keeps them in constant contact—and keeps Jack constantly off-balance. After a passionate weekend together, they can't resist continuing the affair. Jack and Lucas know they're on thin ice. Diplomatic circles are notoriously conservative, and they each know that the right woman by their side makes a very significant contribution to their success. Will they make the correct decisions for both their professional and personal lives? Or will they need to sacrifice one for the other?

ZAHRA OWENS was born in Europe just before Woodstock and the moon landing and was given a much less pronounceable name by her non-English-speaking parents. Being an Aquarian meant she would never quite conform, and people learned to expect the unexpected.

She started writing fairy tales in first grade; the same year she came into contact with her first group of English-speaking friends, a group which would eventually grow to include people from all over the world. On the outside she was a typical only child, accustomed to being with adults most of the time. On the inside, she sought ways to channel her wild imagination.

During the daytime she earns a living as a computer specialist, but it's her former career as an intensive care nurse that tends to seep into her fiction. Maybe this has to do with her weak spot for flawed characters and imperfect bodies, or maybe it's just her sadistic streak coming through. You be the judge.

Visit Zahra's web site at http://www.zahraowens.com/ and her blog at http://zahra-owens.livejournal.com/.